Favors

Carol Bartolet

Copyright © 2006 by Carol Bartolet

ISBN 0-7414-3204-8

Published by:

INFI∞ITY
PUBLISHING.COM

1094 New DeHaven Street, Suite 100
West Conshohocken, PA 19428-2713
Info@buybooksontheweb.com
www.buybooksontheweb.com
Toll-free (877) BUY BOOK
Local Phone (610) 941-9999
Fax (610) 941-9959

Printed in the United States of America

Printed on Recycled Paper

Published July 2006

Dedicated to the memory of Jean Salter Kent,
mother and friend, my inspiration

To Babe!
Happy Reading!
Carol Bartolet

PROLOG

As she approached the spot, the tiny hairs on the back of her neck felt prickly and wet. Skeletons of wrecked cars loomed above and in front of her, the night casting eerie, foreboding shadows. The car bodies, crushed and broken, were stacked in their mass grave. Two A.M...Johnnie's Auto Parts. *Don't be a baby*, she thought, as thick, oozing fear threatened to overlap her thin shield of courage. *I love Ty and he loves me. After all, I am a grown woman. Ty said that.* Shakira remembered his strong, dark arms encircling her willing body, overwhelming, consuming. Passion had brought her here. For him. Recalling moments of his hot, thrusting lust, she inched forward, anxious to complete this task and get back to him. *Look for the red Caddie! It's not squashed yet,* he had said. *Get the package, leave the backpack, and get back quick!* Those were his orders. She knew better than to question Ty. His anger was ugly and violent. The two boys had paid for their disobedience with their lives. *He wouldn't hurt me, of course*, she thought, biting her lower lip, eyes darting here and there towards the darkness. *We're in love! To hell with what Momma said. What did she know? Momma was old and used up; she couldn't understand.* It was easy to sneak out. A lock on her bedroom door wouldn't keep her in. That sissy room all pink and ribbons and bows. *Baby stuff! I'm not a little girl. I'm fourteen, got my womanhood. Not a prissy virgin either. I got a man, a real man...not a childish boy!*

Sighing with relief, she saw the car, blood red even in the moonlight. The chrome grill smiled with broken evil teeth as the headlights, hollow and menacing, stared back at her. The loser in a fight, catching its breath, waiting for round three. *Get a grip, Girl! It's just a car!* Her heart pounding, she felt a hidden presence. *There is no bogeyman!* Gathering strength and courage, she swung the backpack around by its straps and, forcing terror to walk behind her, she approached the car. As she peered into the windowless driver's side, she saw a large manila envelope on the torn seat. She grabbed for it, scratching her arm on a glass shard

i

but not noticing. Hefting the package under her left arm, she tossed the bag onto the seat and turned to run.

Her face smashed hard into something and she shrieked in confusion! A man! Several men! *No! Shit!* Her arm was wrenched so hard from her that the package fell. Another man went to the car, saying nothing.

"Let me go!" Shakira screamed, thrashing and yanking her arm with the strength and agility of a cat being readied for a bath. But she was held fast. They did not let her go. Crying and still shrieking, she saw the men were short, but much bigger than herself. *The Rico Gang!* She screamed louder, hitting and kicking until she was thrown to the ground like a broken toy. Her head hit the earth with a dull thud.

"Shut up, bitch! We gotta check the money! It'd better be right or you and that dog will pay hard!"

Shakira continued to struggle until someone jammed her face into the ground, nose flattened and bloody. One man sat on her back. *Lay down quiet, be still, be calm,* she thought. She could hardly breathe.

"It's here," said one of the men. "Sent a little senorita to do his dirty work? Was he afraid of us? The big man afraid?" he continued, crouching low on the ground and whispering into the girl's ear.

Another man grabbed her arms roughly and pinned them behind her. "Well, where's our tip?" he laughed. Another began pulling at the back of the black girls shorts, ripping the nylon material open with his knife. As he tore the material, he yelled with joy, lips pulled back to display white teeth...teeth and knife both shining in the lunar glow.

An adrenaline cocktail of fear threw Shakira into a rage of earnest kicking and squealing. *This was not going to happen!* Suddenly, hair yanked back, her neck was jerked to hyperextension, almost cutting off her wind! In the fierceness of the attack, she smelled oily fingers and foul grease as fingers covered her mouth. She opened wide allowing a thumb to slide in against her tongue. She bit hard! A scream of pain and anger was followed by a deafening punch that rattled her skull and broke both upper incisors. She couldn't breathe at all! Nose embedded in the dirt and filled with blood, mouth full of pieces of tongue and teeth, she was finally quiet.

Laughing as they took turns, they raped her, punching their erections into every orifice. Stripped naked, she still lay silent. Eyes were open, but shock had rendered the prey into merciful unawareness. Torn car parts became metal intrusions into bloody vagina, anus, and mouth.

Tiring of her silence and lack of fight, the biggest man put his hands on his hips and looked down at her. He appeared bored and totally satisfied with himself.

"Okay, let's go. I gotta get back to my woman and a shower."

The gang took the package and bag and slithered quietly into the night, still murmuring and poking each other in the ribs as they walked. Their game was over. Time to go home.

There was no sound in the junkyard, except the girl's quick raspy breaths. "I'm ...I...lived. I'm not killed..." She tried to get up, but her head swam with fuzzy stars and a roar like the subway tunnel. She fell back to her knees. First resting, then crawling, she found her clothes. They were hung neatly on the side mirror of the red car. Shakira heaved herself towards the door and sat propped against it, breath sounds gurgling from fractured ribs, now threatening her lungs. Struggling, she pulled on her shorts, then her shirt. Blood began to soak through the cotton right away. Holding the window, she pulled herself up. She couldn't think. "I wanna go home. I gotta find Momma!" As she found another portion of youthful strength, she began to walk, using a rusty rod as a cane. *Ty will kill them...must go there first.*

Making her way through the two alleys, back to her drop off area, she limped with pain and humiliation. Ty saw her coming slowly, then he saw the blood. He ran toward her, eyes surveying her clothes, her bruises, bloody face and red-streaked legs.

Senses deadened, but relieved to see him, Shakira squeaked out, "They raped me.....they almost killed me!" She fell against him, feeling woozy and faint again, seeking comfort.

"Where's the package?"

"Huh? Wha....?"

Tyrone smacked her with the back of his fist. The girl's blood sprayed his shirt and she fell to the ground, wailing.

"You stupid bitch! I need that package!"

"But...." Her sentence was interrupted by a kick to the kidney. She began to vomit, retching blood and foamy phlegm.

"Shut up!" he shouted, enraged and furious.

Was Momma right? He doesn't love me? But he does, I know he does…he's just mad right now. Shakira could not let go of her fantasy. Broken and bloody, she whispered, "But you said you loved me."

He just glared at her. Maybe he hadn't heard.

"That's how stupid you are. I'm a man; you're a dumb little girl. In fact, I'm taking you home right now. Get the fuck up!"

Right now that was just where Shakira wanted to go. Home. Tyrone took her arm and pulled her up, half dragging her to his pearl white Lexus with the spinning chrome hubs. Opening the back door, he threw her inside.

"Don't lay down…I don't want no blood all over my leather!"

She sobbed now almost inaudibly. Tears washed blood from her face in scarlet rivulets down her cheeks. Yeah, she just wanted to go home.

Tyrone would take her home all right. He would deal with Cortez Santiago and the rest of those Latino bad guys later. He would get his supplies and his money back. He would also thank them for leaving their DNA with a dead girl. He smiled as he pulled up to the well-groomed house. Such nice little gardens, he thought. Fresh paint too. Frilly high society. What was the point?

Once more she whimpered, imploring, "They almost killed me….."

"*Almost* is the key, Darling Girl," he said, raising the Glock to her head. Her eyes flew open in surprise, but there was no time to respond. Two shots were heard in the normally quiet neighborhood as Shakira became no longer useful. Her body was returned as promised, broken and battered, tossed like garbage onto her mother's front porch.

fa vor   n. 1. an act of kindness 2. a small present or token, as at a party

Chapter 1

"Come on, Badger, move your butt before you get stepped on," remanded Emily to the fat, tabby-striped feline on the floor. He was lying in his favorite sunshine spot on the polished hardwood below the shop's bay window. She gave him a gentle shove with her big toe that he ignored in typical cat-like fashion. Maybe he was resting up for his day ahead as official store greeter. Finally, he lazily sat up, stretched, and opened his whiskery mouth into a big cat yawn. He eyed his owner indifferently, blinked twice, strode to another spot a foot away and lay down again. He rolled onto his back, daring his owner to attempt a belly rub, as he tried not to watch her through half-open lids.

"You need to get a job, Mister, besides dusting up the floor and windows with your big hairy body," Emily said softly as she stooped to scratch his chin. She coughed, dry and hacking, as she stood up, and figured the cat had managed to actually find some dust on that puffy mop-like swirling tail. "If I had wanted a feather duster, I could've gone to the Dollar Store instead of the County Pound," she chastised. "And I wouldn't have to be buying 'Cat Chow for the Obese Feline' at Publix either!" Badger just closed his eyes and stretched out even farther, making himself even bigger and longer, oblivious to his mistress's comments. Sighing in exasperation, Emily stepped over the rotund and fluffy mass at her feet and headed to the rear of the store.

On this warm and muggy August Florida morning, Emily Vanderhorn had more important things to do. She stopped briefly under one of the swirling fans, their wicker blades sending cooling breezes throughout the establishment. Emily raised her arms as if to the heavens, enjoying the airy sensation and sighing with satisfaction. She felt the entering coolness fill her sleeveless blouse with billows of comfort. What Emily did not feel were the approaching winds of change. This ordinary day would soon begin blowing her life off course. Not the life everyone saw here at FAVORS...her other life.

Oblivious to the coming whirlwinds, Emily toiled effi-ciently. Except for some unpacking of new inventory and the late-week cleaning she did herself, she was almost finished with her work. The neatly organized storeroom behind the customer area was almost empty; most of the recently delivered boxes had been opened and inspected. Emily was meticulous about her sample items put out for display. They were personally and carefully arranged as new pieces were added. Her clients wanted the best and only the very best. The presentations had to be perfect.

Emily reached for the first of five cardboard boxes labeled "Fragile" that were stacked on the floor at the rear of the store. For some unknown reason she had some special anticipation about this order. She drew the razor-sharp box cutter from one of her apron pockets and deftly sliced the plastic-taped edges of the first box. The box contained several imported English porcelain figurines she was planning to display in the gift area of the store. Each was unique and expensive, beautiful and finely detailed. She paused to admire each one as she lifted it from the foam peanut packing and unrolled it from its plastic bubble wrapped protector. This box contained figures of children at play. An innocent was laughing merrily, mouth wide open on a swing, hair blowing in the wind. Emily could almost hear the happy squeal of delight just by looking at the artist's naturalistic work. Next, she found a figure of a little boy who had a calico kitten sitting on his lap while he teased it with a soft-tipped weed. Emily could imagine the little tail swishing in excitement as it readied to leap at the elusive swaying prey. *So realistic-looking, yet whose childhood was this ideal?* thought Emily. Children and animals were her loves. Never trust adults! Emily had morals. They were just a little different.

She reached for the next wrapped item and began to unfurl it from its cover. A small blond sunny-cheeked girl in pigtails, bib overalls, and holding carrots behind her back, was touching noses with a pretty pinto pony. They were standing in meadow grass filled with daisies and clover. It was so life-like that Emily suddenly could feel the warm summer sun on her own cheeks. Transported unwillingly and feeling light-headed, she felt a familiar humid breeze blowing through rain-soaked cedar trees. Emily could smell the damp, loamy woods near the beat-down shamble of a cabin she had once called home. It was nothing more than a shack made up of discarded sheets of tin roofing and logs and sticks from the forest. Windows and lumber for the porch front had been begged or stolen from the nearby sawmill. Mrs. Emily Vanderhorn did not want to make this return trip. But again it was June 12, 1936 … Waverly, Alabama.

Chapter 2

Nine-year-old Emily Sue McCracken had awakened early and put on the threadbare but clean gingham dress she had carefully hung on the bedpost. After dressing she crept silently to the front of the shack. She grabbed the skimpy broom and quickly whisked off the bent and broken planks on the porch, set the breakfast table with forks, plates, and tin coffee mugs and ran out to the shed. Once there, she was greeted by cackling hens that ran to her feet, circling and scrambling for the few pieces of cracked corn she fed them. As they bobbed, scratched, and pecked the ground, she went to their nests and took out the treasured eggs. She carefully placed them into the front of her dress, folding it up like a sack, and walked slowly and deliberately back to the cabin, bare feet treading softly on the dewy grass. Reaching the front of the shack, soft, dusty soil already warmed by hot morning sun stuck to her wet toes and soles of her feet. She liked the sensation. But, holding the eggs cautiously, she tried to wipe off the dirt onto the old grass mat before entering the sparse cabin. As she peered through the torn screen door, she could see that now her mother was up and making coffee and some grits on the old coal stove.

"That's it?" Mama asked with a disapproving frown, wiping her hands on a flowered apron and opening the tattered door for her daughter. She was pretty in her own way, but years of toil and stress were seen in premature lines on her face. Her hair was unwashed and tied back in a makeshift bun. She was thin and angular but had curves in all the right places, unnoticeable under the unattractive baggy housedress.

"Yes, ma'am, this is all I found."

"How many hens are left out there? No more visits from that varmint coyote, I hope?"

"No Mama, they was all there and hungry."

"Well, everyone's hungry. Now git busy on your other jobs, little lady."

"Yes, ma'am."

Emily carefully deposited the eggs into the wire basket on the old oak table and straightened her dress. She ran out the door as fast as she could. She had heard her stepdad moving around in the other room. She ran to the old cow and begged her not to kick while she expertly squirted the milky streams into the tin bucket. She always liked the sounds the milk made as it hit the bucket and wanted to experiment with different aims and different pressure on the teats. She liked to see how much foam she could make by squirting the milk faster and harder. She knew better, though, and hurried through the procedure with prudence. Careful not to spill a drop, she carried the small amount of thin white fluid back to her mother and Frank.

"Did you spill some? That's all? Not a very good job, Missy," said Frank, who was inhaling the aroma of frying bacon as he scratched his hairy armpits and adjusted his boxer shorts over his large, pendulous belly. He wore a sleeveless wife-beater style undershirt and sat at the kitchen table in the only chair with armrests. To say the shirt was threadbare would have been a compliment. *This is one man who should spend more time covering himself up. No one in their right mind wants to see this at breakfast*, thought young Emily. Shaving and bathing were not Frank's priorities. There was no hot water. Heating water would have meant work gathering firewood or stealing more from the neighbors.

"No, Frank, this was all she would give," answered Emily with nary a glance in his direction. She was careful not to make eye contact any more than was necessary.

"Time to take the old girl with me to work. Maybe buy a young calf in the spring. Maybe could steal one right off the trucks when they unload."

Frank worked at the slaughterhouse one mile down the road from Emily's family. Grady's Meats. Emily hated to think about that. Her mother had cooked the eggs and bacon and toasted some bread. Hot grits were put on the plates with the other food. Emily wolfed hers down quickly and said she had to finish her work.

"Then git outta here, girl. Don't be playin' round neither. Everyone's gotta earn their keep 'round here, ya know," reminded Frank loudly, as he scratched his crotch and adjusted his balls.

Well, what Emily did know was that Frank never did a damn thing around the place except yell at her mama and stink.

One thing she had learned was that keeping herself clean and bathed was worth the extra time and effort. Emily scooted out the door, careful not to let the screen door bang. It was full of tears and holes, but at least kept the dogs and cats outside. Fixing the door was not apparently on Frank's 'to do' list. When Emily's father was killed in a tractor accident, Frank was her mother's desperate attempt to keep the family together. At least he had a job and was willing to help support her two daughters. Frank was really not what you would call supportive, however. Emily still missed the warmth and love from her Daddy, but was resigned to the fact that she must survive here with Frank.

Emily glanced behind her at the ramshackle mess she called home and ducked through the trees towards the meadow. As long as she did her work, no one paid much attention to her. She got to the meadow in less than three minutes. Maybe she would still be there by the fence. Frannie. And there she stood, nose buried in the deep summer grass. A fat spotted pony, gentle and kind, with huge brown eyes framed with long white eyelashes. The pony's head came up suddenly when she heard Emily approach. She was not alarmed, but nickered a welcome and trotted over to the little girl. Emily reached into the pocket of her worn dress and pulled out a handful of the chicken's cracked corn. The little mare nuzzled her palm, careful lips plucking each tiny corn morsel of the offering. Emily laughed as the spiky muzzle hairs poked her hand. She kissed the pony on her velvety nose and laughed again as the hairs brushed her cheek. The pony then went back to eating grass, accepting the girl's presence. Emily brought a small hairbrush that rightfully belonged to her mother and began singing as she brushed the tangled mane. As she worked she fantasized that the pony had wings and soon they would fly away to a castle. She would be a beautiful princess in her very own citadel in a faraway land. A safe place where no one would come into her room unless she said okay. It would have a big moat, surrounded by gators, like here in the swamps of Alabama. At school there was talk about huge gators able to take full-grown deer, grabbing them from the edges of the marsh grass easy as pie. Emily figured she could catch these alligators and put them in her moat. They would be mean and eat Frank and all the other horrible people in her life. The magical pony would carry her up and away to lands of fun and fantasies whenever and wherever she wanted to go. She would be the boss of everything. Things would be fair. Emily would be in control. Maybe she would snap her fingers and bad people would just disappear. If the alligators didn't eat them.

Frannie allowed the pig-tailed girl to climb on her back and sit astride. Emily could then be a Wild West rodeo queen, or Lady Godiva, or a famous movie star riding a beautiful racehorse like Bold Venture or Gallant Fox. The books at school told of many happy girls, famous and rich and smart. And Emily was sure nobody dared to bother them. The pony's back was warm from the July sunshine and her summer coat felt soft and smooth. Lying on her stomach, she stretched her arms to encircle the pony's neck.

"Let's just fly away, Frannie. What d'ya say? Let's go!"

Sometimes the little pony would oblige with a few steps, moving towards greener grass or a particularly tender piece of clover. This was true heaven for Emily. Once the pony actually trotted around the field at her rider's urging, never offering to buck, seemingly at home with the child on her back. All was peaceful and lazy in the morning heat. Frannie's previous owners had given the outgrown pony to her as favor to her mother, in exchange for some wonderful homemade pies. Mama made some awesome pies, even winning awards at the county fair. Of course, Frank had been furious, yelling about how cash would be nice, another mouth to feed, and what did Emily ever do to deserve a gift like that. Frank terrified Emily, but Emily was smart. She knew how to keep out of his way, and did her best to not cause any trouble. She always did her chores and tried to remain as invisible as possible unless she was working. She had excellent grades at school and was reading at the top of her class, but there were no books at home. There was no one here that was ever going to spend any time taking Emily to the downtown library either. Frank just couldn't see the point. Emily also liked to draw. She had one small pencil left from school and spent hours alone drawing ponies and long-haired princesses. She was a pretty good little artist too, at least that's what Miss Nelson, her third grade teacher, had said. One thing Emily knew for sure. She was not going to be like her sister. Jessie had left home at sixteen. She was pregnant and uneducated. Emily also knew the horrible secret of abuse. Frank had been "doing things" in Jessie's bed as long as Emily could remember.

Jessie and Emily had shared a room and twin beds. When Frank would stumble in at night, smelling like sweat and booze, Emily would pull the covers up over her head. She heard the muffled cries and the threats. She heard the creaking bedsprings and Frank's moaning. Sometimes she heard slaps and sobbing. He usually left quickly and she had glimpsed his grotesque figure on its way back to her parent's bedroom. He was so arrogant he didn't even bother to sneak as he slid back to his own bed and Emily's mother. Jessie would cry into the night, and sometimes Emily would ask her to climb into bed with her. She dared not go over to Jessie's bed, as that bed smelled rancid and dusky. She would probably puke. Her sister told her to just shut up and that way she could stay safe. Emily not only feared Frank, but hated him. She had no respect for her mother and determined she would never be the washed-out dishrag of a parent her Mama was. She would be strong and independent. And she wouldn't need any man, that's for sure.

"Why'd you let him hit you, Jess? Why?" ventured Emily to her sister huddled now beside her under Emily's torn and tattered quilts.

"It buys me some time, little one. I'll be out of here soon."

"You can't leave me here alone! You can't!"

"I love you, Emmy. But you need to find a way out. You'll be next. He is the actual devil and Mama can't stop him."

Little Emily had no trouble imagining pot-bellied and unshaven Frank with horns, tail and trident.

"Why don't you tell her?" said Emily with terrified tears rushing away from her long-lashed eyes.

Brushing the wet blond bangs from her kid sister's forehead, Jessie put her head on the pillow next to her face. "I have tried to talk to Mama, you know. She says I am dreaming."

"Dreamin'?" said Emily, eyes wide and astounded by this revelation. She was up on one elbow staring into her sister's face, almost nose to nose.

"Mama will never save you, either, from Frank. She is selfish and afraid and has to protect herself from that sleazy sweat ball. Just shut up and stay safe. You are still the baby for a while. Maybe one of those big bulls at the plant will decide not to git butchered one day and stomp him into the ground."

"Will that really happen?" asked Emily with a hopeful smile, eyes wide with question.

"No, the real world ain't like that. So you will have to plan to take off as soon as you get little nubby boobs, as that is when you will stop being a baby to Frank. He don't care. As long as you got girl parts, he will stick his thing in you. I hate that bastard. I would like to kill him."

"Want me to kill him for you, Jess?" said Emily with a serious look.

Jessie gave her little freckle-faced sister a hard stare and began to laugh. "Okay, Darlin', you can kill him for both of us. But I am outta here."

"Where will you go, will you write to me?" whined Emily, tears beginning to fall and feeling abandoned.

"For the safety of both of us, I can't tell you anything more. Trust me; you'll be the only one who misses me around here. Frank will go back to plunking Mama and that will be it. You will be okay for a while," Jessie promised. "Don't let him take you swimming in the pond without Mama. That was how it all started. He told Mama he was gonna give me swimming lessons. We drove out there to Mason's pond and no one else was there. It was a school day, and Frank said this was a more important lesson than books could teach. Oh yeah, sure. Well, we were out in the water and he kept dunking my head and laughing like it was a big joke. Probably to let me know he could drown me at any time he wanted. Then he would lift me high and throw me up and into the water. It was kinda fun at first. Then we would swim around for a while and he would go underwater and surprise me from behind. He put his arms around me and held me tight. I could feel his hard thing behind me and he reached into my swimsuit from behind. He just kept rubbing and moving. Kept saying it was okay. Yeah, like I would believe this was all part of a swimming lesson."

"What did you do? Why was he doing that?"

"I couldn't do much of anything. I was afraid he really would drown me. He was doing that because he is a bastard, Emmy. A bastard. It got worse. He would put his hand underneath me at my crotch and throw me into the air with his hand. His finger going into all my private places. He would even do that when we were all together for our picnic. Some picnic."

"And I was so mad that you were getting all the attention from Mama's new boyfriend."

"Never be jealous over any man, little sister. That is one lesson for the here and now."

"I hate boys already."

"Anyway," Jessie sighed and continued, "Next he was coming into our room which you know all about. He had gotten worse since Mama married him. It's the beer and whiskey, too."

"Yeah, he gets those red eyes. Yeah! Devil eyes!" whispered Emily clutching her sister's nightgown tightly. "Is that how Mama got those bruises?

"Frank has given Mama a cut lip, black eyes, and knocked out two teeth. Don't you remember the trip to the doctor? Mama broke her arm falling down from the hay wagon? Well, Frank threw her out their bedroom window. I saw it from the dog pen! Frank didn't see me since I was cleanin' up hound poop, but Mama did. Frank got nervous when he saw her arm bent crooked like a hot dog stick. So they conspired up this story and he took her to the hospital. Said he was real sorry to Mama and it was an accident. What crap. He was just worried she might not be his able-bodied servant any longer."

Jessie held her sister in a tight grip and both cried themselves to sleep. A sisterly chat never to be forgotten. But soon Jessie was gone. Just took off during a September night and never came back. And as predicted, Mama and Frank hardly seemed to notice. Emily thought Mama was probably relieved as she wanted Frank to stop banging Jessie. But soon after, Frank began following Emily around.

"Hey little girl, are those titties you are growing under that shirt?" said a leering Frank almost every day, like it was something new he had just noticed.

Emily would just glare back at him. If there were even a vague chance that looks could kill she would give it her best try. A couple of times Frank's thick fingers had made a grab for her but failed to connect. Emily was fast and ran off to do her chores. Her mother had looked on but only from the margins of her vision as she continued to pin sheets on the line in the backyard.

Emily was still dozing on the flat warm back of the pony mare when she heard Frank calling her.

"Emmy! Emmmmmy!" he yelled, sounding gruff and mean, not drunk.

"Coming! I am coming, Frank," answered Emily quickly, as she hopped off the pinto, ducked under the rusty barbed wire and ran quickly down the grassy path towards home.

"I did all my chores," announced Emily with hands on hips, telltale horsehairs covered her legs and belly.

"Well, that's damn good, Emmy. Was just talking to your Mama and we decided it was time for your lessons to begin. Swimming lessons," drawled Frank as he slowly chewed on a piece of hay.

"I already know how to swim!" countered Emily, hands on hips, duly warned by Jessie.

"Well, girl, do ya now? Then tomorrow we'll be going to Mason's pond to take your swimming test. We'll both be seein' what your strokes are like. If you're good, you can be getting' a job as lifeguard when you are older, just like your sister did."

"I don't care to be swimmin' Frank, not with you!" said Emily with a toss of her pigtails and her tiny mouth curled into a defiant snarl.

"Well, well, well. We will definitely be seein' about that!" said Frank, hairy fat arms tensing meaty biceps, eyes narrowing in on Emily with a hard ugly stare. He would have loved to grab her and beat the living shit out of her right now. But he had bigger, better, and more fun things planned for his mouthy little stepdaughter. His flaccid penis began to jump to life just thinking about that cute little body, that brat mouth with the full pouting lips that never knew when to shut up. Yep, he had just the thing for that. He would see that he got his way, no matter what. Frank stomped back into the house and the screen door slammed resolutely behind him. Emily was smart enough to know that Frank had not given up and she was scared and worried.

The next morning Emily was taking the usual thieved cracked corn to Frannie. As she neared the field, she was shocked and horrified to see her pony haltered and being led down the path to the shack. Worse yet, at the other end of the lead line was Frank. Evil exuded from every pore as he walked the willing, gentle pony towards Emily.

"What are you doin' with Frannie?" whimpered Emily, now almost speechless with terror.

"Well, me and Frannie is goin' for a little one way walk. Frannie and Frank, ain't that so cute? Sounds like one of them kiddy books you like to read. Yep, Frannie and Frank. Nice ring to it."

"Where are you goin'? She's *my* pony, you know?" asked Emily as she threw back her shoulders and tried to be as tall as she could, like a cat meeting a foe face to face. She could actually feel the hair rise on her neck.

"Little smart mouth, do ya remember they sell horsemeat too at Gradys?" with a grin turned mean and nasty. "I'm just taking her fat little self for a walk to work with me this nice morning. My little girl seems to not be grateful for me getting' her a nice little pony. A nice fat little pony will make lots of pony steaks and dog food too for our huntin' hounds. Everything and everyone on a farm has to pull their weight, ya know."

"Nooo! You can't!" screamed Emily at the top of her tiny lungs, freckled face now beet red with anger and fear.

"I can't? Just watch me. Come on little horsie, you and me got a date with the blood floor."

Emily went pale and felt sick as she flashed back to the time her stepfather had made her go to work with him to get his paycheck. Said he wanted her to see what he had to do to feed her and the family. Made her stand screaming at the butchering of calves, saw the bodiless, horned heads of steers in huge steel bins. She could still remember their open-eyed blank stares. Worst was the bawling of the cattle as they were forced into the shoot leading to the kill floor, terrified by the smell of blood and bowels. Mercifully then, Frank's boss saw and heard the screaming child and yelled at Frank to get her out of there. Frank was severely admonished and was told if he tried to bring children into the slaughterhouse again, he would be fired on the spot. Emily, though, was already emotionally wounded. She cringed in horror now as her stepfather led the pony down their lane towards the packing plant.

In desperation, she yelled after Frank, "Mr. Grady will never let you kill my pony. I will tell him and he will fire you!"

"Emmy darlin', Mr. Grady is on vacation this whole week. Seems to have went away to see his auntie or something. Don't think he will hear you screaming, or Frannie either."

Emily ran to her mother and begged her to help. "Do something, Mama, do something! For once, help me!" Emily was breathless and wheezing in her pleading, hanging desperately onto her mother's skirt. But her mother was as useless as she always was. The only thing she could do was hug her daughter and share her tears, saying nothing.

"It's not fair! It's just not fair!" Emily screamed at Frank.

"You will find out little daughter that life is not always fair in this world," whispered Mama, holding her tight in a vain and weak attempt to comfort the weeping child.

"Pleeease! Frank, don't do it. Pleeease! I'll be good, I'll do anything!" pleaded Emily, now held in a vise grip by her mother.

"Too late now, Missy. Too damn late," Frank announced as he tightened up the lead rope and tugged the pony along. The unsuspecting Frannie looked back at her small owner quizzically, huge round eyes blinking expectantly.

"Please Frank, I really need the swimming lessons. Come back and we will go now. Please, just put Franny back in her field and let's go now?" pled the crying, hysterical girl.

"Hahaaaha!" laughed Frank fiendishly as he continued along the dusty road, walking with an arrogant swagger and swinging the lead rope almost playfully. "Oh we'll be going swimming all right. But it will be tomorrow. Yep, tomorrow is another day." He was whistling a tune as he sauntered away, not looking back again.

Emily suddenly jumped away from her mother and yelled "Fuck you, Frank, fuck you!" Much to the shock and dismay of her mother who was trying her best to contain the flailing, shrieking child by the wrist. "I hate you, I will kill you, you bastard! I will, I will, I promise!"

Soon Emily's sobs quieted in her mother's arms. Her Mama released her and Emily went to the road and looked into the dirt. Then she knelt down in the dust and ran her forefinger around one small hoof print. It was all she had left of Frannie. A dusty print in the road. As she cried and cried, tears fell with indignant plops into the dirt, making tiny volcanoes as they landed into the powdery dust. Salty teardrops rolled down her face onto her lips. She could taste her hatred and anger. The feeling of unfairness and hopelessness. She would never forget this, never. And now she would make sure Frank never would forget, either. Resolutely, she wiped the tears from her dusty face, rose from the dirt, and went into the shack, this time letting the door slam behind her with a loud crash. Mama watched tearfully but helplessly as Emily walked away, a stricken child. But what her Mama did not see was the change in Emily's expression. Strong determination replaced the weakness of childhood, courage replaced fear, thought and reasoning had replaced the emotional outburst. Innocent baby blue eyes had turned steel cold with calculation. Sometimes life isn't fair. But then, sometimes it is. Life is what you make of it.

Suddenly, heart racing back to the present, Emily rose from the storage room floor. She realized her palms were sweating and she had perspiration on her forehead, despite the cooling fans. She dried her hands on the dust cloth and dabbed at her damp face. Regaining reality, she smiled as she carefully placed the figurine onto the center space in the lighted glass carousel cabinet. This one would have a center stage flourish. A piece full of memories. Maybe she would even keep it for herself. After placing each porcelain sculpture in the lighted case, she ran a piece of shiny moss colored silk along the glass, making waves and mounds of material that were pleasing to the eye. Nothing too extravagant which would take away from the beauty of the figurines themselves, but just give a little enhancement, actually a little enchantment to the lovely display. Now it looked perfect. Little children, little puppies and kittens, and Frannie herself back in green sunny meadows. Once she was satisfied with the porcelain, Emily gave Badger another scoot with her foot and started to rearrange some assorted baskets on the floor near the back of the store. The musical tinkling of the antique brass bell over the front door interrupted the quiet moment. FAVORS had a visitor, an expected visitor.

Chapter 3

"Hello, Miss Em...... How are you this morning?" asked the female voice tentatively, as if testing the air to see who was there to listen.

"Well, look who's here! Ms. Yolanda Grimes! I am just fine, and you?" answered Emily, from the rear of the store. At that same moment her granddaughter Brigetta was entering the back door. Her summer helper. Emily added loudly, "Hold on one second, Yolanda, I hear Brigetta coming in. Got to get that girl something to do since she needs to be busy all the time. Reminds me of me! Brigetta? Hi, darlin', could you get Ms. Grimes and I some iced tea? I just made some peach and it's in the fridge. Also could you check the oven?"

"Hi Granny, Hi Ms. Grimes, I'll be right there with the tea.....You know, my Granny's such a slave driver," replied twenty-year-old blond Brigetta, smiling widely and showing perfect teeth and young full lips. She gave the visitor a wave as she turned toward the kitchenette.

"That child's surely a dream, Emily. You're so lucky. Two great girls for granddaughters. I'm missing my granddaughter so badly. I'm crying all the time. Think I'll ever get over it?" asked Yolanda, sniffling just a little and wiping a stray tear with an embroidered cotton hankie.

"I think soon you'll definitely feel somewhat better, although the sadness and loss will be a long time going. I just can't imagine how I would cope with that. Well, actually, I have a good idea where I would start," said Emily, with a sly wink, and reaching for Yolanda to give her a comforting hug.

"I think I know just what you would do about that, and I appreciate the favor," responded Yolanda with a delicate whisper and touching Emily's arm gently, just as Brigetta came in to the center of the store. She was carrying a silver serving tray with frosty crystal glasses of peach iced tea. Several fresh-baked scones on a dainty rose-trimmed dessert plate smelled sweet and rich. That was another wonderful part of the FAVORS atmosphere;

something was always baking in the little oven. The fans swirled downward with purpose, inviting aromas to circulate throughout the whole buying area.

"You know I'll always have favors," interrupted Emily with a soft smile. "That's why I'm here!"

"Oh, of course, that is why I... we always come to you for our catering needs," stammered Yolanda. "In fact, I'm here to pay my bill for the fantastic baby shower you helped me with. You would think it was the Crown Prince of the Caribbean being born, the way that family was carrying on. But we pulled that sucker off with a flourish! Between your decorations and my good soul food, we are it, girl! There is just no other way to go in this town!" The two older women were grinning and slapped their palms together in a mutual greeting of congratulations.

Brigetta stood and listened to the older ladies bragging on themselves and then went back to the small kitchen hidden at the rear of the store to get a bottle of diet Snapple. True, FAVORS was a great store and she knew eventually and way in the future, Granny Em would be doing all the arrangements for her wedding, when and if she ever found Mr. Right. Now she was perfectly content to go back to nursing school again in the fall and continue the quest for learning. There would always be time for men later on. Look at her older sister, Mikki; she was doing quite well on her own, a top engineer in her field and making lots of money. She could have her pick of men with her brains and beauty, but right now preferred working at the job she loved. Mikki's job and family were what mattered to her. Getting married would come later for both sisters.

Brigetta sipped her drink with a straw she picked from a mason jar in the kitchenette and continued to appraise the two ladies chatting amiably. Yolanda was Jamaican, tall, and very lovely. Her dark, raven-black hair was pulled back tight from her face in a stylish chignon, all elegance and style. She wore a soft blue, sleeveless sundress that dropped just above her small ankles. A turquoise ankle bracelet and matching small square earrings were her only jewelry. Her light brown skin was smooth and wrinkle free, even though she was just a little younger than Emily, maybe early seventies. On the clear unblemished face, Brigetta saw signs of worry. Lines of sadness and lack of sleep were encroaching on territory around her eyes and mouth. But Mrs.

15

Grimes presented an overall picture of timeless beauty, a very classy lady.

Turning now to look at Emily, it was easy to see that she had been fair-haired in her youth, actually a strawberry blonde. Now her head was crowned with silver gray, cut short with curls softly tousled to frame her face. She allowed herself the luxury of a fresh cut and styling every two weeks. She was a good head shorter than Yolanda, but lean and tan, with sculpted muscles that belied her age. Emily wore white cotton Capri's with a white cotton blouse embroidered with pink flamingos with sequin eyes and beaded palm tree accents. She wore flip-flop sandals with a huge silk chrysanthemum atop each foot, toenails painted bright pink. She had at least removed the carpenter's apron to join her customer for tea. Brigetta knew her mom would not approve Emily's outfit. Susan was more the L.L. Bean type. Well, at least Emily had not joined the Red Hat Society, thought Brigetta. She would never have found time for all that. Besides, she loved her Granny Em just exactly the way she was. She could be very controlling, a little outlandish, a little eccentric, but she had a big heart and was lots of fun! Not bad for a seventy-seven-year old widow.

The women were now sitting at the white wrought iron table sipping their tea, huddled together in quiet conversation. As Brigetta dried some coffee cups in the little sink, she couldn't help but admire the lives of the two older women. Both were fit and trim, intelligent, and owned their own successful businesses. They were both wealthy and depended only upon themselves for their welfare. Strong and self-supporting, the way she hoped it would all turn out for her. Then Brigetta saw a check pass from Yolanda to Emily and, strangely enough, also thought she saw some cash, a big wad of cash, in a rubber band. God, just like they were drug dealers or something, Brigetta thought, eyes widening, straining to see. Well, maybe the check was pre-written and the amount had changed. That happened some times. Or else, maybe Yolanda had decided to give her grandmother a big tip. That was not unusual, she supposed, but Yolanda was a good friend of her grandmother's. They usually gave each other new customers, but not extra cash. Shrugging to herself and getting back to her work, Brigetta saw some mail had fallen to the floor. Granny Em's work apron was hanging on the refrigerator door handle, and some of the letters were still hanging out of the pocket. Picking them up, she placed them onto the counter so Emily would be reminded of them. The shop's mail usually came early and Emily was a stickler on getting to it first. There was a small gray envelope but it was empty. Looking around on the floor, she couldn't find its contents. Hoping it was not lost on the main floor of the store, she looked for the return address. "NYC"...New York City? Wondering which friend of Granny Em's lived there, she put the envelope on the top of the other mail, so Emily wouldn't miss it. It smelled feminine and perfumed. Brigetta would ask her about it later and help look for the lost letter. She began to sign for a newly arrived shipment of music boxes to the rear door. Just as she began noticing a cute UPS guy delivered it, she heard sobbing from the front of the store. Wondering what was wrong, she inched forward, peering through the divider of hanging ferns. She saw a tearful Yolanda again hugging Granny Em. Oh yeah, this was about Shakira. Yolanda's granddaughter had been murdered by a dope runner somewhere on the Panhandle of Florida. He had never been caught. He was a career criminal at age twenty-four and was wanted for about a million things. That was several months ago and it appeared that her grief had not lessened. She felt sorry for Ms. Grimes, who had brought her whole family here from Ocho Rios many years ago to get a new start here, supposedly to get away from drugs and crime in Jamaica and then this happens. Yolanda Grimes had the most popular and expensive catering business in the area, CARIBBEAN SOUL. She and Granny Em had worked together for years pulling off the most fabulous parties and celebrations, often in a joint effort. It was only natural the two ladies would seek consolation from each other in times of loss. Brigetta went back to the fridge to get more tea, but when she brought out the pitcher, Ms. Grimes was gone; the little bell at the door was still jingling its good-bye.

"Is everything all right, Granny Em?" asked Brigetta. "I saw Ms. Grimes crying. It was about little Shakira, wasn't it?

"Yeah, Brig, I'm not sure she'll ever get over it. There are just some things you never can get over. That child was always running the streets and getting in trouble, no matter what her momma tried to do for her. And Yolanda did all she could to help her. Paid for counseling, private schools and all that. Shakira just didn't want any help from her mother or grandmother, no way. All grown up at 14 years old," answered Emily.

"But nobody deserves what happened to her, Granny, right?" continued Brigetta.

"Oh no, Darlin', that little girl never got a chance to grow up and get right with herself. Some people do deserve to die, but not a little child. Never a little child," replied Emily with a determined, stone-like face, her eyes suddenly turning hard cold blue. Brigetta went to her grandmother and gave her a kiss. Emily reached for Brigetta and gave her a big long hug.

"Thank you for turning out so great, young lady," said Emily. "You never gave your mom or I a bit of worry."

"Not even when I ran away when I was ten?" asked Brigetta with a grin.

"Trust me. I knew where you were every moment. I also had a pretty good idea how long it would take for you to decide to come back."

The two gave each other a quick grin and another hug. Suddenly at that moment of touching family love, Mrs. Clyde B. Sponseller announced her arrival. A huge woman with orange hair and a purple tent-sized dress was shouting commands to her limo driver outside the front door. She brought with her two white standard poodles. The door was flung open with a crash and the bell clanged loudly into the door jam as Penelope Sponseller made her grand entrance. The huge dogs were jumping and straining at their bejeweled leashes! This proclamation was sure to mean another big occasion to be planned, maybe another birthday party for one of the poodles. Emily ran to the door as if she couldn't wait to hear about the new big event!

"Well, Hello, Bella and Fella, you big sweeties!" exclaimed Emily, as the dogs bounded towards her. Luckily and smartly, the shop's displays were both child and pet proof and safe from all comers. Emily petted and kissed the big white dogs and noted they smelled like Chanel. Probably used the new groomer in town, "Ritzy Pets". She saw their trademark purple glitter nail polish had been freshly applied to the newly clipped doggie nails. Emily did not mind the pets, children, or confusion but had merely rearranged her shop. She grimaced as she saw Fella lift his leg on the door jam. Brigetta saw her glance and discreetly ran to the back for paper towels, disinfectant and deodorizing spray. The shop actually was safe from everything from big purses flopping about, dogs jumping and peeing, or kids with busy gooey fingers. After all, this was how she made her fortune. Emily created

FAVORS. Give the customer good service and good product. Go above and beyond the call of duty and you will be duly compensated. I think that is what they said at the customer service meeting years ago, thought Emily. Give the customer what they need, what they want, and what they can only get from Mrs. Emily Vanderhorn. After all this was Palm Beach and the shop was one of posh Worth Avenue's most upscale and opulent. Everyone who was anyone came to Emily's FAVORS not just for amazing party favors but also for specially designed decorations and gifts.

Mrs. Sponseller cruised the store flinging her multicolored beads from Mardi Gras and fluffing her carrot-colored frizzy hair. "Come on little darlings, you are such smart dogs!" she exclaimed to the staring Emily. "I should have named them 'Mensa' and 'Jeanius'! What do you think, Miss Emily?"

"Oh, I think they have a brilliance of their own. People are aware of that instantly, I'm sure!"

"That is why they're here! Graduation from doggie school! My own babies have graduated!" Penelope beamed with delight and pride as she paraded around the store. She chose several items for the upcoming Dog Obedience School graduation party. Bella and Fella had barely passed the novice class but their accomplishment would be celebrated surely in a most extravagant manner. She proudly confided to Emily that specially made caps and gowns were at this very moment being customized for both poodles. After spending over $6,500 on trinkets, favors, decorations, and special ordered jeweled collars for the dogs, Mrs. Sponseller graciously said, "Emily, I would love for you to join the celebration! You can even have a seat at the "owner's table."

Emily quickly responded, "I will try to make it, but I am not real sure about my schedule since I am taking a little business trip soon." Since this was part of the customer relations policy maybe she would send Brigetta, she thought sneakily, or better yet, talk Susan into going. Mrs. Sponseller said to watch for the engraved invitations to arrive that would be personally signed by each dog's footprint in gold ink. *I can hardly wait*, thought Emily sarcastically.

"Hey, Brig," Emily called to the back of the store after Mrs. Sponseller and her entourage had left, "Can you and Mikki watch the store and Pink Flamingo for me? I need to be away for a week or two." Brigetta was disposing of the soiled towels in the trash can by the back door. She didn't answer.

Emily took out the card from this morning's mail and reread the address. "Ridgeway Apartments, Bldg 4, Citrus City. P.S. I am in my eighties. I cannot do this any more. YOU cannot do this any more. The debt is now considered canceled. But good luck! Always grateful, M."

She quickly stuffed the note back into her pants pocket, giving it a little pat. *Yes, Margaret, this is my last time too, we are both way too old for this!* This last bit of information was vital. Now the waiting was over and she could move ahead with her plans.

"Where are you off to this time Granny, meeting Prince Shahid in Vegas again for a quickie, huh?" responded Brigetta, as she dried her hands and began to apply some lotion. It was a common theme that the girls shared with Granny Em when their mother commented on all the money Emily spent on the girls. Emily had once responded that she was the secret concubine of a Sheik and he sent her millions in return for her sexual favors. The girls, being high school and grade school ages at the time, roared with laughter while Susan was appalled. It had remained a standing joke among them.

"Yep, the old guy is horny again. You know once they've had me, there is no substitute. Ever since I refused to join the harem, he has wanted me all the more. And remember the belly dancing classes? My allure in unending, Darlin'!" continued Emily, enjoying the game and lifting her shirt to do a little belly dance around the display of lingerie. She picked up a red feather boa and swirled it about her chin, trying to look alluring and sexy. Both of them began to laugh until Emily had a fit of coughing and had to retreat to the tiny kitchen. There she got a fresh iced tea and calmed herself while both women continued to giggle off and on.

"Granny, are you all right?" asked Brig, truly concerned. "You've had a bad cough for awhile. Are you sick?"

"God, no. Me? I never get sick. Look at this gorgeous body! Does it look unhealthy?" retorted Emily. "Probably got a feather down my throat."

"Well, I know you look better than most women twenty years younger, but really, Gran, have you been to a doctor lately? You look just a little tired," responded Brigetta.

" I see Dr. Getts on a regular basis. He, of course, wants my body like all other men! But, seriously, I feel fine. Probably some allergy to some new Florida pollen. I'll be fine, I promise," said Emily, reaching for Brigetta's hand, giving it a pat of reassurance and taking another sip of tea.

"Okay, so then will Mikki be in town or what? I heard Mom talking to her last night, something about Dad's birthday, I think. Aren't you going to be here for that? We are going to celebrate that he is going to actually be home for a few weeks," asked Brigetta.

"All the better time for me to be away for my trip. Just doing some merchandise shopping and going to a few seminars in California. I love your Dad but he needs to spend time with you girls and since all of you will be here, I can trust the shop will operate in full swing. I have the greatest confidence in your business abilities," continued Emily.

"Yep, you know we can handle everything here. No problem. When will Mikki get here?"

"Your sister arrives this weekend and has a few weeks of vacation. I can't wait to see her, and won't leave until we get to all spend a few days together. You both have been so much help to me, you just don't know. I love you girls all so much."

"By the way, I found an empty envelope on the floor back there…you had better check and be sure you haven't dropped the note."

"Sure, I'll check. See? You always are on top of everything!"

Emily had plans that were on a specific time schedule, and arrangements had been in readiness many weeks in advance. She had just needed confirmation of that address. Now to proceed as per project scheme. Planning and prioritizing came easily to Emily. Making and managing money were learned skills in which she had become quite accomplished. *Not all favors are done for free. Justice does sometimes come with a price.* No one knew that better than Emily. She was proud to admit to all of that. But it wasn't modesty that left a main part of her talents shrouded in secrecy. Emily had vowed that her much loved family would never know quite all about her life and activities. The security and safety of all family members relied on that.

Chapter 4

As Emily drove home, her head filled with Joseph. Her husband and confidante. She still hadn't quite forgiven him for dying. So much more he had to offer. Another example of life's unfairness.

But with his help, she had bought the building, started the shop from bare bones, and thrived. It had helped carry her through without him. *I'm still mad, though, Joe!*

The shop specialized in items representing the popular Victoria'sn era and also coastal living. Emily had always loved the sea and all the ocean's creatures. To her, the waves and sand, the smell of ocean air, represented God Himself. Antiqued lace swags, elegant long strings of sea pearls, and hand-made table coverings were chosen with huge satin bows. Mostly for weddings and anniversary parties. A small table display was overflowing with heirloom-style purses for gift giving and special occasions. Emily particularly loved the crushed velvet bags with sequins and beads. Joseph had given her a similar purse as an engagement gift.

Clustered in a corner, a few hanging garment racks held translucent lingerie just perfect for bridal showers…or perhaps the mistress of the moment. For the brave and adventurous, thong bikini panties in iridescent shades, fur-trimmed bed jackets, and animal print pajamas in wild surreal patterns hung on scented satin padded hangers. No, FAVORS wasn't an ordinary store. The gift bags with silver logo cost the owner over six dollars each and that was her wholesale price. Adding the opaque silver tissue paper and satin bows and streamers, the gift-wrapping could be just as elaborate and beautiful as the gift itself.

Turning onto the beachfront road, Emily had to pass the Yacht Club, Marina del Mar. She smiled as she turned the wheel of the Jag towards home and recalled the planning and decorating of Sam Treatenburg's 102-foot vessel for the seemingly simple elegance of cocktails and an intimate dinner for two. The drinks and meal were followed by the marriage proposal and presentation of the three-caret diamond ring from Tiffany's & Co., a store just a block away from FAVORS. The yacht had been converted from bachelor pad to fantasy fairy tale ship, with no detail being missed. Tiny white lights were strung from every passageway, just enough that when the main spot light switches were turned off, the boat became a wonderland of beauty. Swags of pale pink sheer were arranged to look like waves and attached sand dollars and tiny shells helped create the illusion. Pink roses were placed in giant porcelain clamshells, lying open as if in invitation. Aromatic rosebud petals were strewn along passageways and on the couple's table. Emily's favorite and most fun part was the wine and cocktail bar. It was covered in waves of blue, then white, satin, rolling to the floor in puddles around the corners of the bar. Atop the bar swam a sparkling pair of ice dolphins, hand carved early that morning, which stood over three feet tall. With the beams of sea blue lighting fixed in their base, the dolphins appeared to leap from the ocean itself. Dangling from the open and seemingly smiling mouth of the larger dolphin was the Tiffany box, holding the priceless blue-white diamond ring. *I would have married him myself. Too bad she said yes.*

Ahead the pink home loomed, awakening and welcoming, rising out of the sand dunes. Emily pushed the security codes into the box, and the heavy iron gate groaned and swung open.

The shop has been a real help to me, thought Emily, as she urged the car towards the garage beneath the house. Most of Emily's customers were either repeat clients or referrals from others who were quite satisfied. Emily was happy to be of service. She loved to decorate and had been artistically creative since she was a child. The fact that owning the small but exclusive store had provided her a fantastic living was not a surprise to anyone in her community except perhaps her daughter. Her only child, Susan, a Yale graduate, was married to Wall Street wizard, Michael Walsh. Her daughter and son-in-law lived very comfortably here in the same community. Emily herself had funded the trust funds and college tuitions for the two granddaughters totally from FAVORS receipts. Susan, though a loving daughter, had once scrutinized her mother's business and at a time had wondered how Emily could afford her lifestyle by selling party decorations. But Susan had seen first hand the gorgeous effects of Emily's handiwork when both granddaughters' high school graduation parties were hosted by Emily's FAVORS. She then realized that the prices others were paying for the extravagance just might be substantial. Emily never talked about her income, but was certainly living well. A lucrative store and a sprawling beachfront estate. No one in the family could argue with the facts.

Emily spent all of Saturday preparing her home so it would be comfortable for the "house-sitters." The girls liked snacks and wine coolers and for the pool to be heated to 88 degrees. She placed freshly laundered sheets and towels in their bedrooms and fluffed the pillows in the dryer. She even added some lavender linen spray to their bedding as an extra touch. Emily's beach house, "Pink Flamingo," which she referred to as a cottage, was really quite a mansion. She loved it like any other member of the family. The estate home on the Atlantic was painted a delicate pink with majestic, white Corinthian columns announcing the entryway. A wide marble staircase led up to the huge front doors. The doors had been imported and were made of teakwood and etched glass. The door's side panels were engraved with seahorses and other marine creatures that welcomed each visitor as they approached the outer foyer. A sparkling crystal chandelier lit the stairway to the front door. Windows and balconies were everywhere and almost all the windows could be opened. Emily had insisted on that during construction, as she loved to smell the sea breezes, hear the sounds of the rhythmically crashing waves, and the piercing calls of seagulls. The 9,000 square foot home and gardens occupied a full three acres of Atlantic beachfront property, completely gated for security and entirely and lushly landscaped. Emily had done most of the garden work herself, having an artist's eye for color, shape, and texture. Giant pink and white oleanders bloomed everywhere along the boardwalks to the beach. *They're poisonous, Mother. Well, of course, Dear!* Crape myrtle, sago palms, lantana, even lovely climbing roses seemed undaunted by the fact that they lived precariously by the salty sea. Wavy stalks of sea oats covered rolling dunes along the planked wooden walkways accessing the beach. Except for the trees she had contracted into the design or the immense palms she had added to the entranceway, she could take pride in the fact that this house was all her own work. The Pink Flamingo was her pride and joy, full of her life and its secrets. Secrets that the big wonderful house would never offer in betrayal. It presented a safe haven that enveloped its loving caretaker with sturdy stucco walls, not imprisoning but protecting.

Inside, the home was private, yet welcoming. A contemporary seaside spirit invited both entertaining and seclusion as it bent to the will of the mistress. Pink and white-flecked marble from the stairway entrance edged its way into the house, a shining spectacle of reflection and light. Dazzling ocean views from breezy porches and balconies seemed to invite guests to sit and sip a cold drink. Thickly padded lounges and wooden deck chairs painted in pastels meant relaxation and luxury. Sitting there for hours with a good novel, watching dolphins in the sparkling turquoise water on their way north or south, Emily could forget all her worries just looking out at the sea. Feeling its waves come and go as naturally as her lungs moved air in and out, she could almost become hypnotized into feeling well and happy. In fact, she felt happy and at ease most of the time now. At her age, there should be time to reflect and enjoy life.

Early Sunday morning, Mikki arrived from Orlando and made time to spend with Granny Em and Brigetta at the beach house. On Monday, Emily, Susan and the two girls went to lunch at the country club, played a little tennis and even met friends at a polo match for drinks and fun. Michael arrived that evening and had taken them all out for his birthday to his favorite seafood restaurant. He beamed with pride when escorting his entourage of beautiful women. Living in a penthouse in New York did not make up for the time away from his family. During these infrequent but wonderful times at home, he relished every moment. He was never eager to return to the Big Apple by himself. Sometimes Susan would accompany him back to the city and they would see all the Broadway shows, stay out late, and act like newlyweds again. Sometimes the whole family would go to New York to see Michael. Brigetta and Mikki were likely to be found in the all nightclubs, dancing the evening away. Sometimes Granny Em even joined them on their evenings out clubbing, since she could boogie with the best of them! Those nights they would all retire to Michael's apartment, but only after sandwiches or even breakfast at the nearby deli. Michael would soon be going back to work in New York, but not until he had enjoyed every moment with his family in Palm Beach.

Tuesday afternoon, the girls volunteered to drop off their Granny Em at the airport in Ft. Lauderdale. She had promised them the keys to the Carnival Red S-Type Jaguar she had bought last year. Emily had opted for a sporty five-speed manual transmission that was specially installed. Then she had taught both girls how to handle the custom performance-built car. Four hundred supercharged horses all painted red. Yeehaw! Emily had always loved horses anyway. The comfy ivory leather interior with wood grain trim held all the bells and whistles that could be ordered or installed. Emily loved the GPS system. It was great for impromptu road trips. The girls loved the premium stereo system and filled the CD holder with all their favorites. As they tooled down the highway toward the passenger drop-off area, Emily warned the girls not to argue over who got to drive where and when. After all, there were other cars in the garage for each to use. Each granddaughter had been given a BMW of her choice for high school graduation, so it was not like they were "car poor" or anything. For college graduation, Mikki wanted to keep her BMW she had received after high school and so was awarded a nice condo in Orlando near her firm. They were both so loved and pampered by their Granny. Not spoiled though, thought Emily. And both girls woke up on the same planet each morning. Definitely not the Paris Hilton ditzy clueless types, these kids were smart, appreciative, well educated, well mannered and beautiful. Maybe she was just slightly prejudiced, but they were great girls.

In the secured passenger drop-off area, Emily made a flourish of grabbing her ticket from the console. She then quickly grabbed her two carry-on bags from the trunk and kissed the girls good-bye, waving the ticket in her hand. After a brief good-bye, the girls both ran laughing from the secured area towards the driver's side of the red ride waiting with trunk still raised, keys now in Mikki's hand, and jammed their butts simultaneously into the seat.

"Girls!" Emily admonished, but couldn't help but laugh as she sauntered off towards the sliding doors to the lobby. They will work it out. Sometimes they acted like they were both still back in high school, but they had always been best buddies. They never fought for real. In fact, the girls were so busy arranging their seating in the car that they never seemed to notice their Granny Em slowly heading towards the "Rentals" sign arrow. As they pulled away, Emily had watched, but did not see Mikki glance back, just a tinge of worry crossing her face. Emily said a little prayer and began to shred her ticket for California, placing it in a trash receptacle. Laughing about the girls had brought on another bought of coughing. She headed for a drinking fountain and popped two Tylenol. *Miserable headache, must be coming down with something.* Near the car rental area booths, there was a bank of large storage lockers. Emily quickly found the small key in her change purse, tucked in beside the small gray card that had come in the mail. The key slid into the lock easily as Emily nonchalantly glanced around. The locker door squeaked open revealing a long bag, almost like a golf club bag, and another military issue duffle bag. Emily grabbed up both items and heaved the shoulder straps into place. Hauling the heavy items, she approached the Hertz rental counter, wearing tennis shorts and her Oakley sunglasses. Ahead, she saw the clerk, a young Hispanic man about 25 years old, whose name badge read Miguel Cruz.

"*Buenos tardes,* rental for Kensington, please?" she asked.

"Number 52, row 7, green Taurus, Mrs. Kensington," the clerk said, as he handed her some forms, maps, and information packets. "The return is marked 'open.' Is that correct?"

"Yes, I'm not sure how long I will need the car, but I have prepaid for a week on my VISA. You got that, right?" asked Emily.

"Got it right here, *Senora.* Are you new to the area, just visiting?" he asked cordially, as he passed some forms to Emily.

"No, not exactly, I live in Florida; just need a rental for a while. My car is being repaired," responded Emily.

"I see your address is listed as Naples. You drove over here and then your car broke down, huh? We see a lot of that. Usually it's the Yankees who have cars not prepared for all the heat. Those cars just dry up and die. Good for the rental business though. Have a good stay anyway," said Miguel Cruz, as he motioned for the next customer in line.

"*Gracias,*" replied Emily as she turned away picking up the heavy bags. Emily snatched up the keys and paperwork, left the air conditioned rental booth, and headed for the shade-covered car pick-up area. As his customer left the building, the desk clerk left his window and customers momentarily and went to the table at the rear of the office.

Raising the receiver, he dialed a cell phone number, reaching an automated voice mail. He said, "It is 2:05 PM. The person I believe you are interested in has checked out a car in the name of Kensington. She will be leaving in a green Taurus. No return scheduled. Hope this helps you. *Adios.*"

Emily quickly found the Taurus, tossed her bags easily into the trunk, and headed for the gate. After showing her rental agreement, Emily was on her way. Now she felt a little overheated. Another scorcher. Glad to be in the car's blasting cool air, she turned all the vents her way, and cranked the fan switch all the way up. Emily was talking to herself and cursing that maybe she had to take better care of herself. That would be all she would need, to end up in some God forsaken hospital, who knows where. But she pushed the radio dials and was soon singing along with Shania Twain and feeling better. Maybe it was more hot flashes. *Does it ever end?* Menopause marches on. Hot flashes, power surges, just a damn hot day. *Women's work is never done*, she thought as she accelerated the Ford up the ramp onto the Florida Interstate, heading north.

Chapter 5

It was the second day since Emily had left the airport in her rented Taurus. She was getting used to the automatic transmission and had stopped trying to use the nonexistent clutch. On the Tuesday afternoon of her arrival, she circled Citrus City to get her bearings. Streets, alleys, parking lots. Emily thought of this as a reconnaissance mission. She felt she knew enough about the town by 6 P.M. and drove to Scott's Self Storage. She punched in the numbers to the gate's keyless entry and turned the car toward the rented garage. She had chosen a rental space near the rear of the storage facility. Angling the car into the small space, she flipped on the light switch and closed the door. The boarding house she had picked was only a block away, but before she walked there, she needed to make some changes. After a quick mutation in clothing and identification, she picked up her rolling suitcase from the trunk and headed out the driveway, locking the car in the garage for safekeeping.

Down the street, the sign for Chez Louise Room and Board was freshly painted and the house looked well kept. It was a large white Colonial with a huge wrap-around porch, complete with cane-seated rockers and a swing hanging by chains from the ceiling. It was cheap and in the center of town, and catered only to women. The room she had rented was small and inconspicuous to match her new circumstances. She was now poor and reclusive Mildred Carr. She had all the paperwork and ID to prove it if needed. She signed in with Louise Chartrel and paid in cash for a month in advance as she described her bus trip from Atlanta.

"Your room is upstairs on the right. The bathroom is across the hall. There are two other ladies up there, but the bathroom is big and there is plenty of hot water. I just got a new heater for the water tank and it works great! No complaints so far!" announced Louise cheerily as she put Emily's cash in her cigar box. "If you need anything, just come down here to my room or the kitchen. We include breakfast with your room, so often you can find me over there," she continued, pointing to the large dining room. The room was covered with wallpaper portraying huge magnolias on a cranberry background. There was a large picture window and old French doors leading to the porch. Moss draped oak trees and a recently cut lawn could be seen outside. Someone was trying very hard to make a go of this place. Emily saw the prior grace and beauty of the ancient Old South home.

"This is all quite lovely, Ma'am. I am sure this'll be just fine," said Emily as she gathered her suitcase and began to pull it up the old planked stairs. She found her room and unpacked a few items, setting them on the dresser. The bed was large and concave, but the sheets smelled like they had been dried outside in the fresh air. There was a ceiling fan, but no air conditioning. Emily pushed open the window and an immediate breeze entered the room. She moved the solitary upholstered chair to the window area and sat down to catch her breath and think. The sunlight at the window was filtered through the huge oak tree, making the room bright but cool. This place was almost too nice, but it would work for what she needed. She pulled out the box of vinyl gloves from the suitcase and put on a pair. She also put a shower cap over her hair. No prints, no DNA. If anyone happened to see her in the room in this getup, they would write her off as a strange old lady and that was just fine.

For days, all went well and as planned. Finally on Saturday she had gone to her P.O. Box at the Citrus City main branch post office. She found the package waiting for her as she had ordered. Carrying it back to her room, she placed the carton on the table and began to slice open the box. Not using a box cutter like at the store, she deftly pared open her parcel with her lipstick case knife. This was a weapon that resembled an ordinary tube of lipstick. However, this one won't be found at Walgreen's cosmetic department. It contains a built-in knife that screws up to the top like an actual tube of lipstick. The knife blade extends to one and one-half inches. Excellent for self-defense, self-protection, or self-preservation. With a few deft slashes through the cardboard, the umbrella length box came open easily and Emily unfolded the plastic wrapped items. An aluminum blowgun, measuring about 49 inches in length and three eights inch in diameter was revealed. A small box encased within the package revealed a piece of rubber. This was the mouthpiece to attach to the blowgun. Several five-inch darts resembling hatpins were folded into brown waxed paper. Under test conditions, this blowgun had an effective firing range of 30 yards. At this distance, a sheet rock target was penetrated one-quarter inch. At 15 yards, 400 pages of a telephone book could be penetrated with extreme accuracy. When discharged, the ad in the mail order catalog had read, there would be little or no sound. This carefully concealed weapon would fit nicely into her tripod cane, hollowed and made to order. Emily pulled the cane from her duffle bag and inserted the weapon into the bottom of the cane, then carefully replaced the rubber foot. The extra glass vial of toxic venom would fit nicely into her other lipstick tube. *A girl just can't have too many lipsticks*, mused Emily to herself. Just a quick dip into the brown glass vial, load the dart, fire, and it would be finished. She was not worried about missing her target. A neck shot, close to the jugular would be all it would take. If all went well, she could be home by Monday night and regain ownership of that bright red kitty cat of a car.

On Sunday afternoon she packed her worn fanny pack with a few other items. One thing, a pen and pencil set in appearance, was quite a bit more. The mechanical pencil contained not lead but a spring loaded steel spike. An excellent stabbing instrument patterned after the "lancet" used by the Office of Strategic Services. The innocent looking matching pen could easily be purchased mail order. It was called "The Guardfather" and reputed to go from "locked to cocked in 1/250th of a second with a press of the pocket clip." It cost only $29.95. A nice price to pay for a very useful ballpoint pen. The shaft was four inches long and spring loaded like the pencil. Emily's additional "just in case" item included a Chinese spinwheel that consisted of eight nails each measuring about three inches long and welded together to form a pronged device. When thrown through the air, it would hit a target in much the same way as a dart.

On her second day in town, Emily had found and bought an old bike at a local junk store. Work on the bike was done late at night. She had it locked to a small cedar tree behind the boarding house. It was a simple task to alter the handlebars, now loaded with a single shotgun shell on both ends. The handlebar would serve as the barrel of the gun. The shell could be fired manually by depressing a bell that would release the spring-loaded firing pin, driving it against the base of the shell. This, of course, was quite noisy and usually tossed the bike rider sideways with quite a jolt. A ride-by shooting was not really Emily's style, but being prepared was a motto for more than just Boy Scouts. And it was always good to have some simple back up plans. Emily decided not to insert the firing pin until she reached the apartments that were her final destination. She didn't want any kids to drive off in the loaded bike and inadvertently try to ring that bell. No, that would not be good. Emily also carried with her an extra gas cap wherever she went. It was especially handy for road trips. One-tank trips took on a whole new meaning when Emily was the driver. This gas cap did actually hold fuel in the tank, but also concealed a dagger. The blade was welded to the chrome cap. Under normal circumstances, this weapon was well hidden, but easily accessible. *Heaven help anyone stupid enough to try to hijack this little old lady at the gas pump*, Emily thought, smiling to herself at her own brilliance. Planned so well in advance like everything she did, Emily did not expect anything to go even slightly wrong.

The mistake was so simple and yet so stupid. After earlier surveillance of the area, Emily donned her best costume of homelessness. She had to cringe as she put on the dirty flowered blouse and oversized elastic waist striped pants. *Yikes!* she thought, as she looked in the bedroom mirror. She could not stand being dirty, something learned in childhood, but had managed to put on the well-worn dirty garb. She rubbed a tiny bit of garden soil onto her elbows and knees and smeared it around. Well, she certainly was quite a mess. A garish smear of red lipstick painted an almost clown-like smile onto her face. It was all a familiar part of becoming another person. She gave her hair a bit of a toss just for good measure. Emily popped two more Tylenol and two swigs of generic cough medicine. It was now almost 8:30 P.M. and battalions of mosquitoes would be out in army-like forces. She allowed herself one more reflective glance in the door window on her way out. This horrible outfit would be all the insect repellent anyone would need, she decided. Gathering all the needed items together, she went out the back door, picked up the bike from the side of the house and started out pedaling slowly through the darkening streets. Toting the small bag and cane and riding a bike, she was just part of the everyday scenery. She quickly neared the south group of apartment buildings about a mile away. It was fairly dark as she arrived, but she knew where she was going. More winded from the bike ride than she expected, she leaned the bike against an overflowing green trash dumpster and attempted to catch her breath.

"Stay there, Trigger," she breathlessly commanded the yellow rusted bike, as she patted its worn vinyl seat. "I'll be right back and you be ready to high tail it outta here, okay? Hey, and be on the look-out for bad guys!"

Emily edged her way in a slow, ambling walk towards Building Four. To anyone bothering to glance her way, she looked like an old woman searching the grounds for cigarette butts or lost coins. Though her head was tilted down, her eyes looked up. She needed to get to the roof. She saw the fire escape ladder and glanced around for observers. There were none. She grabbed the bottom of the high ladder and pulled. Though rusty, it seemed sturdy enough. She climbed and it held. Reaching the top and throwing her weapon over the roof edge, she crawled over the top. While preparing her equipment, she fingers slipped and a vial of toxin bounced off her grabbing hands and landed on the tar roof with a crunch. It was then she realized she had forgotten her bag at the bottom. What was she thinking? She needed the extra vial in the lipstick case. She began a careful but hurried journey back down the steps. Her first error in judgment in a long time, she would later recall. A nagging cough, a fever, and poor judgment all added up to a fall from a ladder. She was about eight feet from the ground when her left leg, balancing on a step, suddenly crashed through the brittle iron rust. She felt a streak of pain jab her right knee as she slipped and lost her grip. She fell headfirst and hard, her last thoughts being a self-depreciating reprimand, "*Amateur!*" But she had fallen in complete outward silence, no scream or yelp of pain. Perfect control, a learned conditioning, even in the disaster of failure. Lying in the black stillness, unconscious, she never heard the rescue squad, sirens and flashing lights, helpful anonymous images that would carry her to safety and assistance.

Chapter 6

Citrus City's only hospital was temporarily quiet at 6 A.M. the next morning. In room 311, a large east-facing window was slowly allowing Monday to come inside. Soft streams of early Florida sun peeked tentatively through slightly parted drapes. Vague shadows gently touched the sleeping patient as if to see if she was yet awake. Surrounding her, the practical enameled walls and the freshly waxed floors were both see-yourself-shiny. The Styrofoam pitcher of icy water and the small plastic cup with bendable straw had been recently refreshed. Despite the clean simplicity which showed care and concern, there were no flowers on the bedside stand. There were no cards or photos on the wall-based bulletin board, no get-well banners, or florist shop balloons. The life contained within the cool chrome rails of the hospital bed was silent and still. The only sounds were the intrusive bleepings of monitoring equipment. A worn but freshly laundered cotton hospital gown covered the patient's chest, but the ties hung loose at her neck. From her left shoulder poked an array of tubes and wires connecting the frail looking body to life itself. The elderly female patient had angular facial features, good cheekbones, and slightly freckled skin that, even in illness, looked fashion model clean and clear. Her short gray hair was now tangled and unkempt, but bore signs of a good cut and recent styling. Fingernails had been stripped of polish but were meticulously manicured and filed short with smooth cuticles. Yet so far the new admission to Bed 2 had been alone and unclaimed.

Abruptly the heavy hospital room door opened and two staff members entered from the awakening corridor and approached the bedside. "Her breathing seems okay now, Kate. How was her night?" asked Dr. Bob Belmont, medical resident, standing and yawning as he merely glanced at the still woman. After his one-second appraisal, he and the nurse carried on their conversation as if the patient were not only inanimate, but also invisible and deaf. The two hospital employees did, however, manage to gaze appreciatively into each other's eyes, smiling, and at first only barely noticing the bedfast old lady and the monitors.

"Well," continued the nurse, breaking the trance, "after the Lasix, her rales and wheezes began to quiet. Temp is still up, about 101, despite the Ancef drip. We have been infusing since about 11 P.M. when they brought her up from the ER. She was temporarily lucid enough on admission to say there were no known allergies. Has been awake off and on, more off than on, though." Katherine Bingham, R.N., the night shift supervisor, continued, shrugging her shoulders and sighing, "I just don't understand it. They found her near Ridgeway apartments, unconscious and lying on the ground near one of the outside fire escapes. Not exactly a haven for the homeless over there. It looked to the paramedics that she had fallen while climbing on the ladder to the roof! I guess that was how she sustained the leg wound. She apparently gashed it open on a rusty step on the way down."

Pausing to pull back the sheet, exposing the leg in question, she continued, "You might take a look at it. Took 24 sutures just to get it approximated. Did quite a number on her right knee."

The doctor looked at the thick rolls of gauze holding the bandage together and began to pull on latex gloves from his jacket pocket. He carefully lifted the edge and shined his small medical flashlight under the wrappings. "Looks like another excellent job from ER," Dr. Bingham announced. "Nice blue sutures, and except for some scarring, should heal reasonably well."

He pushed his glasses back up his nose, asking, "Was there an ortho consult? I would wonder about any internal tears or damage to the joint."

Katherine took the gloves from him and tossed them in the trash receptacle, answering, "Think everything looked good. Alex Morrell was on call last night, so we can double check with him."

"Good, Morrell is the best. I'll be seeing him later for some golf anyway."

Sighing with perplexity, Katherine continued, "I just don't get it. She was wearing a rag-tag Goodwill outfit that even my bingo addicted grandmother wouldn't touch, old Nike tennis shoes and had a big old flowered purse full of weird junk, like a pen and pencil set in a nice case, screwdriver, lipstick case labeled "Passion Red" ....you know, bag lady style. It just doesn't fit."

"Well, Oh Sheltered One, there are bag ladies in this little crappy town, you know. Maybe she thought she could sleep safely up on the roof. She's just another lost soul who lives on McDonald's dumpster munchies. What doesn't fit about that?" queried Bob. "Other than the fact that the Ridgeway area is drug central, I mean."

"Dearest Doctor Bob, are you going to bother to further examine the patient? Or even read her chart, like my nurse's notes, or the ER report? This should especially interest you…. Your patient was wearing underneath all that carnival style, Victoria's Secret iridescent pink glam bra and matching tap panties. Not your everyday bag lady undies, would you say? This was like $100 worth of lingerie, not to mention that her legs and armpits were clean-shaven. Her skin is smooth and not dry and cracked like we usually see with street people. Probably well-lotioned by Giorgio or something. Now what cardboard box has all those latest amenities for personal hygiene?" retorted Kate.

"Wow, could you show me the evidence, or maybe tonight you could model something like it? I had better get the full picture, I can tell. I really love those see-through numbers, with lace, too. Maybe a thong? You know, so I could get the full understanding of the situation. It could help me be a better doctor!" responded Bob, with a lecherous grin, peering over his wire-rimmed glasses.

"I just knew you would say that, you are such a perv! Seriously, this lady mumbled that she was 70 something years old. Obviously she came from somewhere where someone was taking care of her financially. But we checked all the local nursing homes, assisted living centers, group homes, and no one has had any walkaways," said Katherine. "And of course, no ID of any kind."

"Ok, ok, always worth a try. Wish you would let me take you to dinner some time though," said Bob as he began to more closely examine his newly assigned patient, "and I love blue, no padding, no underwires?"

"Uh huh, right," Katherine groaned. "Let's worry about the patient this morning, okay, Doctor Bob?"

The small and delicate looking woman under the sheet was breathing quietly. The doctor took out his stethoscope and listened carefully. Her respirations were shallow but lung sounds showed some improvement from the prior ER reports. Further examining, the doctor actually pulled his hand back in surprise! Expecting soft flaccid muscle tissue, he was shocked at the hardness beneath his inquiring fingers. Her body showed not emaciation or wasting as expected, but firm, toned muscling. Even more surprising was the presence of continuing tan skin …all over. No tan marks! Well, wherever she came from and whoever she was, she certainly did not get that bronze color from living under I-75, thought her doctor. Dr. Bob Belmont could not help but become immediately more intrigued about his Jane Doe patient.

"Hey, Kate, I think I figured it out. She was climbing to the roof for some nude sunbathing when she fell!" offered Dr. Belmont at a whisper, glancing slyly at Kate from his peripheral vision, while placing the stethoscope here and there on the patient's chest and abdomen.

"Yeah, that's what I always do, go tanning in the middle of the night. That always works," countered Nurse Bingham, suppressing a laugh while avoiding direct eye contact with the doctor. She could smell his after-shave and she just wanted to grab him, pull him close, and inhale deeply!

"Well, maybe she wanted to beat the early morning crowds?" suggested Dr. Belmont with a silly smile on his face, as he again stood erect and put his stethoscope back around his neck.

Kate groaned and just rolled her eyes.

After completing his exam, Dr. Belmont left for the nurse's station to write orders for blood work and review the ER chart, lab and X-ray reports. Kate left the room to continue her morning patient assessment rounds and get ready for report and shift change. She was thinking that Bob was always clowning but in actuality he had a lot of concern for his patients. She really liked that about him. The fact that he was handsome, intelligent, and also liked her was a big plus. He was built like the college quarterback he once had been, with dark curly hair, and very dark brown eyes. Those eyes, thought Kate, with the thin rimmed glasses, so sexy, so radiating intelligence and kindness. Sooner or later, maybe they would find time for each other away from the hospital. Kate's request for transfer to the day shift had been granted. She smiled to herself as she thought that soon she would actually have a life.

Room 311 was again relatively quiet. Pudgy Helen in yellow scrubs from housekeeping was outside the door, ready to begin the daily mopping of the floors. The large cotton mop slopped noisily into the disinfected water and Helen began swishing it from side to side across the floor. The smell of Lysol began to permeate the room. The chatter of employees, muffled by sounds of nurses pushing the rattling medication carts in the hall, could be heard, subtle and vague. Numbly, and as if groping her way through a fog, the patient began to regain her full sense of consciousness. Lying quite still and not daring to move, she assessed herself from the inside out. She had listened quietly to the voices of the doctor and nurse, feigning her total comatose state. Now, cautiously and at first just mentally, she did a head to toe appraisal of her body. Everything was there, no missing body parts. Everything was movable but stiff. *Damned arthritis!* There was a little pain in her right knee and most of all, extreme fatigue and a headache that wouldn't quit.

"Think, think, think! Don't move or give anything away. Become aware of yourself first. You seem safe, but until you know, lie still, think quietly…feel…sense. Survive," thought the patient as she listened to the sounds in the corridor. "I am Mildred. Good, continue to get that brain in gear. I am simply Mildred Carr. I was feeling a little woozy and I fell. Rusty piece of scrap iron they call a fire escape. Think, think, think! God! I fell while doing an important favor! Shit, shit, shit! Oh no, where is my …?" Her returning thoughts and awareness had sent her heart racing into a sudden machine gun rhythm! Immediately a warning beep rang loud and she instantly knew! "Right, I am in a God damned hospital! Control! Get control! That would be fucking grand, set off alarms, they come in to do CPR, start hooking up paddles, all set to zap the hell out of me! Better look alive quick, just be careful!" As in everything else, Emily Vanderhorn had great internal control, a learned technique, very handy in many a precarious situation.

The alarm had set off a code call for the third floor and the medical team streamed quickly into Room 311 like ants on a dead bug, armed with a crash cart loaded with needles and filled syringes of various drugs that would kill you or cure you. The planned attack was squelched when the small lady in Bed 2 squinted open her bright blue eyes and murmured, "Where am I, honey?" in her best old lady raspy voice. She even threw in a bit of an Alabama Southern drawl for good measure.

Eagerly Nurse Kate jumped right in, "Remember? This is a hospital, dear. You have a touch of what we believe is pneumonia and you fell."

The nurse took the patient's small hand in hers when she was answered with a blank stare. Those eyes were very hard to read. Cold blue, like hardened steel, yet sparkly bright and ready to offer cheer and laughter? Who was this woman? What paradox was hidden here? The nurse was instantly both confused and intrigued, but ready for any mysterious challenge.

"Do you remember falling? You hit your head and you had a little fever. Who are you?" Katherine continued, anxious for answers. That was just the beginning of the flurry of questions Kate wanted to ask, but knew to let the tired woman go slowly. She gently touched the old lady's arm with her other hand to show her concern. She too, then felt the surprise of the underlying hard musculature, as she gently stroked the soft, tan skin.

"Of course, I know who I am, but I just forgot for right now," responded Emily in her most sweet and mellow tone. "Do you know who you are? Hope so, otherwise not much hope for someone your age," she couldn't help but add while scrunching down in the bed to appear even more small and fragile. May as well have a little fun while she was here.

Nurse Katherine's eyes first widened, then she smiled, her own green eyes crinkling up with a pleasant awareness. The little lady was quite okay for now. "I am Katherine Bingham, your nurse," answered Kate.

"My name is Mildred, Mildred Carr," added the patient with a haughty attempt at indignation. "And I am really tired right now. Wake me up for breakfast!" And that was about all the information she was going to share right now. Bits and pieces, little by little, lies would be fed to the staff to be greedily absorbed, just enough to buy escape time. Emily then closed her eyes and went into an apparent sleep mode, meaning "Bye-bye, see'ya" to the hovering and plainly astonished staff.

Kate smiled at the newfound attitude of her new patient. Then she waved everyone away and back to his or her stations to await a more dire "Code Blue." Efficiently she disconnected all the monitor equipment per Dr. Belmont's recent orders. Then she automatically began to arrange the sheets and pillow on Mildred's bed like a mother hen with a newly hatched chick in the nest. At least her new charge was feeling better. And soon they would have other information. Nurse Bingham knew in time she would have someone to call. A family member, a friend, maybe even a spouse would soon be coming to Citrus to claim their dearly beloved.

Maybe one of her daughters was a sales clerk or even a partner in Victoria's's Secret... maybe at the Orlando store where she herself shopped. Right now Kate wanted to get the night's green scrubs off her tired body and get home to bed. She hurriedly walked towards the staff lounge and locker area. No sign of Dr. Belmont. He had been paged to the ER soon after leaving Mrs. Carr's room earlier in the morning. Arriving at the staff dressing area, she began to strip off the pants and top. Alone, she appraised herself in the full-length mirror. Not too bad for thirty-something. She was still proud of the image in the reflection. Reddish brown hair pulled back in a neat ponytail, smooth skin with the nose and cheeks faintly tinted with those Irish born freckles, and a tall thin physique. Maybe she and the good doctor could become a great team, even away from Citrus City Hospital. The day shift would soon be hers and she could hardly wait.

Back in Room 311, Emily was now fully aware. She remembered she had fallen near an old building wall and rescuers had assumed she was attempting to climb the fire escape. She recalled that actually she had slipped as she was coming back down the ladder to retrieve an item from her bag. The ladder had fallen apart beneath her foot. Not a very well maintained piece of junk, she had noted. How can a landlord get away with failed building inspections? *Guess I will have to sue*, she smirked to herself. She had been heading up to the roof all right, trying to fulfill her obligation to society. Her work ethic was such that a minor illness and a little shortness of breath would not let her stray from her carefully laid plans. Timing was everything in her career. She remembered becoming dizzy after trying to hold in a coughing spell. Her throat had felt like she had swallowed a dozen duck feathers. Just try not to cough with a tickle like that. Impossible. The fever had been there for a few days and she had taken some Tylenol to help that. Must have been the cough syrup that made her mind less than clear. She remembered feeling more than just a little boo-boo brained. No wonder half the kids in the nation were now sucking down cough syrup for a joyride. What next? Soon there would be warning labels on bananas. Was there anything that was actually safe for you anymore? Anyway, how stupid to fall there of all places, she thought. Caution and extreme agility were tools of her trade, and she was good at it. Just finish the favor and she would have been home. It wasn't that she didn't like doctors or didn't take care of herself. It was just a bad time and the wrong place. She should have been at the lovely Beachside Clinic with familiar Dr. Getts, instead of here in this small Florida town, home of more than just a few douche bag dopers. There would be lots of explaining to do unless she could think fast and get well enough to get out of here quickly. Pneumonia? This turn of events was foreboding. Emily was not used to failing, either physically or in her career. Obstacles yes, failure never. The new plan would consist of being the slightly incompetent patient, hiding her return to wellness, and disappearing at the earliest convenience. Going back to the rooming house on Jackson Street, although temporary anyway, was no longer an option. A new non-compromised set-up would have to be put in place to finish the favor as promised. It wouldn't be hard. This place was just so convenient. But tracking of Social Security ID, asking for Medicaid numbers and other intrusions into her identity just couldn't happen. She had to make sure of that. So far her lack of responses had been noted, she was sure, as some sort of dementia, caused either by Alzheimer's or from her illness and fall. But that had been the reason for her success so far. She was just an elderly, sometimes confused woman who used a tripod cane. Wondering then where the cane was, she saw it propped handily by the small locker in her room. She would have to remember to grab it on her way out. It would be sure to come in handy later. Now that the cane's enclosed aluminum blowgun had been left on the roof, Emily would have to order another from her catalog supplier. That was but a minor inconvenience for now. She smiled and turned in the bed, pulling the sheet over her shoulder, trying not to stretch or bump the painful knee. It still amazed her what could be found through various militia magazines like "Soldiers of Fortune" and the even the Internet. It was nothing to see ads for "sound suppressor products," "laser sights," or "new and interesting arms." Online stores were available to sell everything and anything, no questions asked and safely delivered to any P.O. Box she desired. And there were lots of those. Addresses everywhere in and out of the country. She smiled as she thought it was sometimes hard to even keep track of herself, so how could anyone else find her?

Back at the third floor nurse's station, Mrs. Carr's pneumonia was the current diagnosis being discussed. There were some areas of consolidation on her chest X-ray that Dr. Belmont was hoping would clear with the antibiotics, specifically the Ancef. But the densities were of some concern. With wandering street people one always considered the possibility of TB, and Mantoux skin testing had been started. The congestion in her lungs was working some havoc on her heart, which was strong but under some stress. Getting rid of excess fluids should help her breathing and ease the workload of her heart. The laceration on her leg was long and jagged but definitely not life threatening. Any infection there should be also helped with the antibiotic treatment. A precautionary tetanus booster vaccine had been given in the ER. The leg would just need some time to heal. Luckily for Ms. Carr, the bone and cartilage of the knee was not damaged. The best thing now was a schedule of rest and controlled walking to improve circulation. For now Mildred Carr would remain a hospital patient. As her mental and physical condition improves, she will be probably considered for nursing home placement, thought Bob. Ms. Carr had not as yet given a home address, so she was probably just a nut case on the loose. Who knew you could find confused elderly these days climbing up three-story ladders? That was probably how she kept in shape, running up and down fire escape ladders, he thought to himself. He had just heard on Fox News of a couple that left home to go to their daughter's house for dinner at 5 P.M. just a few miles away. Three days later the State Police hundreds of miles away found them, out of gas, parked by the side of the road just outside of downtown Atlanta. Until then, their daughter had no clue that there was that much mental deterioration. Like Mildred, they, too, would need 24-hour security. Surely Ms. Carr had relatives who might not even know where she was. Perhaps further information could be pried from his patient once she was on the mend. He felt confident that Kate was the nurse for that job. She had previously worked on an Alzheimer's unit for years and was patient and kind. She could elicit memory recall from even the most unfortunate victims of brain deterioration. Besides, this would give him another reason to meet with Kate. He loved that sort of consultation work. Maybe they would discuss the case over cocktails at Oceanside Grille. That is, if she ever had time off when he was not on call. At least she would soon be on the day shift. He couldn't have felt happier than when she told him her transfer had been approved. Now there was double the chance they could be slugging down Margaritas and rolling around in the sack. Some day. He felt she was interested, but work came first…for both of them.

Emily was again motionless in her faux sleep. Churning inside her brain, plans were made. She could stay here long enough to regain strength. She would leave during the busiest part of the hospital day, maybe tomorrow or the next day. She would slip out unnoticed, fading into the warm sun and hurrying traffic flow. Her captors had deemed her well enough to disconnect the monitors, so she was no longer leashed to the bed. Just a small hanging bag of iv fluids was attached to her left arm. Once she was energized enough to assure getaway, she would just walk out. Shuffling nonchalantly down the baking hot sidewalk to her safe haven, she could quickly reorganize, finish up and go back home. There she would find family and friends, her beach house, and her cat. She looked forward to the return of days of normalcy. Sometimes the life of Mildred Carr, the derelict with a fascinating wardrobe, was just too stressful. It was time to retire. If only someone would take over the responsibility. Too much cerebral activity was wearing her out and soon sleep was no longer a pretense.

All of the morning staff had now arrived. Darla Simmons, one of the nurse's aides for the West Main Medical wing, brought breakfast to her bedside table at 8 A.M. sharp. She was a spiky-haired blonde, cheery girl who looked like she graduated from high school yesterday, but in actuality was probably about Brigetta's age. She had a pimpled face and looked like her hair needed a good shampooing, but she brought with the food a wide grin. Service with a smile was the best thing to happen so far. Not exactly room service at the Ritz, to which she was more commonly accustomed, but it wasn't too horrible. Actually, Emily realized she was starving. She hadn't eaten much of anything for the last three days.

"My name is Darla and I'll be your server today," joked Darla pleasantly, setting the tray on the bedside table. "Usually one of the kitchen waiters brings in the trays, but since you are new, I thought I would meet you."

"How nice," replied Emily, trying to size up the girl.

Emily smiled back at the almost overly cheery girl and felt her stomach growling with anticipation after smelling the faint odor of food. After being propped by the raising of her electrically operated bed, she grabbed the chilly metal bedrails and pulled herself up. Darla added an additional pillow for support and opened her condiments for her, chatting incessantly as she placed pads of butter and tiny containers of jelly on her tray. After Darla left the room, Emily surveyed the covered dishes like a kid at a birthday, wondering which gift to open first. A small bowl containing a poached egg hidden under a small saucer cover, a piece of butter-soaked white toast, grits, and a small glass of orange juice was apparently the Sunshine Special of the Day here. The nagging cough was back between bites, but Emily managed to greedily eat some of her meal. Then she fell back, resting on her elevated pillow, exhausted from the effort, dozing. She could feel grits stuck to her chin, but she was suddenly too weak to lift the napkin to wipe it off. She remembered seeing "old people" in nursing homes with food stuck on their faces and dribbled down their clothes. Heaven forbid! With a renewed last effort, she found the napkin that had slid down under the table into the sheets. She dipped it ceremoniously in her water glass and carefully removed the stuck and now drying food from her face. Maybe old and sick people get too tired from chewing and that is the reason for Jell-O. You can actually suck it in between your teeth if you have to. Another mystery solved.

This is so weird, she thought. *I never feel this tired. I usually eat like a pig, run like a maniac all day, and then become a social butterfly until 2 or 3 A.M But things will soon be back to normal. Pneumonia is treatable and you get better.* Always feeling herself a lucky person, Emily was cautiously optimistic about her newly organized plans for the future. Watching the mesmerizing slow drip, drip, dripping of the iv solution leaving the hanging bag was like counting overly lazy liquid sheep, and again she dozed. True, Emily was lucky. Except that some luck was good and some luck was bad.

Chapter 7

This morning was the time for the good luck. Soon Darla was back at Emily's bedside table gathering the breakfast tray. "Good, you are able to eat! That means soon your iv will be disconnected," the nurse's aide announced with certainty. "Then you can just take a pill instead for your infection."

She helped Mrs. Carr with the call light and flipped on her TV for her. Darla also helped her patient with a bath consisting of a pan of warm water and washcloth with a small bar of soap.

"You don't have showers here, Missy?" asked weary Emily with a sigh.

"Yes, but that's when you are stronger. You got a pretty big conk on the head, you know!"

Emily reached for the back of her head and found a good-sized knot which was sore but not what you would call a ten on the pain scale. Emily had a great tolerance for pain, just not a very good tolerance for anything that held her back from what she wanted and needed to do. She responded, "Yep, I feel a small bump. Nothing much to worry about though. I'll be up and running by this afternoon, you'll see."

"You seem to forget you were knocked out for about the whole night! Probably a concussion if not a skull fracture. Not only that, your leg is all bandaged up and you can't get that wet."

Emily finally conceded to the fact that she would be doing her bath in the corner chair while Darla put some clean sheets which smelled liked the hospital laundry on her bed. Emily had to admit that she felt much better and more awake after her bath and being able to brush her teeth. Climbing back into the bed required some effort. Her leg felt like it had been used as a prop in *The Texas Chain Saw Massacre*. She found the call light and TV controls dangling from the bed railing within easy reach. She decided to stay awake as long as possible and not spend too much time napping. Talkative Darla had left to further her bed-making skills, so Emily started flipping through the meager selection of stations available. She could learn about mammography, learn about a new program called "Eldercare," or view the usual major channels. There was also a local TV station and Emily decided to try that. Emily was soon propped up, clean and comfortable, watching the local morning news, a bit groggy from the effort of eating, but not for long.

Suddenly she sat straight up, her eyes flew open in surprise! A police scene appeared on the screen and none other than Tyrone Dupris was shown being dragged from his Ridgeway apartment by a bevy of excited and yelling officers. They all wore SWAT insignias, helmets, and flak jackets. Dupris was obviously wounded but not dead. Mildred felt her heart race again and she strained to pick up every bit of information being relayed. She quickly grasped the chrome bedrails and pulled herself up and forward, all her attention focused on the newscast. She turned the volume control as loud as she could without bringing attention to herself. According to the news reporter's explanation of the situation, more police had been called when Tyrone, a man known to be more than just a common bad guy, was seen running in the parking lot. He had been startled by the commotion caused by police and emergency vehicles that were there for a Ms. Mildred Carr and her injury, not originally for him. He had spooked and taken off running back to his cousin's apartment and that directed the attention of law officers to the fleeing man. Tyrone's guilty conscience had caused him to run right into the squads called to the scene for the medical emergency.

"With several warrants for his arrest, Tyrone Dupris was running for the safety of relative Chink Black's efficiency when spotted by Lt. George Sanderfield. Sanderfield, who was on an earlier, unrelated emergency call to assist a responding ambulance team, immediately recognized him. Sanderfield chased the fugitive to his cousin's apartment on the third floor where Dupris barricaded himself. The SWAT team was called, a gun fight erupted, and Dupris was shot!" reported Ted Krantz, local newscaster from WKAV. Krantz spoke on with more details and then turned the spotlight to local weather.

For Emily, this was a gift too good to be true! Maybe this was her lucky day! Finally things were going her way once again! The detailed follow-up television story had reported that Tyrone Dupris was suspected to be a known peddler of drugs who targeted school kids. To say Dupris was a nasty bastard would be a huge understatement. His idea of a good business deal was selling to elementary kids and using them as runners for his enterprise. Dupris was accused of killing at least two young boys when they didn't perform their duties to his expectations. He had reportedly given them both heavy gold chain necklaces and then strangled them with the jewelry. Dupris used a fourteen-year-old girl for sex until he was bored with her, then he allegedly shot her and put her body on her mother's front porch for emphasis. *Yeah, Tyrone, we all know what a bad dude you are*, thought Emily. This story was fact. Emily also knew there was a chance Dupris might get off. The biological samples found on and in the body did not belong to Dupris. But Emily had no problem with blaming him for Shakira's death. No problem at all. The lone patient in Room 311 knew the little girl's grandmother, Yolanda, very well indeed and therefore the whole sordid story. Dupris was wanted statewide but nearly impossible to find since he had terrified the entire local African American community. Even Dupris' drug buddies were afraid of him. Most had an idea where he was, but no one had dared open their mouths.

Emily flipped down the sound button on the TV once the newscast was over, but left the video idling in case of updates. She couldn't afford to miss a moment. Emily felt quite revived and rejuvenated by this late news. Now that Tyrone Dupris had been shot, Emily needed to know his condition. Had he been brought to this hospital? He must be here, unless he was airlifted to Orlando or Tampa. *Let's hope we have better ways to spend our tax dollars than helicopter rides for murderers.* Anyway, there was no mention of that on the news. She rang her call bell. Darla scooted quickly through the door with a look of exasperation on her face.

"What is it, Ms. Carr? Are you okay?" she asked, as if she had been interrupted in the middle of something more important than making beds.

"I'm feeling much better, but I am really scared now!" said Emily while trying to tremble realistically. "I just saw on the news that some bad guy had been shot and I was thinking maybe he is here in this same hospital with me!"

"Oh, don't worry Ms. Carr, he is here all right…lots of commotion last night, I understand, but he is under armed guard!" answered Darla in her most soothing manner. "We don't really have anything to worry about." She began to pat her patient's knee in an attempt at comfort, feeling important now that she was able to tell the patient something new and interesting.

"But where is he? What if he is close by and gets away?" whimpered Emily, her eyes huge with supposed fear.

"He's on the floor below us and there is at least one cop at the door at all times. I went to see for myself! I am a very nosey person; at least that is what my friends say. So I try to find out everything! You know, inquiring minds want to know! Also I peeked by the guard and he is pretty shot up I guess. But as a precaution, he is shackled to the bed, both hands and legs, too!" continued Darla, excitedly telling what she knew. "He is still running his trash mouth though, so they must not have shot him in the head! What a bastard! Hope he dies, but he probably won't. Some lawyer will get him out and back into society. God, I sure hope he croaks!"

"Well, I don't really feel safe, honey. Could you be sure to shut my door? And my bathroom, does it lock from the other side?" asked Emily.

"Those bathrooms are safe, Ms. Carr," said Darla reassuringly. "They serve two rooms, but lock on each side. There is no one in the adjoining room right now, so the bathroom is all yours. With the census so low you probably won't get a roommate either. Many of the citizens of this fine town are 'snow birds' and are all gone for the summer. You can be safe and sound in a private room with a wonderful view of our staff parking lot! You can just pretend you are at the Hilton! You can lock the door on the adjoining side if you want, in fact, I can do it right now for you. Will that help you feel better?"

"You are a darlin' little girl, helping a poor ol' lady feel safe and comfortable. I can lock the door myself a bit later. Maybe you would take a walk with me after a while, when I am feeling stronger? I would feel good if someone was with me," pleaded Emily, in her most helpless voice.

"Oh sure, Ms Carr, they won't want you out walking by yourself until you are stronger anyway. Wouldn't want you to fall! And we have to be careful of your stitched up leg. We'll just get your cane this afternoon and go for a nice little stroll. I'll come by after lunch and see if you are ready to try it, okay?" offered Darla.

"That would be grand dear, if you're not too busy. See you later then," said Emily. "By the way, can I order some favorite foods for my lunch? Maybe that would improve my appetite."

"Oh sure, the dietician will bring around a menu for you. Also, I think one of the nurses will be by soon to disconnect you from the iv. Then you will be free as a bird, just be careful. Remember you have a nasty cut on your knee. Seeya later," said Darla, leaving the room with a small wave.

Emily breathed a huge sigh of relief and when she heard the big room door swing and click shut, she got up. Feeling just a little wobbly, she headed for the bathroom, limping a little and dragging her iv pole. She saw for herself, no one in the adjoining room. She also quickly checked her cane and bag and found everything in working order. This would be too easy. Emily always had a quick revision ready for her plans and they were usually very successful. After scoping out the room, she hopped back into bed. A surge of adrenaline was giving the patient a new burst of energy. Soon an R.N. from the day shift arrived and took out the iv needle and bandaged the insertion sight. The patient was now free to travel, unencumbered by tubes, bags of fluid, or annoying beeping alarms.

After lunch of some unidentifiable meat…was it beef or pork?…who knows? … Emily again rang for Darla who was there in a few minutes. She had been carrying noon trays back to the carts for return to the dietary department.

"How was your lunch, Ms. Carr?" asked Darla.

"Oh quite wonderful, but I'm not really all that hungry now," responded Emily. "Do you think you would have time to take me out and about? I'm feeling like I need to move my legs a little. Arthur-itis, you know. Try not to get old, honey."

"Getting up and around is the best thing for you, so let's get you moving!" replied Darla.

Soon the shaky little lady with cane in tow was headed down the hallway with her arm holding Darla's elbow. An extra gown was wrapped around her back to front at the patient's request. "Am I all covered up? Don't want to give all these doctors a thrill they ain't paying for, you know!"

"Don't you worry, Ms. Carr, I'll protect you!" laughed Darla. "In fact, later we'll see if we can get you some pajama bottoms to save your little tush from all those prying eyes!"

Emily quickly cased the hallway as they walked, including the situation of the nurses' desks, report area, medication carts, laundry room and stairways. They slowly moseyed down to the lounge area where they sat to rest. The leg was sore, but maneuverable. Talkative Darla wanted to know about Mildred's family and where she lived. She hated to lie to the young girl who had been so helpful, but self-preservation came as easily as the misinformation she began to feed her avid listener. She was sure this was going to be passed on, so had to remember just what tall tale she had been spinning. She actually had a repertoire of three or four stand-by faux family situations that she could embellish as needed. On the way back, she coaxed Darla to take her to the elevator and down to the second floor.

"Honey, maybe if I could see the security downstairs?" coaxed Emily cautiously. She would definitely feel better if she could see for herself the armed guard situation at Tyrone Dupris' doorway. Darla thought it would be okay and told the nurse in charge they would be going downstairs for a brief walk.

As soon as the elevator doors swished open, Emily saw a vigilant police officer sitting by Tyrone's doorway. He wore a navy blue uniform and cap and sat in a folding chair watching the few visitors in the hallway, arms folded in a protective stance. He was about 30 years old and fit. Uniformed Division. No FBI in sight. But they were not going to place a fat, lazy cop here, she decided. But his shift would be over soon, and she would see what the night would bring. Hospital doors would be locked securely for the night and there would be no need to restrict the passage of visitors. The officer nodded vaguely to Darla and went to the nurses' station for a refill on his coffee.

"Don't worry; he is always right there in sight of the door. And look inside, Ms. Carr, Mr. Dupris is strapped to the bed. He is not going anywhere. I asked and they said he was shot in the kidney and has a lot of pain, so I doubt if he wants to get up and run away right now!" Darla confided.

Darla was surely a curious creature. This was not always a good thing. Right now it was working well for Emily. In her apparently innocent glance into the room, what Emily saw were some leather shackles of hospital issue that wouldn't hold a wiggling 2 year old, let alone a hardened criminal. True, both arms and legs were locked tightly to the bed and the patient was now sleeping. Or was he? Was probably dosed high on morphine, but the state of his mind was something Emily would have to consider. Now Emily saw the pink sticker on this patient's door. "Allergic to Penicillin!!" So Mr. Dupris has a bad reaction to penicillin! He could even die and wouldn't that be too bad. This fact only confirmed what Emily already knew. She knew every last detail about Mr. Tyrone Dupris. For days she had known exactly where he was and pretty much what he was doing on a daily basis. She always thought it was interesting that people with one allergy often had many others. Bad DNA or something. Well, this was one mean dude that needed to be taken out of the gene pool entirely. Of course Dupris was alone in the room, which did have a window. He was covered with a crisp sheet and his head was turned towards the windowed wall. Emily envisioned his well-abused dong under that white sheet impaled via catheter to a bag full of bloody urine that hung from the rail of his bed. *Couldn't happen to a nicer guy*, she speculated. Another quick glance showed Dupris' room, 244, had the same setup as hers on the third floor. A shared bathroom.

"Could we go back now, Sweetie? I am getting a little pooped out," asked Emily. "Let's go this way, so I don't have to see the killer criminal anymore, okay?"

Emily turned down the hall, glancing nonchalantly into the room adjoining Dupris. Not only occupied, but it held male patients in both beds who were chatting amiably. Not too sick unfortunately, but could be awaiting surgery in the morning if her luck prevailed. A small hurdle for Mildred Carr, as she had jumped much higher obstacles in that particular persona.

Darla watched as her charge scuffed along beside her. She had noted earlier there was something vaguely familiar about this woman. Not that she had seen her before, she thought, but the lady reminded her of something in her past. Well, maybe her own grandmother who had died 3 years ago in a nursing home. It was probably just the situation that sent her mind back to those days of visiting her Meemaw at Live Oak Plantation Rest Home. Darla had spent many a day taking care of the old woman, hoping to get a large inheritance. As it turned out, there was no money at all. Huge medical bills had quickly depleted her grandmother's resources. Darla was always looking for a scheme to make some quick money. She had become a nursing student mostly to try to meet and marry a rich doctor. At least that was her ambition. Or perhaps one of these old fogies here at the hospital would take a shine to her and leave her millions. One never knows, she thought. Her class at the university in Tampa was full of other nursing students, most all hoping to make a difference. The only difference Darla wanted was a change in her own situation. Darla had taken this summer job near home as a nursing assistant just to stay in contact with elderly patients and make a little money for school.

But for now, this weird old woman would get all of Darla's attention. Her goal was to find out all the information the nurses wanted about this patient. This would put her in a good light with the supervisor and possibly get her some better assignments than bed making. And Darla could be quite persistent when she needed to be.

"Here we are Ms. Carr, back to your private suite," said Darla. "I will be leaving soon but will be back tomorrow to see you and we can walk again if you want."

"It was the best trip I ever had," responded Emily. "I think I'll just rest a while in my chair, please."

Darla helped her into the old, comfortable overstuffed chair by the window, placing a worn thermal blanket over her lap and legs. "Please shut the door on your way out. I will be getting a nap soon and can get myself back into bed," said Emily. "Thank you so much for all your help."

"Oh, any time Ms. Carr, but it was nothing. Glad to be of service!" beamed Darla, happy to be getting the confidence of the new patient.

Darla soon had clocked out and was on her way to her nearby apartment. As the door shut, Emily was already up and checking out the area outside the window. Not much ledge there and as she tried the latch, she found the window was frozen shut. Probably to avoid those jumpers and law suits, she mused. *You have a painful and terminal illness. Okay, good-bye, and a final leap...au revoir, cruel world*, she thought. That would definitely appeal to those who wanted a fast way out. No chemo, no drugs, no pain, no surgery...just a quick slam into the blooming jasmine and sago palms below and that was it. Not a bad way to go, really. As for herself, she would be willing to suffer a little pain to buy just enough time to say good-bye to her family and get her affairs in order. Yes, those affairs, what a surprise that would be to her prudent and fastidious daughter. Susan would never approve, no, not in a million millenniums.

So the window was out, but that was just a thought anyway. Her original but revised plan was best, but the riskiest. Quickly she went to the waste can and happily found that the maid service around here was not up to par. She snatched up what she needed and raced to the bed with it, placing it inside the pillowcase. She jumped, startled, as the door swung open and Helen again moved into the room with rags and spray bottles this time, dragging a large trash container to the doorway. She greeted Emily with no more than a grunt and proceeded to empty bins, and spray clean the bathroom. She moved slowly, apparently not noticing Emily climbing slowly into the bed and under the sheet. *A good time for a nap*, thought Emily.

After a salt free turkey dinner, Emily asked for the pajama bottoms suggested but forgotten by Darla. The afternoon aide brought them without comment. She was polite but not very friendly.

"Don't want my butt hanging out, you know!" explained the patient, as the aide left the room murmuring something. *Bet she won't be back to offer an evening back rub*, surmised Emily.

Emily switched on the news and channel surfed looking through the local and statewide stations for any breaking news on Dupris. She was relieved to hear that Dupris could not be transferred to any sort of jail facility due to his condition. She didn't really think he was movable in his situation, but one never knew how the judicial system would work. Emily sat in the bed with the lights out as she listened to the hallway noises. Once the afternoon shift departed around 11 P.M, things got much calmer. Nurses were talking quietly and working on charts, she thought as she listened through the slightly open door of her room. Once the night shift nurses started taking their breaks, Emily would be up and moving. She knew she would have at least twenty minutes before the evening rounds began. She had to be back in her bed before anyone came to check on her.

Chapter 8

Around 2 A.M. Emily was still and quiet for a few minutes, just listening. The hospital seemed to be sleeping. She rose carefully from the bed and slid silently to the tiled floor. She sat on the edge of the chair and pulled the hospital issued paper slippers onto her feet. Her injured right knee protested slightly but bent enough to allow the makeshift shoe to cover her foot. Quickly and silently, she went to her locker and bag, found a screwdriver, a pencil, and a few other small items. She picked up the pilfered empty iv bag from under her pillow and exited Room 311 via the bathroom, locking the door behind her from the inside. Adjoining Room 309 was shadowy and empty, the door to the hallway fully open. Emily crept to the door of the adjacent room and slowly closed it just a bit more. Using her key chain sized mag light, she found the used sharps container on the wall nearest the bathroom. She grabbed the screwdriver and used it to deftly and soundlessly snap the plastic safety latch on the right rear of the box, prying open the lid just enough to see inside. Using her mini light and her tweezers, she was able to grab a small insulin syringe and pull it out. *Too small*, she thought. She dropped the tiny syringe back into the box and tried again. This time she was able to reach a 5cc syringe with needle still attached. Then she replaced the lid into its previous position. No one would notice any tampering, she thought to herself. She pulled two new vinyl gloves from their holder on the wall as she went back to the bathroom. She flipped on the light, closing the door to Room 309 behind her and locking it. She tossed the iv bag and tubing in the sink and she began massaging the residual fluid into the bottom corner of the bag. Then she jabbed the syringe needle thru the plastic bag into its contents, withdrawing a full syringe of liquid. She hoped a teaspoon would be enough. But then, that was the glory of back up. A fail-safe job. She carefully placed a cap she had found earlier on the floor by her bed onto the needle. Then she placed the bag into the trashcan, covering it with some rumpled paper towels. Placing the syringe, gloves, and small tools into a holster-type wallet, she quickly strapped the little bag onto her waist under the pajamas. Then she flipped off the light and crept back to the door of Room 309.

Suddenly remembering her cane, she went again through the bathroom and grabbed it. She could hardly play the part without all the props. But then she desperately hoped she would not even be seen. Back at the door she squinted out into the corridor while holding the edge of the door, her eyes barely visible. Nurses were murmuring over a chart at their station. The hallway was totally empty and the lights were dimmed for patient comfort. Emily exited with the stealth of a prowling panther on the hunt. She found the stairway door almost reflexively and quickly leaped down the steps, running down to the second floor with her cane under arm. She felt no pain in her leg as she zoomed downward. All stiffness was gone. She was amazed that she was scarcely out of breath. Adrenaline moves the world, she thought. But next would be the touchy part. She knew the staff laundry was just around the corner, and so waited until the night officer went towards the desk. He was heard speaking low to the nurses there. When a call light buzzed, the nurses' attention momentarily went to the other end of the hall.

"You nurses ever eat anything bad for you?" the cop queried. "All I ever see you girls eat here are carrot sticks and yogurt. Don't you ever call out for pizza? Maybe I should bring donuts tomorrow night, glazed or jelly? How 'bout it?"

"Listen Al, you know all of us are on a diet except Jenna and she tries to eat healthy. Not all of us care to indulge in cholesterol bombs. We have to maintain our girlish figures! We have to trap all the men we can while we're still young and gorgeous! Of course, if you brought chocolate...!" replied Jane Beck, second floor night supervisor.

"Yep, a box of Godiva would work for me," chimed in Susan, her assistant. "Don't bother to bring us a box of generics from the Dollar Store, either...none of those ten pounds for a buck deals. No thank you, Al. We are divas here, you know, only the best calories will hit our hips! Otherwise it just isn't worth it, honey!" They all laughed quietly and never saw the flash of movement down the hall near the linen room.

Emily was still listening to the banter when she almost invisibly rounded the corner of the laundry room, quickly removing the hospital pajamas and putting on a pair of green scrubs she found on the shelf. She rolled up the waist to a thick wad so the pant cuffs wouldn't drag. Then she placed her PJ's on a shelf, carefully folded and obscure, just in case. Now she was ready to go to Room 244 and meet Mr. Tyrone Dupris. Dressed in employee garb, she was much more vulnerable. If caught, she could not claim "old ladyitis". She would be found out as an impersonator and the hospital would not take kindly to that sort of security impingement. Although timing was much of every success, she had only ten more minutes to make it back up the stairs and into her bed. The nurses on her floor would soon be doing checks on their patients. Now Emily was beginning to feel that familiar tingle, and just a single drop of sweat formed on her brow. She inched forward and quickly slithered into Room 242. The two men were, thankfully, sleeping. Please be good sleepers, she hoped. She knew one thing; they were both great snorers. It was like stereo, snores dueling in the night for some unknown award. In the morning they will both claim the other one snored so loud he couldn't sleep. Emily was familiar with that routine. She used to be married to a champion. The bathroom connecting the two rooms was Emily's next stop. Sliding silently by the sink and toilet, and opening the door to the darkened Room 244 and the notorious Dupris, she felt the surge of power and control that would get her through this venture and back to safety. Every nerve was keen and alert. Ears listened, eyes became panoramic lenses, and everything focused on her goal. There he was, bad man Tyrone Dupris. His eyes were closed and slight whistling emerged from his flat and swollen nasal passages. Perhaps his nose was broken during the fight with police. His face was marked with a rainbow of puffy colors visible even in the dim light. Small bags of fluids were piggybacked into larger bags and were hanging from iv poles at the bedside. The output collection container gathering bloody urine still sagged heavily from the bottom bedrail. There was now over one liter of ominous dark reddish brown tinged liquid. Dupris was a dark-skinned black man and he glistened with perspiration as he slept. His hair, braided into dreadlocks, was damp and matted against the pillow. The sheets, once crisp and fresh, were now rumpled and dank, while the stench of illness pervaded the room. He was not a bad looking guy, Emily thought, for a child killer. A huge scar on the left cheek only made him look more foreboding, but not ugly by a long shot. Here was a man who had so much potential at one time.

He had good parents, both a mom and dad, a rare commodity in this day and age. The family was educated and, it could be said, middle class good citizens. There was a lot more to the story of Tyrone Dupris, but now was not the time to contemplate his family tree. As with most favors she did, she wanted a personal touch, a reminder as they were sent on their way to hell. The officer assigned to Dupris' door was still discussing the benefits of a pastry-filled life with the nurses. Dupris' door was open but not the whole way. Just enough for a little light to enter.

"Dupris!" she whispered huskily. "Dupris!"

"Whaa...? Who...whaa?" Dupris mumbled in a medicated stupor, still not awake, but turning towards the shadowy figure by his bed.

"Shssh. Be quiet. I am a nurse. I work here. Chink sent me to see you. Just whisper. I got word from your homies. Shssh," said Emily in a very hushed voice. Emily had already punched the needle thru the dripping tubing to the prisoner's arm and was slowly injecting the contents of the syringe. She began to pray then that Tyrone's immune system would do her work for her. "Roll over on your side. I have to take your temperature. You may have a fever, the doctor says."

"Who th' hell are you, Bitch?" replied Dupris, but in a quiet manner, intrigued now that maybe someone was here to help him out of this predicament. "Chink don't know no white lady players, especially old ones. You a nurse? Pretty old, ain't ya? H'ain't seen yo here befo'. "

"Listen, Chink is ace kool. Chill, Dog," continued Emily in a harsh whisper. "He was down at the glass house, dis'n' the nation. Just for you, man. Trying to get you out; nobody will drop a dime on you. You're safe for now. Chink may be a base head but he is blood with you...told me to tell you."

"Okay, I fooled out and landed in here. Gotta get out," said Dupris quietly and with some sense of desperation. "Can't stand it here. Gotta get gone. Make another gig. Another posse. Venge. Can't stand the pain, sucker shot out my kidney, man. Why another butt temp, man? They just did it a while ago." Tyrone naturally did not trust anyone, especially this old white bitch, but at this point he had nothing to lose. He would get help from anyone stupid enough to bail him out of this predicament. He definitely was not planning on going to prison. After all, he didn't deserve that. He was just trying to make a living.

"Temp must have been high, Dude," Emily countered as she put on the Latex disposable gloves. "Hurry up now, roll over just a bit."

Dupris grimaced with his bruised and swollen face, then rolled painfully but obligingly on to his right side, facing away from Emily and the door. Emily quickly opened her specially ordered container from lunch, and dipped and swabbed the pencil's eraser end in it. Then with as much grace as she could muster in the situation, she poked the rectal preparation into the unsuspecting butt hole of Tyrone Dupris. After giving it a quick twirl to dislodge the coating from the pencil end, she removed it right away. She then placed it inside her removed glove and tucked the wrapped pencil back into her bag.

"Damn quick, ain't yo'? Can you get me a four-five? Tell Chink I needa four-five. Gotta get outta here..." slurred Dupris. "What's the hot line, am I gonna live? Didn't have no fever early. I do feel sick though and lots of pain."

"Dupris, Chink sent rock in a needle to help you. Just relax, like you are on the pipe. Relax and enjoy the ride," said Emily. *Yeah, like I am going to get you a gun and drugs, you fucking bastard,* she thought to herself. Anger, cold as ice seeped into her, feeling more like an annoyance than an emotion at this point.

"Did you stick me man? I do feel a little funny," murmured Dupris faintly. "Not like beamin', like sick. Hey, my butt is burning, Man, and I gots the itches. You didn't use no Latex gloves did you? It's on my chart, Man, I'm 'lergic to that stuff, ya know!"

Emily was so surprised she almost laughed out loud. *Latex, too? How did I miss that one?*

"Shssh! This stuff always works like that. Be quiet and I'll be able to get more for you, but you gotta lay still and not make a noise!" ordered the shadowed silver-haired nurse in green scrubs. As the old woman turned to leave him, she bent low to his face. Dupris couldn't see her well, but his earthly focus had begun to fade.

"Hey, Dupris, did you ever hear of kissing your ass good-bye?"

"Say wha'?" he moaned.

"Well, you bastard, think of this as your ass kissing you good-bye!" Emily whispered coarsely as she turned to go. Dupris was unable to respond. His throat felt very tight and his breath came in short wheezes. Suddenly his eyes rolled back and an involuntary loud gurgle came from his throat. He began to seize, with arms and legs violently and noisily jiggling the metal bed frame! The shackles held him tight, as they seemed to engage the bed in a frenzied dance of convulsive, clanging movement. Foaming froth began to spew from his jerking lips as blood began to leak from his nose and tongue. Emily exited fast through the bathroom as the patient's monitors began calling out familiar alarm signals in short loud bursts. Emily waited in the adjoining room right behind the hall door, afraid the two snoring patients would awaken amid the confusion and noise. But they slept on. Presumably, the glory of sleeping pills. Nighty-night, all. As the Code Blue was paged on the overhead speakers, Emily listened as the rush of code team members raced to Dupris's bedside, confused and unaware of what was causing his problem. Glancing at the hall clock, Emily saw she had only three minutes to be back in bed. Then, like an hour glass, Room 244 filled and the hall emptied, as she dashed shadow-like back to the laundry closet and quickly changed back to patient garb. She tossed the scrubs into the canvas bag used for soiled and used uniforms, careful to place them on the bottom of the tangled careless pile. No one noticed the pajama clad woman reenter the stairway and bound up the stairs as if defying gravity. Nor did any one see her then carefully steal back to Room 309. There she redeposited the syringe and also the peanut butter clad pencil through the lid of the sharps box. The gloves she sent swirling down the toilet, with a prayer not to clog up the drain. She ran through the bathroom, raced to the locker and replaced the tools into her bag. She quickly set the cane in the corner and jumped between the wrinkled sheets, now breathless. The code was still being paged, as well as a Dr. Hampton, Emily heard from the hall speakers. Her heart was racing, but she felt immediately calmed and began to relax mentally, using an old Yoga technique from the past. She was perspiring just a little from the tense situation. *Try this on Fear Factor!* she challenged to the world in general. This will get the old fight or flight system moving. Now she was feeling a little weak and nauseated. At least there was no coughing spell this time.

In the quiet, she suddenly realized there was something wet on her right leg. Shit! Emily jerked up to a sitting position to examine the damage. She pulled the cord on the light over her headboard. Pulling back the sheets once again and pulling up the pajama leg she gaped at her knee. The bandage on her wounded right leg was soaked thru and was oozing blood. Damn! What if it had leaked on the way back up the stairs? The pajama leg was also smeared with fresh red stain. It was too late to go back and retrace her steps. She slipped back to the bathroom and took off the pajama bottoms. Grabbing paper towels, she pressed the gauze-wrapped wound and held it tight. Hobbling back to her room, still holding pressure on the bleeding mess, she stuffed the bloodied pajama bottoms into her bag in the locker. She was relieved to see that the oozing had stopped and blood was drying on the bandage, turning a dark brown now. Emily suddenly yanked the light cord, plopped back on the bed, and began to snore. Just then, a nurse peeked in. Seeing her patient apparently sleeping soundly, she decided to return later to check her blood pressure and temperature. After the nurse closed the door, Emily carefully limped back to the bathroom and flushed the telltale towels down the toilet. She then crept back to the bed, leaving the sheet and blanket off her leg. Soon it would air dry and if she held it still, would stop bleeding on its own. She couldn't risk reentering the hall and absconding with fresh rolls of gauze to do the job herself. Tomorrow, nurses would rewrap it and scold her for bending her knee too much. She would explain to them how it happened. When trying to sit on the john, she slipped and hit it on the side of the toilet paper holder. Of course, she didn't want to bother anyone, so just went back to bed. As long as there were no drips on the stairs to explain, she would be safe in her lie.

Down on the second floor, Tyrone Dupris was urgently yanked from his restraints as doctors and code team members attempted to pound and poke him back to life. Dupris' problems came from within. Antibodies had been formed when originally presented with the penicillin used to treat Dupris's last bought with gonorrhea. For those unlucky individuals with highly allergic and sensitive immune systems, these same self-created fighters were now ready to attack all comers. Emily had known about the severe penicillin and peanut allergies from careful research and questioning Brigetta. Once there is an allergic reaction to penicillin, her granddaughter had stated, a person is more likely to have a reaction to other drugs in the penicillin family and to drugs in the penicillin-related cephalosporin family....such as cefazolin, like Ancef. Emily had read her own I.V. fluid bag carefully. She was quite fastidious. If the grave drug-induced immune response didn't kill Dupris, she knew the peanut butter would do the job. She had learned from her granddaughter's nursing books and a quick double check on the web that people with severe peanut allergy couldn't even kiss someone who had eaten peanuts until several hours later! She had also learned that the rectum is great place for absorption, for instance, the reason for the use of rectal suppositories. So, after the immediate onslaught via intravenous bolus injection of Ancef and concurrent rectal absorption of peanut butter, Dupris's body responded in a very civil and proper manner. It killed him from the inside out. Emily still smiled about the unknown Latex allergy. Another failsafe bonus. The doctor's recorded findings would include edema and sudden cardiac and respiratory arrest. Apparently his kidney was damaged so badly that it was a main contributor in Dupris' demise. Treatment with lifesaving drugs had failed and an autopsy was ordered by the county medical examiner. But as Tyrone's limp and lifeless body was lifted onto the coroner's gurney for transport to the county morgue, no one shed a tear. The reaction was surprise perhaps, but not grief. Cops quietly chuckled to themselves, but only in private, about saving money on a trial, years of appeals, and incarceration. Everyone except his publicity-seeking, greedy lawyers thought young Tyrone Dupris had done the world a favor by dying.

Chapter 9

Emily slept amazingly well from 3:30 A.M. until the morning trays bearing breakfast arrived on the third floor. Darla was back on her shift and jiggled her patient who was just blinking herself awake, "Quite the sleepy head this morning aren't we? Pancakes today, just like Perkins!" The offering looked and smelled wonderful to a hungry woman who had been up half the night.

"Sure, I'll bet they're really good," answered Emily. "Lots of syrup? I love syrup and butter! Got any more peanut butter? Just pile that stuff on my toast and I am a happy camper."

"Will see what we can do, Ms. Carr. Are you feeling better today? You seem to be in a pretty good mood! Ready for another walk?" asked Darla, glad to see her patient in such a good humor and ready to eat. She learned in nursing school that a good appetite was a sign of improving health.

"Well…I had a little accident last night in the dark. Went to the bathroom and banged my leg a little. Could the nurse come and bandage it this morning? The doctor hasn't been in yet and I would like to have it all cleaned up before he gets here," requested Emily innocently as she pointed to her knee under the sheet. "Also, remember those pajama bottoms you promised me?"

"Oh sorry, I'll get them right away. Let's see the knee. We'll get it all fixed up soon," Darla said as she lifted the sheet and saw the blood encrusted bandage. Her eyes popped open in horrified amazement as she viewed the damage. "And you said you did this how?" she asked suspiciously eyeing her patient.

Seeing the shocked expression on the aide's face, Emily tried to downplay the situation by maintaining her calm demeanor and pooh-poohing the whole thing. What could be so unusual about a bloody wound? After all, this was a hospital, wasn't it?

"You weren't out running around on your own, were you?" queried Darla, with another doubtful look in her squinting blue eyes. With raised brows she stood back with arms crossed as she stared hard at her patient.

"No dear, I just banged it up slightly and it started to bleed a little," answered Emily, trying to remain as casual as the circumstances would allow.

"Looks like more than just a little, Mrs. Carr. Now I hope we don't have to put a guard on your room too," she quipped. "I'll have the nurse come in right away and try to repair the mess. I am sure you'll be fine, just a little too much action! In fact, it looks like you were the loser in a big knee-kicking fight!"

Soon a new and unrecognized nurse named Caroline entered with a tray full of dressings and began to carefully unwrap the blood-crusted gauze. She examined the wound and found one of the stitches near the kneecap had pulled loose. "Well, Mrs. Carr, we will just have to strap you down if you don't behave," she joked. "Actually we can just apply a steri-strip to hold those edges back in place. No need to do much else. You'll have to be extra careful now with it until it gets a chance to start to heal. No more aerobics classes this week! Also no jumping, singing, dancing, judo, or anything else, just to cover all the bases. Got it?"

"Okay, I promise. I will just lie here and decompose in complete silence," answered Emily. "Really now, I'll be a good girl."

Darla soon was back in the room with the pajama bottoms. She wanted to spend time with her patient after the wound had been cleaned and rebandaged. Nurse Bingham had requested that Darla try to find more information about Mrs. Carr. Financial services were requesting some data for billing, as to be expected. Darla was a natural choice for this since she was so talkative and had an insistent way of inquiring.

"Ms. Carr, you haven't told me really anything about your family. Do you have any children? Grandchildren? I am a nursing student, you know. I live in a nearby apartment and have a new kitten named Bubbles. My mother gave it to me. Said I would learn responsibility. The cat is a real pain, always scratching up stuff and that litter box! Phew, it stinks! But I want to take her back to the dorm when I start back to school in the fall."

Eager to interrupt the barrage of chatter, Emily said, "At cat at school? Do they allow that?"

"Probably not, but she will be okay in my room. She'll be alone a lot, but she's just a cat so she won't care. If she meows too much I will just duct tape her mouth during the day when I am gone or something," said Darla, laughing fiendishly.

"I hope not. That would be cruel. Maybe you shouldn't have a kitten if you won't have time to take care of it and love it," said Emily.

"Oh, I like it all right. It's kinda cute, but you have to remember, it's just a dumb animal not a person or anything. That's what my daddy always said anyway."

"Sometimes daddies don't know squat," said Emily with a frown and furrowed brow. She was now worried about little Bubbles. Well, at least it was a distraction from her own troubles.

Darla continued to talk, oblivious to Emily's animal welfare concerns, "I am just working here for the summer and then back to school for the fall semester. I think I want to be a Pediatrics nurse, though. I love the kids. I keep thinking I've seen you before, maybe…"

At that last sentence of continual patter, another alarm went off, this one in Emily's head. Where had she been seen before? This young girl was about the same age group as her grandchildren in Palm Beach right now. Brigetta, too, was in nursing school but was home for summer break. God, she missed her, as her mind took a trip back home for a moment. She was probably sunning herself at the pool, reviewing her microbiology or anatomy. The girl was a real scholar. Not that she missed out on the fun or boys. She was absolutely gorgeous, very attractive, and lots of fun to be with. Tall, yet curvy, she could have been a model. Long, shiny, straight, almost-white blond hair, clear skin and absolutely huge blue eyes. But she was very serious about her studies and sports. She had been quite the tomboy, scaring her mother by climbing trees to the top branches and waving at her through the window on the third floor sewing room. And she loved her Granny Emily Vanderhorn. Granny Em had taught Brigetta to drive, allowing her access to any of the cars garaged at the Pink Flamingo. They shopped together at exclusive shops at Worth Avenue, financially able to shop at Saks and Tiffany's. But their greatest pleasure was shopping discount stores and finding bargains. They would giggle girlishly when complemented at the country club.

"Oh, Emily and Brigetta, you girls really know how to shop for the cutest clothes! And those handbags, are they Gucci? Brigetta, it must be so nice to have a Granny that can afford to take you to all the best shops!" were common remarks from Mrs. Grace Hawthorne, snobbish bridge club president.

Little did they know that the fashion may or may not be from Saks or in fact, any other exclusive and, they thought, over-priced store. Their biggest secret joke was that shopping at Wal-Mart, Value Mart, or outlet stores gave them great joy. The fun of finding a marked down cashmere blazer and coordinating silk scarf for less than $25 was a thrill known to both of them. A shared confidence that drew them close. Two women bonded by the bargain-shopping gene.

Brigetta loved answering, "Oh, we go to all the very special, secret places for all the best bargains, Mrs. Hawthorne. Granny Em knows them all. She takes great care of me!" Then the two would walk away just waiting for that ideal moment to burst into gales of shared laughter.

Emily had always helped Brigetta study, asking nursing test questions, practicing chemical equations and learning lots herself. They would sit by the side of the pool at the Pink Flamingo and go over and over the exam questions. Wine coolers on ice and chips with cheesy salsa were the official study snacks. Brigetta always got A's and Grandma learned all about anaphylactic shock. Quite the symbiotic relationship. It was always handy to have medical personnel in the family. Brigetta had even mentioned going to medical school to become a surgeon instead of being a nurse. Well, the girl could certainly do whatever she put her mind to, just like me, Emily thought. Her second granddaughter, Mikelle, was also greatly missed right now. She was older, having completed college three years ago. She accepted the novice engineering position at a top firm right out of school and was climbing her way to the top. This one was also gorgeous and statuesque, tiny waisted with curves in all the right places. Her hair was a dark golden auburn and her eyes were sea green. She had dark lashes and brows, giving her the aura of a gypsy. She made it through engineering school at the top of her mostly male class. Being the only female at her office was far from intimidating for Mikki. She was a very determined young woman. Emily had always thought that she was the one relative most like herself. Very strong-willed and ambitious. Basically she was a hard worker, but also unwilling to take crap. Older and more experienced than her younger sister, she, too, had her life on track. Though more introverted than Brigetta, Mikki also had career goals that had not yet included getting married and starting a family. There would be no "glass ceiling" for Mikki as she would just crash her way through and laugh as she heard the tinkling of broken glass.

Nothing would get in her way, and in that, Mikki and her grandmother were exactly alike. It was comforting to Emily to know that Mikki was helping Brigetta at this moment, staying with her at the Pink Flamingo to keep an eye on the house, her cat, and also the shop. Susan and Michael would have some precious time alone at home. This also gave the girls some time together as they would camp out in their favorite guest room, stay up late talking about guys, and watch chick flicks all night. She really missed both girls and her daughter. Susan was quite a prude at times, but was like a mother bear when it came to her kids. Emily was sure Susan would protect and support her family at any cost. Loyalty was an inherited family virtue. What she needed now was to get back to the life of Emily Vanderhorn. She needed to see her family and get back to her store....have a normal, but of course, very rich life. Thinking herself truly very lucky, Emily's mind had wandered into dreams of life at the beach and country club.

"Ms. Carr? Hellooo? Did you hear me? I think I have seen you before," repeated Darla, rudely shaking Emily's arm.

Jolted back to reality and an unpleasantly fearful sensation she didn't like, Emily quickly responded, "Oh no, Honey. There is just me in my little room on Jackson Street. No family. Hope you do well in your studies, though." Cautiously she asked, "Where do you go to nursing school, Dear? I am sure you will be a wonderful nurse."

"The university in Tampa, I graduate in two more years. I just love it. There is so much to learn and the other students are really a fun group. You know, you look like someone I saw at freshman orientation. Oh well, lots of people look alike, I'm learning. Just so many chromosomes to go around, right?" said Darla.

"I guess I am just one of those generic people that some-one is always going up to and saying, 'you look like so and so'...happens all the time," responded Emily quickly. "I must have a 'universal face.'"

Horror shot through her thoughts, as she had just realized where and how Darla might have seen her. She had attended an orientation tea for nursing students at the university with Brigetta and Susan. Darla was probably there. Well, there was no way Darla would be able to put Mildred Carr and Emily Vanderhorn together. But it just might be time to get out of Dodge! Where was a good fast horse when you needed one?

Chapter 10

"Ms. Bingham? I just was talking with Mrs. Carr in 311, and she mentioned she lived on Jackson St. Thought you would like a few more clues," reported Darla at the mid-morning mandatory staff meeting. Several nurses and aides were clustered around a small table in the floor's break room, sipping steaming coffee from thick-handled porcelain mugs. "How is she doing, anyway?"

"Hey, good for you! Maybe we can get someone in here to help with discharge and going home. Did she say anything else? Oh, and yes, she is doing okay so far, I think. Still waiting for some reports. Dr. Belmont will be in later this morning and go over everything with us and also with the patient," responded Kate.

"I've also noticed that Mrs. Carr is much more alert, in fact, she even seems smarter than she was yesterday," continued Darla.

"What do you mean, smarter? You know that when people are sick they are often not running on all cylinders. Maybe that's it?" asked Kate.

"Well, it's more than that. Sometimes, now I am not sure, but it seems like her Southern drawl just disappears and she is using bigger words. It's almost like she is a different person for a while. Could she be schizophrenic or something? You know, a double personality?" continued Darla.

"Well, schizophrenia doesn't mean two personalities exactly, but stranger things than that have happened around here. Who knows? I plan to talk more with her later on today," answered Kate. "At least we know now that she's not homeless, has an actual place to go home to."

"Yep, Jackson Street," said Darla her face beaming with pride.

"Well, I'm glad you were able to find out that information, Darla. Good job!" praised Kate.

"Not only that, but--now this is really weird--I think I may have known or met her before," persisted Darla, now on a roll and wanting to make more points with one of the head nurses.

"Known her from where? Now that wouldn't be too strange, since you live in this county. How do you know her?" asked Kate.

"Well, I don't *know* her, but just think I have seen her before. This girl I go to nursing school with comes from a very wealthy family. I mean lots of money, so everyone knows her. She came to orientation with her grandmother and mom. I could swear this woman is her grandma! They look identical, I mean except that we thought Mrs. Carr was a street person. Maybe they are related or something, I don't know. I just know they could be twins!" Darla prattled on.

Feeling that this was just a bit overboard, Kate suggested Darla move on to report on her next few patient assignments, reassuring her that they would discuss it more at another time. Since Kate had happily been switched this month to the day shift, now she was eager to see her patient, Mildred Carr, during waking hours. There was much more she wanted and needed to know. She didn't think Darla's observations would amount to much, but wanted to continue to explore the mystery. After the brief staff meeting, Kate went back to her desk in the work area.

Dr. Belmont walked slowly up to the nurse's station, reading a chart as he went. "Hi, Kate. Well, bad news for our mystery patient. It seems Mrs. Carr has a possible tumor in the lung. Left lower lobe. We need to go talk to her and schedule a biopsy. The prognosis may not be good, but we'll wait for the full reports before we toss her in a grave," said the doctor.

"That bad? Gee, you are not usually quite *that* negative, Bob. What is going on?" said Kate, now genuinely concerned.

"Big tumor, probable not operable, but maybe we can use some chemo or radiation. Don't know yet, as we have to see what we are dealing with first. It's in the lung though, that much for sure. Didn't she have 'no' marked on the smoking part of her history?" continued Dr. Belmont.

"Yep, said she had smoked before, though. Not sure when she quit," said Kate. "Are you ready to go see her now?"

"Well, hate to be the bearer of bad news. Hope she's not the type to shoot the messenger," he said as he flipped through the pages of lab and X-ray reports. "Let's get on with it. Coming?" He picked up the charts and helped pull out Kate's chair as the two left the conference area to see the patient.

Their patient was reading a newspaper as they walked into her room. Emily knew from the paperwork hanging from his hands, and the grim look, that the doctor did not have good tidings. He had brought the results in writing so the unlucky patient would not doubt the doctor's words. Disbelief was a common reaction to this type of information. She suddenly felt a glob of fear in the pit of her stomach. But Emily had never been one to walk away from any tense situation. Therefore she scooted down into the bed and just pulled the sheet up over her head, still and corpse-like. Maybe they will just go away. Maybe this is all a bad dream.

"Okay, Mrs. Carr, we can still see you. The news is not that bad, really!" reassured Kate.

Mildred inched the sheet down from her face and stared directly at her lynch mob. "Well, spit it out. Don't leave me hangin', folks", demanded Emily, as she forced herself to sit up again and face them.

"You have a growth in your lung and we need to do a biopsy. That will let us know what it is and what we should do, Mrs. Carr. It could be a number of things, but until we know for sure we can't begin to treat the condition," said Dr. Belmont.

"There. That wasn't so hard. Just say it. That's the way I like things. No need to pussy foot around. But, it's probably cancer, isn't it?" asked Emily.

"Of course, we can't say for sure, but it could be. We need to go ahead and order the biopsy. I have to call in the chest specialist to care for you, okay? Nurse Bingham has all the necessary paperwork for you to sign. We just need your permission and to locate your family," continued Dr. Belmont.

"Yes, Mildred, we need to call in your family so they can help you through this difficult situation. No one wants to be alone in a hospital, I know," added Kate.

"You're right, I don't want to be alone, but there's no one to call. Just do the biopsy and let's get this show on the road. How 'bout this afternoon?" replied Emily.

"Well, I'm glad you are eager to get going on this, but it will be tomorrow until we can schedule everything. We will get right on it, though. By the way, when did you quit smoking, Mrs. Carr?" asked Dr. Belmont.

"That's right, blame the damned patient. I haven't smoked since I was thirty, Dr. Belmont. But I know the risks, and I have been under a lot of stress in my life, so let's blame that, okay?" Emily said sharply, eyes rolling back and throwing up her hands.

"I'm sorry Mrs. Carr. The extra history is just helpful in these cases. I didn't mean to upset you any more than you are. I promise we'll get some answers for you as quickly as possible," said Dr. Belmont. "I am really sorry that we don't have happier news." He reached for the stethoscope around his neck and began to place it on Emily's chest. He listened carefully as the patient tried to breathe deeply for him without coughing. As he stood up, he gave her a pat and a thumbs up sign before he left the room.

Soon Mildred Carr was signing lots of hospital papers promising to be a good girl and not sue, pay her bill somehow, and not curse while under anesthetic…or something like that. As everyone left her room, she felt the aftermath of the detonated bomb. But true to form, she did not, could not, fall apart. Instead she began to think and plan. This was the method of coping she always used.

Running her fingers through her short curly hair, she scrunched her eyes tightly shut. She had not allowed many tears in her life, and this was not the time for them now. Feeling sorry for herself was not a reason to cry. She would get through this for her family. They needed her and she needed them. But what to do now? She had been planning to leave the hospital tomorrow, have Brigetta take out the stitches from her knee next week, and get back to the shop and home. Back to normal. Mission accomplished. Now this! Never having any real problems with her health, this was all quite a shock to absorb. The "Big C" was not in the plan. Emily hated kinks in her well thought out plans. And she especially hated for things to happen over which she had no control.

Within minutes, Emily had been forced to make the quick decision to have the biopsy and find out the actual diagnosis. Then she would plan from there. No sense in going crazy until the official word of doom was spoken. For now, she would lie low and keep those nosey questions at bay. Now she could hide under a veil of despair and anger that would, of course, prevent her from giving out any more information right now. She had been set up financially under an indigent plan and she would need to reimburse the hospital somehow. Maybe an anonymous grant from an anonymous benefactor. Shit. What else could possibly happen today? If only she could talk to one of the girls. If only her whole life was not a big secret.

Just then, as if on cue, the door burst open, and unwelcome Darla came rushing in to the room. "Mrs. Carr, I just heard you are having a biopsy tomorrow. Are you okay? Can I do anything? I should really find some family for you. This is not a time to be alone, you know," she gushed out, rapid fire.

"I am fine, dear, and there is just no one to call. I'll be all right, you'll see," responded Emily, feeling like a patient who needed to reassure the medical staff.

"Do you want me to sit here for a while and talk? I have a few minutes now," asked Darla.

"That's okay; I know you have lots of other people who are really sick to take care of. I think I just want to rest now for a while," said Emily, trying to gracefully tell the girl to get out.

"Well, I am going to go through my orientation pictures when I get home. I swear one of the ladies with Brigetta Walsh was her grandmother and she looked just like you. I will even bring in the photos to show you. I'm going to show Nurse Bingham too. The similarity is just uncanny. I can't get over it. I'll look for them tonight. Well, then, seeya tomorrow, Mrs. Carr. Have a good night and don't worry about tomorrow," said Darla, turning around to head for the door and waving a good-bye.

Well, now I do have something to worry about, little Missy, thought Emily. *Curiosity had killed more than just cats.* She had initially liked using all the extra attention from Darla to her advantage. But now, she was becoming a burden. A dangerous burden. There was no way her family would be drawn in to this and her life be exposed. Darla had helped her find her way to Dupris, but now her usefulness was gone. In fact, she was becoming a destructive force, almost as bad as the cancer cells she knew were now creeping about her lungs like alien invaders from Planet Death.

As Darla exited the room, Emily was concerned. She felt relieved to see her go, but wondered what the girl would come up with next. Peering into the hallway through the doorway, Emily could see Helen from housekeeping had stopped Darla. Helen was pointing into the room and down the hall and grumbling. Such an unhappy soul, did she ever smile, thought Emily fleetingly? She decided then and there, no matter what, never to become a crabby old bitch no one could stand, miserable and horrible to be around. Tomorrow was another day and maybe things would be better.

The next morning's testing was scheduled to begin early. Emily had not slept well, as a million thoughts and ideas had wormed their way through her brain. She had finally willed herself to sleep about 2 A.M. She awoke with uncharacteristic baggy eyes and an ill-tempered demeanor. She dragged herself to the bathroom, washed her face and gave herself a hard stare in the mirror. *Well, Emily, you look like shit,* she told her reflected image. *So you had better not start acting like shit! Get a grip and get your act together.* As far as Emily was concerned, the inconvenience of the testing should be just a small roadblock on her trip back home.

Soon a pleasant black man, who identified himself as William from Radiology, rolled in a wheelchair and helped the patient into the sling-like seat. Releasing the brake from the wheels and adjusting her legs onto the footrests, he announced that she should be prepared for an excellent trip. "I have a superior driving record," he joked. "No fatalities this week!" Emily was glad to find someone cheery to brighten her day as she rolled along, her lap and legs covered with a thick white cotton blanket. They soon arrived intact as promised after an elevator ride to the lower level of the hospital. *Probably have the morgue down here too,* thought Emily. The cream-colored walls were barren, except for exit signs, room markers, and clear plastic corner protectors. The halls were lined with waiting patients in wheelchairs or on carts. Most were connected to I.V. bags and dripping fluids. Some wore nasal cannulas for oxygen, their faces pale and lips blue, their breathing loud and strained. A man still in torn dirty jeans lay moaning on a gurney with obvious road rash visible on his left arm, protruding from under a sheet. The other arm was wrapped in layers of gauze that did little to conceal the blood oozing through the bandages. Cuts and areas that were beginning to bruise covered the entire right side of his face, swelling already starting to close his eye. Maybe a car or motorcycle accident, Emily thought, as she viewed the patterns of injury. That was what they always said, she reminded herself, no matter how bad your situation, there will always be someone worse than you. She mused over the fact and realized there would also be someone at the end of that line of thought. The person who was at the end of the chain and actually was the worst off person in the world. Of course, they probably wouldn't be in good enough shape to even realize it, thankfully.

It was finally Emily's turn to go back into the caverns of darkness and metal monsters to begin the series of tests. A C.T. scan was done of her chest and abdomen to evaluate the full extent of the tumor and to look for any spread of disease. A needle biopsy was done, guided by C.T. scan where a small portion of the abnormal mass was obtained. Emily was glad she wasn't required to have the bronchoscopy today as it made her gag to just think about it. Two of her friends had told of their experiences with the scope going thru the nose to the lungs and it had made her cringe. Emily's mental make-up was great, but she didn't want to deal with any more medical torture than possible.

From this point the tumor, if cancerous, would be staged and its extent determined. There would be more tests to come. Then would follow the decisions about treatment. Emily already knew about the difficulty of cure for lung cancer. The survival rate was not good, even with aggressive therapies. She knew her outlook was poor and began to think back to her childhood. That was not a thought process she often allowed to enter her mind. Emily knew she was at high risk for lung disease even though she had quite smoking a long time ago. She began smoking in childhood, the developing years. Smoking and stress, well, those were big ones on the cancer risk list. The facts that she had kicked the habit and now lived a healthy, active life were pluses. She tried to calm herself as visions of her youth came creeping back. Not pleasant memories. If she had lung cancer, there would be another reason to hate her parents from hell. She began to feel hot with anger once again, palms moist with sweat, involuntary tremors in her arms and legs. *Stop!* She screamed internally. *Don't go there, it's not worth it!* Slowly the cogs of her mind stopped spinning out of control and calmness returned. Stress and smoking. Oh no, she would never be the poster girl for the ideal childhood. But then, she would never be nominated for the ideal child either. *Thanks for everything, Frank and Mommy Dearest*, she said to herself sarcastically. She was eleven when she took up smoking. She was nine when she killed her stepfather.

Chapter 11

After spending yesterday blaming alternately herself and then her parents for all her woes, Emily resolved to get on with what was left of her life. That part of the testing was over and now she awaited the jury result. Soon, and right after a breakfast of soggy Corn Flakes, the harbingers of bad news were in to see Mrs. Carr. She was told the tumor was definitely cancer. Emily had watched them approach with a numb, almost out of body experience. This could not be happening to her. A very, very bad dream. Maybe the days of bad luck were ahead.

"Well, what are we going to do with this, people?" Emily asked haughtily, still sitting bravely erect in the bed as the verdict had been delivered.

"The tumor is large, but operable. So even though that sounds bad, there are some positive aspects, Mrs. Carr," said Dr. Belmont, with Kate at his side. "The tumor is non-small cell cancer and it is stage T3. That means we can still do some surgery to remove it, then follow up with more treatments. The best news is that we don't think the cancer has yet spread. For the size of the tumor, that is amazing in itself. If you get lucky, with the surgery and radiation or chemotherapy, you could do reasonably well. There are, of course, side effects that we will discuss, but the good news is that there is hope for your situation. If you are willing to follow through with all the recommendations, we may give you many more years. There is never a guarantee, however, and lung cancer is a tough one for sure."

"Doctor, I am not a weenie, but I admit, this does scare me. A lot, actually. I need time to digest all of this," answered Emily. She was feeling not quite as lucky as she felt a few days ago.

"Time is of the essence in this case, Mrs. Carr, although I understand your concerns. We'll go over all the treatment options with you in detail, but I want the surgery scheduled as soon as possible," responded Dr. Bob.

"Will you do the operation?" asked Emily.

"Oh no, we need to get your chest specialist and oncologist to go over the results, examine you, and take over from here. There will be a few more confirmatory tests, I'm sure. We want the best result, you know," said Dr. Bob.

Emily was now feeling a little sick and out of control. God, she hated this. Several of her peers had bouts with diseases and one or two had died. Now she felt great empathy. Oh well, this was it. No sense in whining about it. She was more worried about the technicalities of the whole thing. Now her family would have to know somehow. She couldn't just stay here and have major surgery, get out of bed, get in the car and drive back home. She needed time to think, time to plan. Her life had taken worse turns than this and she had survived. Just a bit of bad luck. How she missed her family. What to do?

Dr. Belmont and Kate left the room as bleak looking as they had come in. Grim Reapers, Emily thought. Soon her luck must change. Bad luck always ends and things get better. Silent and alone with her thoughts, she began to figure out a plan. Suddenly her room's heavy door swung open and Darla burst in. *Not again!*

"I just heard the news and I am so sorry. I want to be of help in any way. I tried to find those photos last night but I ended up on the couch. Bubbles needed to cuddle up and we both fell asleep before I knew it! I just wish I could help you through this, Mrs. Carr," Darla gushed.

"Please, I will be fine. And I told you, there is no family to worry with. Please, you can just help me by bringing me ice water or maybe a TV Guide or a magazine. I really appreciate you, Honey, but I am fine," responded Emily.

"We just can't let you lie here all alone, so I will be in to see you any time I can get away. Maybe I can be your family for now?" queried Darla.

"Sure, fine. That would be nice," said Emily, thinking, *please just go away and let me think.*

"Okay, what can I do for you now?" continued Darla.

"Well, you could get me a local newspaper to read, dear. I would really like that. I still like to know what is going on around me, you know," answered Emily. *That should get her out of my hair for at least a few minutes. Now go play somewhere else!*

"Sure!" Darla exclaimed excitedly. "Be right back! I'll even pay for it myself at the gift store. I know you don't have any money, but I'll be happy to do it for you!"

Emily thought she saw a glint of questioning in the girl's statement about the money. As if she expected her to contradict what she had said about her financial status. Emily was careful not to relay anything in her facial expression except pure gratefulness. Anything to get her out of here. *What I need from you, is time alone to think.*

Examining her options, Emily ran over the checklist. There was an open return date to Palm Beach, but the girls would begin to worry if she was gone too long without calling or checking in. The car rental was also an open date with the credit card in Janice Kensington's name. She had the Taurus as long as they were being paid. Badger was home with the girls, but Mikki would have to be getting back to Orlando soon, leaving Brigetta alone at her beach house. Susan would still be busy with Michael until he went back to New York. Her household bills were paid automatically through the bank, so no worry there. She could just go back home and then see Dr. Getts, telling him about her cough. He would then reorder the tests and give her the bad news once again. That was Option One. Option Two or Plan B would be to have everything done here, just call home and tell everyone she would be gone for a while as she was sick but okay. She didn't think that would go over too well with the family. Such worry warts! Option Three would be to have the surgery that should be done quickly, recover enough to start the chemo or whatever tortures were in store for her, and then go home. She would tell Dr. Getts she had been diagnosed out of town and he would refer her to a local oncologist to continue the treatment. Even then, her family would not need to know right away. She didn't want them to worry. If the treatments failed, or if her hair all feel out, she could break it to them in her own way. Otherwise she would get well, at least for a while, and things could continue as before. She might continue doing her favors, although it was definitely time to retire from this type of endeavor. Running the store brought her great joy and peace, although not quite the excitement she was used to. That's what she would do. Have the surgery here, and see what happened after that.

The next morning Emily was seen by Dr. Sam Rogers, oncologist, and Dr. Ed Waterson, thoracic surgeon. The operation was scheduled for three days from today. That night, Mildred Carr and Emily Vanderhorn began to pray as the one person they were. Something she hadn't found to work in years past, but now she was willing to try everything. *Please Lord, let this go smoothly. I can die, but don't make this a mess for my family. I don't want them to have to try to figure all this out. Why is Granny Em here? What was she thinking, what was she doing?...just let me get through the surgery and back home. Well, God...over and out, 10-4 or whatever. I know I have no right to ask anything, but just this once. Please. I am not a totally bad person, really!*

The halls were darkening and voices more muffled as nurses and staff went about their nightly duties. A sign--NPO after midnight--was hung at the end of her bed, and an aide came in and took away the pitcher of water. She got hungry and thirsty right away. That was funny how that worked. She felt the Band-Aid on her arm from the blood draw and licked her dry lips. So this was it, all part of the final countdown. More tests in the morning, no breakfast, more needles and prodding. Not much could be worse than this. In all her life, she had a zillion scary moments, but this was the topper. Her life was in someone else's hands, not her own. She literally had no control over the testing procedures, the surgery, or the outcome. Not a pleasant sensation. Maybe her luck really had run out this time. Totally.

At just after midnight the phone by her bed rang, jarring and jolting every nerve suddenly awake. Who could that be? Maybe a wrong room number? What was wrong with the switchboard, putting through calls at this hour?

As she shakily picked up the phone and tentatively said hello, true terror made her blood run so cold that her bones hurt. The voice at the other end was the sum of all her fears.

The voice urgently whispered, "Granny?"

Chapter 12

Oh shhitt! "Umm, ...Oh, hi Darling. How did you know I was here?" Emily questioned, trying to sound nonchalant. "And where are you, Mikki?"

"You know, I should be the one asking the questions, Gran, because I am just a little concerned. What in the world were you thinking?" responded Mikki with a tinge of anger in her voice.

"Wellll, it's a long story, young lady, and I am old enough not to need a babysitter," said Emily. Sweat, real sweat, was now flavoring her armpits, as her mind raced. This would be a hard one to get away from. *The best defense is a good offense?*

"To answer your question, I'm across the street on my cell and about to come up to your room!" announced Mikki. "Don't you think it would be best to detail this situation in person? Moreover, in private?"

"You can't just walk in to the hospital and come up the stairs at this time of night. They will think you are a terrorist or something," Emily said, vaguely hopeful that she would just go away. Emily was now sitting up at the side of the bed, legs dangling, almost as if ready to run.

"Sure Gran, I would make a great Osama, but people get sick at all hours of the night at a hospital and no one will keep me from visiting my old, sick Grandmother, now would they?" continued Mikki with more than just a hint of sarcasm.

"You just don't know the problems you will start. It will be a very bad idea, Mik, just trust me on this one," pleaded Emily.

"Granny, you're not the great secret you think. I know you're using another name and you will soon be telling me why and how and for how long. I can promise you that. I want all the answers and you will soon be giving me all the answers," Mikki said with much determination.

"I have never heard you speak to me like this, and I must say, I don't like it, Mikelle," said Emily, her spirits floundering. What to do now? She could see there was no stopping her granddaughter. This was just what she did not need now. A few nights before major surgery and she had to deal with Mikki and her questions. There were lots of stories she could invent, but the Sheik story had ended when the girls were in Junior and Senior High. Now she had to move on to bigger and better things.

"See you soon, Mikki," said Emily in the flat dull tone of resignation.

"I would think you would be glad to see me, Granny. I'll be right there," answered Mikki solemnly.

Emily quietly hung up the phone, dumbfounded for the first time she could remember in her life.

Downstairs, at the front desk in the brightly lit lobby, Mikki announced herself as the granddaughter of Mrs. Mildred Carr, Michelle Smythe. The beautiful young woman got more than a subtle stare from the elderly gentleman who volunteered at night. As this vision of a woman approached his desk, he almost dropped both his crossword puzzle and glasses.

"Whoa, what was this?" he thought, startled out of boredom and complacency. He wrote out Mildred Carr's room number on the visitor pass with shaky fingers. Citrus City was not used to this type of woman gliding around late at night. She looked like a movie star or model. He tried to not ogle openly, but he was smitten with instant adoration. He would have given this young gorgeous woman the world if she had just glanced his way. Mikki smiled her biggest and most flirtatious smile and pursed her beautiful full lips, offering an air kiss of gratitude.

"Thank you so much for letting me go up to her room at this late hour. But her surgery date is fast approaching, I just knew you would understand," she said seductively, her large eyes peering through thick, dark auburn eyelashes.

There was further heavy appraisal as she walked away towards the elevator. The security guard was just returning from the cafeteria with black coffee in a lidded white cup.

"Wow, Jimmy, who was that?" he exclaimed, looking back over his shoulder.

Both men watched mesmerized as the low-slung jeans, cropped T-shirt, and high-heeled sandals went through the opening elevator door. She turned as the doors began to close and gave them just a hint of a tiny wink, as she flipped her hair back over her shoulder.

Jimmy and Hooch both stood staring, mouths agape, almost salivating. Neither could speak for minutes.

Hooch, then, suddenly came to his senses. "You did check her out, didn't you? Where was she going? Who is she, a model? Who is she visiting?" he questioned, rapid-fire.

"Just someone's granddaughter. An old lady having surgery in a couple of days and the chick drove all day to get here. Couldn't say no to that, could I?" answered Jimmy, shrugging his shoulders.

"Well, no, we couldn't say no to her anyway. My answer would be yes for about anything she wanted from me," Hooch smirked, as he scratched his crotch.

"Yeah, Hooch, they all want you. Sure. Right," said Jimmy. "I have seen those flocks of birds just chasing you all over town."

"No reason to get sarcastic on me now, Jimmy. Just admit you would want her too!" said Hooch.

"I may be ancient, but I am not mummified. I still keep the old woman happy," said Jimmy, grinning and thinking about his Viagra prescription.

Hooch laughed and said, "She'd probably be happy if you just leave her alone and not snore too loud, Jim Boy!"

Both men went back to reading their puzzles and magazines and drinking coffee from disposable cups. Mikki headed for her goal of Room 311. She slipped steadily through the elevator doors and with a familiar cat-like stealth, flowed silently through the partially closed door to the room, closing it tightly behind her.

"Here I am, *Mrs. Carr*!" she announced with triumph, throwing her arms above her head as in a victory celebration. Seeing Mikki, Emily Vanderhorn was again smitten by her granddaughter's beauty and poise. She couldn't help but smile and feel inner joy at the sight of family.

"Well, Granny, what do you have to say for yourself?" queried Mikki, leaving the closed door and rushing towards the bed. She leaned over and kissed her grandmother on the forehead.

"I am sick and I am in the hospital?" answered Emily, suppressing a smile.

"Good. That's a great start. A smart alec answer unbecoming a woman of your stature in life, but a great start. Keep going!" Mikki demanded, standing beside the bed with arms folded.

"You seem to know everything, so why don't you tell me what you do know. Maybe then, out of the kindness of my heart, I will fill you in on some missed details. Will that work for you?" Emily responded with her eyes scrunched up elfishly.

Mikki stood towering over her grandmother at the bed-side. She glanced around the room and grabbed the corner easy chair, pulled it to the bed and dramatically plopped down. She dropped the Louis Vuitton handbag unceremoniously onto the linoleum. Flinging her long auburn locks to the side, she eased back into the chair, arms on the worn rests. Then she lifted her long legs, kicked off the Gucci sandals, and placed her feet between the bedrails onto the mattress.

"Okay, now I am comfy and ready to have our little chat, Granny. As a favor, I will begin," she announced.

"You are oh so kind to me, Dear Grandchild. Please do begin to talk. This conversation is bound to be so enlightening. I can't wait," responded Emily, enjoying the banter. She was grinning inside, despite her fear. Family was here. She felt annoyed, yet happy to see her. Curiosity begged for answers so she steeled herself for what was to follow. Just what did Mikki know? This week was just not going her way.

Mikki, once comfortable in the worn chair, got back up and helped Granny Em raise the head of her bed. She adjusted her pillows for her and gave her cheek a gentle touch.

"I was so worried about you. You may be a pain in the butt, Granny, but I was terrified driving here," said Mikki.

"I'm sorry. I just didn't want to bring the family into all of this mess. I am having surgery in a few days for cancer. It's in my lung. Does that suck or what?" said Emily.

"Granny, I know that much. That's why I'm here. I happened to pick up a call at Mom's house from a girl who works here, a Darla? She told me she thought you were a relative of Brigetta's. She got the phone number from the nursing school directory. She just called on the chance that we knew you and didn't know you were here. Of course, I denied everything, said I had never heard of you and that Brigetta's grandma was in California. That is why I couldn't tell Brig yet, since I didn't know what was up with the assumed name and all that crap. So, the jig is up, Granny. The word is out, and here I am," continued Mikki. "And by the way, my new name is Michelle Smythe, your wonderful and concerned granddaughter. Sooner or later, this Darla person will put everything together. I was there at the freshman tea too, you know, but sat with my friend Gazelle.

Remember? If she starts looking through her pictures, she may add this all up. That is why you need to tell me what is going on and why we are sneaking around like secret agents."

"That Darla is the nosiest girl I know. Besides you, that is. Why couldn't she just have left things alone?" asked Emily.

"Don't worry about her. Let me worry about our 'new identities' and Darla," said Mikki.

"I was planning to have the surgery and get better enough to come back home. I would have been fine, you know," responded Emily.

"Oh yeah, you're doing great, just great. All alone in a place that is almost like a foreign country and ready to have life-threatening surgery for a life-threatening illness. All alone. Nothing like sharing things with the family, Granny. That's not right. You know it," stated Mikki, a little tear forming in her left eye. She quickly got a tissue from the bedside stand and wiped it away. "God, where do they get these things? They feel like sandpaper." as she blotted more tears which were now free flowing.

"You may not have noticed, but this is not a Five Star Resort exactly. And by the way, just as a warning, the butt paper is even worse," Emily quipped.

Mikki smiled through her tears and regained some composure. "I was so worried. And now, I am so glad I came. Didn't you want to see us?"

"Darling, you don't know how much I've been thinking about all my family in the last few days. This has been a nightmare extraordinaire. Unbelievably awful. I'm very glad to see you. But I know you want answers to a bunch of questions you have every right to ask," continued Emily.

"Oh no, Granny, what ever would give you that idea? Just because we supposedly put you on a plane to California and now you are here in Citrus City? Gee, why would we want an explanation for that? Actually, I think it has been a common occurrence with you. But why would we want to know, after all, you are just our Granny. Our dear Granny Em we all love and cherish and miss," responded Mikki, sitting back onto the edge of the chair.

"Do I detect a bit of sarcasm, Mikelle? I am truly sorry for everything. Really. It's just that some things are best unknown. In fact, I couldn't tell you everything for safety reasons. It was for everyone's protection. Take my word for it," said Emily, now wiping a tear herself.

The two women hugged for a long time. Then Mikki pulled out two bottles of cranberry Snapple from her insulated lunch bag she had packed for the drive. She unscrewed the tops, stuck a straw in each, gave one to Emily and plopped back down in the chair, feet once more propped on the bed. "You are allowed something to drink, right? What does NPO mean?"

"Maybe... No Pissing Outside?"

"I'm sure that's it," answered Mikki, narrowing her eyes.

"Well, I'm sure it won't hurt me. I'm really thirsty anyway."

As Mikki watched Granny Em suck down the juice, she was sure it was not allowed. Granny Em was enjoying it too much. Soon the whole bottle was nearly gone. "Well, Granny, we have all night, Mikki continued. "And don't say you are tired and have a big week ahead in the operating room. You will be sleeping all day of the surgery, unless they have some weird sort of anesthetic they use out here in the boondocks. Maybe they just pop you on the head with a pitchfork handle. Either way, you'll be out."

"I thought you came here to give me tenderness and sympathy. Okay, let me just drink my juice while I concoct my story."

"No story, Gran, no story. I want the truth and nothing but the truth. I'm a big girl and I can handle it all."

Emily sipped slowly through the straw while her mind raced through thoughts, compiling stories and images and sorting. Some went to the shredder and some were organized into credible ideas. She watched her granddaughter who returned her look without flinching. The two sipped their drinks and read each other's eyes.

"Gran, don't even think that you will get away with it," stated Mikki.

"With what?" responded Emily with feigned innocence and her best angelic expression.

"I can see the wheels turning now. Put away the halo! You are thinking about how to get out of this and what you will tell me. We are both grown ups and it is time for truth or dare."

"Okay, okay. I am just trying to figure out a way to best say what I need to tell you. That's all."

"Bullshit, Granny. You're gonna try to tell me some big ones, and I know it. Only this time the old Sheik story is not going to fly. I'm ready for the real stuff here and now. And by the way, you are a captive here in your chrome bedrails and I am going to guard you. You are safe with me, but you will talk."

"How did you ever get so bossy? You are starting to sound like your mother, and we know how much fun she is."

"We are not here to have fun. We are here to figure out the rest of your life. Let's get on with it."

Emily noisily sucked her straw at the bottom of the glass bottle, trying to drown out Mikki's words. Mikki just sat watching her from the cushy chair. There would be no getting rid of her. She was here for the duration.

"Okay, you know I have cancer. This week I have surgery. By the way, what ever happened to patient confidentiality? HIPPA and the Privacy Act? That Darla has a damned big mouth and a too, too inquisitive mind," said Emily.

"Gran. What happened? That is what I don't know. Darla said you were climbing a ladder to an apartment building in a really bad section of town. Now, we all know, that is not something most grandmas are doing, especially mine! Or so I thought. What is up with that?" said Mikki with emphasis, ignoring the question about privacy. "Also," Mikki continued, "my fashion-wise, excellent shopper Granny is thought to be a penniless bag lady? I mean, this is really a good one. I don't know if one night is long enough to even begin this conversation, but we are going to give it a good try."

"Does Brigetta know I am here? What about Susan? Any-one else?" asked Emily.

"Just me so far, Granny, but how long do you think that will last? They think I had to go back to the office for some unfinished contract I had to dream up at the last minute."

"Oh, so now you are a liar, too? I don't feel so bad, being the only fibber in the family."

"Not quite the same, do you think? Please get on with it," responded Mikki.

"Yes, actually I was climbing a ladder and fell. Got a nasty cut on my leg, by the way. Want to see it?"

"You are stalling. I am waiting."

"Such a persistent child; always were," continued Emily. "Anyway, someone found me as I apparently had passed out or something. I had some pneumonia and a fever. That's it! The fever caused me to do some weird stuff!" she tried, watching Mikki for signs of belief.

"Sure Granny, what was it? 110 degrees and it caused sudden brain dementia? You didn't seem that sick a few days ago when we dropped you off at the airport! Remember the airport, where most people go to actually get on planes and go to their planned destinations? You know, the places they tell their families about? You did have a little cough. In fact, you have had it for a while."

"Oh Geez. Well, no, I did not get on the plane. I decided not to go."

"I got that much. Please go on," demanded Mikki.

"You know, you are pretty harsh on an old lady who has cancer and is about to have major surgery!" said Emily, looking hurt and turning her head on the pillow to look away from Mikki's face. When Mikki said nothing in response, Emily moved just her eyes back, still facing away.

"You are right," exhaled Mikki after some time in stand off. "Just give me the basics and let us get through this operation. I guess you will be able to tell me everything later. Are you going to be all right? God, I am so worried about you."

Grateful for the temporary reprieve, Emily turned back to her much-loved granddaughter. "Thank you. I promise I will tell you everything later. Really. I will."

Their hands met. Mikki took her grandmother's petite age-spotted hand and held it in her own. Both hands had long slender fingers. Her own was well manicured, with professionally applied French tips to the nails. Granny's nails were cut short, practically so, with a hint of clear polish still visible. Granny wore no jewelry now, of course. The back of her hand had several large bluish marks, from I.V. needles, Mikki supposed. The skin was warm and slightly damp. Their touch was tender and binding as blood related fingers gently entwined, and softly squeezed.

"I love you, Granny," whispered Mikki. "I will always love you, no matter what you tell me. Trust me in that. In fact, I have an idea of why you are here. Brig and I have had lots of time together at your house to talk."

"Well, I can't wait to hear your synopsis. But I love you too, and I do trust you. I will trust you. We are family," murmured Emily. She then felt a sense of peace and also fatigue. As their embraced hands rested on the sheets, she gave Mikki another little squeeze and closed her eyes. There would be time to deal with the future later. Right now, the big obstacle was the tests and the surgery. The tumor. Staying alive. Mikki was here holding her hand, literally, and all would work out eventually. Emily's head fell back against her pillow. Mikki's face lay across the older woman's arm, the lowered bedrail allowing them touch and closeness. Both women felt the waves of tension begin to ebb away. Sleep was awarded like a prize as the combatants agreed to call a momentary truce, in fact, an allegiance. The room was again dim and quiet, this time peacefully so, as soft sleepy breathing replaced the persistent interrogation.

Chapter 13

Mikki awoke before dawn from her curled up position in the chair, rose and stretched. In the darkened room, she glanced over at Emily and saw her eyes were still closed. She crept to the bathroom to wash her face and give her hair a quick brushing. She was getting a little nervous about her Granny's upcoming surgery, but was determined to remain calm and confident for the patient's sake. She covered the Snapple bottles under paper towels in the trash container. She didn't want to be tried and convicted of giving restricted fluids to a patient listed NPO, even though it was just a little after midnight. Today's testing would probably not start on time anyway. She silently crept back to the chair where she had spent the night.

"How come you're up so early?" said Emily, so quietly she caused Mikki to jump.

"Didn't think you would hear me. I had to pee and wash up," answered Mikki.

"That john sounds like a typhoon approaching! How can anyone sleep through that? Anyway, I was awake off and on through the night. Just a little scared, I guess," said Emily.

"Granny, you're a tough old bird and you'll probably scare the cancer cells right out of you with any luck. Really, I think you'll be fine. This is a challenge for all of us, but I think you'll be fine."

She helped Emily to the bathroom and back and then tucked her back into bed. Dawn was approaching and light was coming thru the window and from under the door as hallway lighting was turned up. Just then Kate came through the door carrying a basket full of sterile wrapped needles, tubing, syringes, and I.V. solutions. She flipped on the room light after softly calling the patient's name.

"Mrs. Carr? It's time to wake up. We have to get you ready for your tests this morning," said Kate. She was suddenly startled to see the form in the corner of the room and stopped in surprise, mouth falling open.

"Hi! My name is Michelle Smythe. I am the granddaughter. I came in late last night," said Mikki quickly announcing herself. "I was here as soon as I heard."

"Oh, I am so glad! Mrs. Carr was insisting she had no family! What a great relief! I am Katherine Bingham, the nurse supervisor for this wing today. I usually work nights and was the night charge nurse when your grandmother was brought into the hospital. We were all so concerned about her having this surgery and no one to call or talk to. So nice to meet you!" said Kate, beaming with the pleasure of relief.

Kate apprised the stunning young woman who had risen from the chair with hand extended to greet her. Now she knew why the older woman might have had the fancy panties. Probably a gift from the family, who seemed to be well to do, if this young woman was an example. She saw the emerald and diamond ring on the middle finger of her right hand and the Tanzanite and Australian opal pinky ring on the left hand. This was an absolutely gorgeous and well-dressed young woman. Another puzzle piece, though helpful, that did not quite seem to fit. One thing for sure, she did not want Dr. Bob Belmont to spend too much time with this apparently single female.

"Nothing to eat or drink after midnight, right, Mrs. Carr? Well, we have to get another I.V. started for the rest of the scans, Mrs. Carr. I have to ask you to leave for a few minutes please, Ms. Smythe. Just policy while we start her line. Would you want to go get a coffee or something? Our cafeteria is open all night and starts serving breakfast very early. You can come right back in as soon as I'm finished," said Kate.

"Oh sure, I'm useless without my jolt of caffeine, so I'll be right back, Granny. Don't run away 'til I get back, now?" said Mikki with a wink.

"I would really like to talk to you, too, Michelle, if possible, when you get back. Or else we can wait until your grandma goes down to Nuclear Medicine. Maybe you could help with the paperwork and straighten out some confusion we have?" requested Kate.

"I don't know how much help I'll be, but I'll be glad to speak to you about my misbehaving grandmother," responded Mikki as she continued out the door and down the hallway to the elevators.

"Aha! We have caught you! Someone tracked you down and that is great! I was so concerned about you being alone with such a big worry coming up. Don't you feel better now that Michelle is here? How did she find you anyway? Did you call her?" asked Kate as soon as she was alone with her patient.

"You're right. I feel better. Yes, I finally called her. I just didn't want to bother my family."

"I knew it! We have so many people who feel like that! I, myself, find it hard to understand, since I would want my whole family to be with me. It's like it's their job or something. They wouldn't feel right if they were left out. We have to admit they love us and will be with us through anything, good or bad," continued Kate.

"Well, I felt Michelle would want to come, and I felt guilty having the government pay for this when some of my family could be footing my bill. I called her on her cell phone and next thing you know, she was here!" explained Emily. "And yes, I was very glad to see her, once she actually had arrived."

"Where does she live? Around here?"

"Oh no, she travels a lot around the state and even out of the country but her home is in Orlando", said Emily, telling a half truth at last. Now she would need some private time with her granddaughter to get the whole story straight. That was what was so nice about working alone. There were no conflicting scenarios. No chances for twists and turns, lies becoming entangled.

"That was one reason I wasn't sure I could even contact her, since she travels. Then I thought I would give it a try and here she is! I was lucky she was not out of the area, I guess."

Intrigued, Kate asked, "Does she model underwear by any chance? I know this is a weird question, but I was guessing that was where you got the Victoria's Secret lingerie. She, of course, is beautiful enough to be one of their models!"

"Thank you, yes, she could have been one of their models, but modeling was never high on her list. My Michelle is strictly business oriented. Her mind has always been fixed in finance and numbers. So you are a good guesser! She is a sales rep for Victoria's Secret and I get all the samples that she can get for me. Isn't that great! A little old lady like me getting to wear fancy panties!"

"Wow, pretty and also brains! What a combination! Guess she has a lot of boyfriends?" asked Kate hopefully, wishing that Michelle's dance card would be booked full.

"She does her share of dating, but no one special right now. Guess she has been spending a lot of time with her job. You know, trying to make it to the top before she settles down with a husband and family," answered Emily, fully knowing why the nurse had been asking. "You are quite pretty yourself, Nurse Bingham. Are you dating that good-looking Dr. Belmont? Now there is a nice catch!"

With a little blush Kate responded, making a note about the superior observation abilities of her patient, "I really like him, but with both of us here at the hospital much of the time, we can't seem to find a spot for just the two of us outside of these walls. Now that I am on the day shift, we are hoping to be able to work something out sooner or later."

"Make it sooner, Kate. You'd be surprised at how fast time starts to get away from you as you get older. It's a real bummer, I must say!"

"Well, I'm sure trying. I know that a career is important, but family always comes first for me, too. And I am so glad your granddaughter's here for you now. I know I would just die if my grandmother was in the hospital and I couldn't be there."

"Always remember your family ties. They are the people you can count on when you need them to be there for you."

Kate nodded in agreement as she began unwrapping the needles and tearing off the tape she would use to secure the tubing to her patient's arm. "Just a little prick now," Kate said she slapped at the small blue veins in the back of Mrs. Carr's hand. Soon the needle was deftly inserted and Mrs. Carr was again connected to an I.V. bag of fluid hanging by the bedside. "Someone will be back soon to give you an isotope injection before they come to get you for the scan. It will probably be at least an hour though. Right now I am going to go get some TED stockings for your legs. They will help prevent blood clots from forming in your legs from all this bed rest and after the surgery. Once we get you up and moving again, we can take them off." She quickly did a visual measurement for size and left the room to get the hosiery. At that time, Mikki reentered the room. Her make up looked fresh and her pretty face was again glowing with youth and a big smile.

"Mikki, come over here quick! Guess what! You sell Victoria's Secret!" Emily whispered to her granddaughter as she pulled her quickly to her, latching on to an arm as Mikki ventured towards the bed.

"I do?"

"Yes, and of course, you are wonderful at your job!"

"Just how did you come up with that one?" asked Mikki with her arms crossed in accusation.

"It just fit the situation."

"Well, Granny, what's our story and let's stick to it?" asked Mikki with a conspiratorial look as the two put their heads close together. They quickly reviewed and revised a believable abstract of untruths capable of being repeated without loss of credence. They made it simple and beyond questioning. The two were related but hardly ever spoke, they devised. They came together as a necessity only when old granny got herself into trouble. Then someone in the family would bail her out of the problem whether financial or situational. That was their whole relationship. They didn't know much about each other, but were there as support when needed. They didn't dislike each other but just chose to live independent lives. Grandma was an eccentric. That much was probably true. The best way to tell a story was to take a truth and embellish it. One part truth, a zillion parts lie.

Kate popped back through the door with a new package of the desired leg wear. She even showed Michelle how to apply them, though she didn't know how long the woman would stay with her grandmother. "Not exactly the latest in lingerie fashion, are they?" grinned Mikki as she examined the coarse, white opaque elastic stockings, holding them up as in a demonstration technique. The hose were applied and Kate instructed the two on why they were needed.

"Shall we talk now or later, Michelle?" asked Kate, when they were finished.

"Well, right now I would like some private time with my Granny, please. We haven't seen each other for a long time, you know?" answered Mikki, still smoothing and straightening the stockings.

"Oh sure, of course. Well, it'll be a little longer. They called from Nuclear to say your testing has been delayed because of an emergency that just came in."

"Well, I hope I don't come back looking like a night light!" stated Mrs. Carr brightly.

"Don't worry, they haven't had any glow-in-the-dark patients lately."

"I don't know much about the medical field or medicine, or surgery," lied Mrs. Carr. "But I am sure I can trust this hospital and my doctor. You said he is a specialist." That part she was hoping was true.

"See you both in a while," said Kate as she gave a little wave as she exited the room.

Mikki got up then and went to shut the door tightly. "Gee, Gran, maybe if you glowed a nice neon green, I could find you more easily! What d'ya think?"

"Funny, but that's my line. Seriously, Mikki, what if Darla comes in here and sees you? I really don't want her to figure out who I am. I can't explain everything right now, but I can tell you, we don't want that to happen. It would be disastrous for the whole family."

"Part of me doesn't even want to know why you are saying that, but I do know I have to believe you. I'll go out to see your nurse in a while and tell her no visitors please, excluding all but only necessary staff. We could move you to another room. In fact after the surgery, you may be going to the post-surgical area for your recuperation, right? Darla shouldn't be on that floor, but as nosy as you say she is, she may come down to see you, especially when she hears that a granddaughter has made claim to you. She probably will assume it is Brigetta, even though I told her we never heard of you and our grandmother was in another state. Another state of mind would be more likely."

"Now is not the time to be cute," said Emily with a sigh. "We really have to figure this out and quickly, before they come and give me some knockout shot or something. She just can't find out. She could be trouble. The girl was quite useful at first but now is a giant liability."

"I understand, Granny. I get it. Don't worry. I have it under control," stated Mikki. "By the way, and don't lie to me, I have to know just one thing."

"What?"

"Was the reason you came here, hmm, …was it anything to do with Tyrone Dupris?"

"Shit."

"Shit is not the answer. Please. Just tell me. A simple yes or no. Then we can get on with the rest of it. Please Granny, trust me, your granddaughter, to help figure this all out for us. Just tell me," pleaded Mikki, as she began to pace the side of the bed while looking up at the ceiling.

There was a long silence. Then a few tears began to fall, first from Emily, then from Mikki.

"I thought so. But, please just say it. Please, please, please."

"You already must know. So, yes, that was the reason. How much else do you know?" said the now tearful Emily. "I always wanted to shield the family. No one was to know anything. This is so dangerous. Please, Mikki, no more questions, okay?"

Mikki was now dry-eyed and had regained her composure when a technician with blue scrubs and a blue hat covering her hair came into the room.

"Just a few questions, Mrs. Carr," she said as she read the patient's wrist band, "then I am giving you a small injection to help us visualize the area of the surgery. Your doctor has ordered it for you, okay?"

She again asked the granddaughter to leave the area as she pulled the curtains, gave an injection into the Y-shaped I.V. terminal, and asked the questions on the necessary forms. After obtaining some permission signatures, she swished back the curtains around the bed and was gone as quickly as she had come in. Again, Mikki went to the door and pulled it completely shut, wishing silently that the injection was truth serum.

"Granny, everything will be fine. Just get through the damned tests and surgery and we will talk some more. Just keep remembering that I love you and we all love you. No matter what. We will all stick together and do what's best. Know that above all else," said Mikki.

"If you only knew the whole thing. Maybe you would understand, maybe not. I'm not the person you think I am. Even so, I always loved all of you. My family always did and always will come first. That is what you need to know. That is really all you need to know. But I'll tell you everything. I promise. I guess I owe it to you. They said I may be on a ventilator and won't be able to talk for a while after the surgery. But we'll talk when I get back from this morning's tests. Really."

"I'm counting on it. I know more than you think, but lots of it was speculation. Now I want the facts, Ma'am, nothing but the facts," Mikki quipped.

Suddenly the door was crashed open and in stalked Darla with a huge grin on her face.

"So, Mrs. Carr, you have been found out! As soon as I heard the news, I came running in to see who your relatives are that have come to your rescue," announced Darla triumphantly, arms crossed and tapping her toe as if scolding an errant child.

"Yes, here you are. As you can see, I am trying to have a private conversation with my granddaughter Michelle before I go for more tests," retorted Emily.

Mikki stared quietly with cool eyes at the overly energetic young woman who had rudely burst into the room. The darkening green irises beneath the long dark auburn lashes were issuing a warning that went unheeded by the precocious Darla. Even after finally seeing the glaring but silent granddaughter, Darla continued to chatter on and on.

"I did find some pictures from the nursing school tea that I had told you about. So I called Brigetta from home last night. Her mom told me that she and her sister were staying at the grandmother's house while she was out of town. So then I called to talk to Brigetta and got her sister instead. I was told their grandmother was in California on a business trip."

"So Darla, why are you telling me all of this?" asked Emily. "As you were told, you were off base. Now I would like to talk more with my real granddaughter, Michelle, rather than discuss some perceived notion you have formed."

"Okay, sorry. It's just that something really funny is going on around here. First you have no relatives, then I call for Brigetta and soon a granddaughter shows up. Not only that, I was talking to Helen from housekeeping and she told me she saw blood spots on the stairs. They led right to your bathroom from the hallway, too. Why would you be out running up and down the stairs in your condition? Somethin' just ain't right, Mrs.Carr."

"Blood? Well, it surely wasn't me! You know you had to help me even go downstairs in the elevator. I had to use a walker. I use a cane to walk every day!" Emily said quietly, appearing to be not the least upset with this revelation.

"Yes, that's what's weird. But I do remember that your bandage was blood soaked in the morning. Where you cut your knee. The morning nurse told me she had to put some steri-strips on it to replace some pulled stitches."

"My, my…you sure get around. Well, don't worry about it too much. Everything is fine now. But I do need some alone time with Michelle if you don't mind?" said Emily icily.

"I am really sorry. I am out of here. We will talk more later. Hope all goes well for you, *Mrs. Carr.*"

Darla exited the room as quickly as she had come in, slamming the big heavy door closed with a swish and click.

Emily looked pale and small now. She was seeing her world unravel in front of her eyes, in front of her granddaughter's eyes, which was even worse. She began to unconsciously wring her hands in a methodical motion, as a worried look began to cross her face. "Just what I needed today. Darla Simmons. I surely wish she would shut the fuck up," announced Emily.

During the whole "Darla experience," Mikki had remained silent for two reasons. First of all, she didn't want to take a chance that Darla would recognize her voice from the phone conversation. They had spoken for several minutes while she let Darla prattle on, telling her all the information she needed and giving none herself. Second, she felt a huge perfusion of anger penetrating every cell in her body. She did not trust herself to respond in a manner that would be perceived as any more than annoyance. She went to Granny Em's bedside and kissed her soft downy cheek.

"Not to worry, Granny, not to worry," she guaranteed, as she wrapped her arms around the small neck and hugged. "You are safe with me. I will take care of you. Always."

Again the door swung open and this time a gurney banged its way into the room, scraping the door and the wooden handrails on the wall. A cute, blond male X-Ray technician who said he was here for a passenger was pushing it. He had no trouble loading the small elderly patient onto the cart, covering her with blankets, and putting her hair into a paper cap, all with barely a glance at the lovely female at her bedside. The women kissed good-bye and exchanged smiles and knowing glances. *Must be gay*, they both were thinking. It was unusual though, since persons of any sexual orientation usually could spare a glance at a living, breathing sculpted work of art like Mikki. Oh well, Mikki thought to herself, impressing a man was the least of her problems today of all days.

The tests lasted four hours and Mikki waited in the family waiting area with a "Cosmo" opened to a page on make-up on her lap. Her eyes pointed towards the model on the colored sheet but her mind was racing to a million other places. Granny had really done it this time. What had she gotten herself into? What Granny Em did not know, was that Mikki had been keeping an eye on her for quite some time. When Miguel from the car rental had left a voice mail on her cell phone, she was not surprised. In her teenage years she began to have time alone in the Pink Flamingo when Granny took off to "visit the sheik." Wandering through the mansion on the ocean, she had childish curiosity. Certain things did not fit together well about her Granny. Granny never spoke much about her life before she met Granddad, in fact, had always avoided the subject. She knew her Granny had made her own business and had married into a fair amount of money. But other than the fact that she was raised in the old South by family other than her parents, she knew relatively nothing about her. She mentioned spending some time at "the farm" but nothing much else. She went to college at a private school, she would tell the girls. They had joked it was the "no-name" university and Emily would say she was always hiding from the school so they wouldn't find her address and request constant alumni donations. The secrets were a big curiosity for both girls, but their mother also remained mum on questioning. Susan seemed unconcerned about her own mother's background.

"She raised me to be a lady, sent me to Yale, and taught me to survive in a man's world. Why would I question that? And you girls shouldn't question anything either. Look at all she has done for you," Susan had admonished her daughters.

And it was true. The granddaughters would never need anything that wouldn't be given. True, their own father was an excellent provider, but Emily granted anything extra or special. During their school days, even their rich kid friends were envious of their life. They all loved to tell stories of their times at the Pink Flamingo, the well-known expansive beachfront estate. Sometimes Emily would let them have sleepovers at the home and a multitude of girls would descend on the scene with their favorite CD's, their favorite pillows, and loungewear. Granny Em would usually let them order pizza, wings, and salads delivered in huge boxes and the place would be loud with dancing all night long. The only rules were that no boys were invited over, no late night phone calls, and they had to stay in the house itself after midnight. Sometimes they would all go down to the beach around dark and James, the gardener, would set up a teepee-style bonfire by the waves. Teen girls would race to the water's edge and grab the precut roasting sticks, cooking their hot dogs and flaming marshmallows until the midnight curfew. What they didn't know was that Granny Em always had at least half a dozen armed security guards on her property lines surveying with paid watchfulness. They remained discreetly out of site, but were always there and working. The guards knew there was no fooling around with the safety of Mrs. Vanderhorn's grandchildren and their friends.

After the outside activities were over, the game room was opened and the masses of female giggles descended into a room surrounded by walls lit by neon guitars, flamingos, and alligators. There was a sparkling, mirrored globe for a lighted strobe effect and a hardwood dance floor. For more fun, three pinball machines, four virtual reality racecar screens, a traditional pool table and card tables were set up. There were even slot machines which paid an occasional surprise token redeemable for gift items in Emily's shop. Mostly the girls would get a choice of lingerie as their award or some glitter body lotion that was also sold at "Favors." There was a massive bar and stools where Mr. Max, a security officer turned babysitter/bartender, served fountain drinks. He always wore a tuxedo-printed T-shirt and top hat for these occasions that was a big hit with the girls. Other favorites were root beer floats and virgin Margaritas. It was fashionably cool for the girls to moan and groan about the lack of alcohol but many felt secretly glad there was no pressure to indulge.

Mikki and Brigetta were glad their grandmother was so different from the blue-haired matrons at the country club. Their Granny was strict but not structured. She was as spontaneous and fun as anyone could possibly be. But Granny Em was not all sugarplums and cotton candy. Mikki had seen her in action many a time. People learned quickly that Mrs. Emily Vanderhorn would not be put into situations where she was at the disadvantage. Mikki smiled at the recollection of the businessman who became the "target" instead of the "target-or". Granny had hired a man's firm who had quoted a price for complete replacement of the brick cobblestones in her circular drive. The quote was fair, but this was an expensive contract. When the job was complete, an invoice was presented to Emily for almost double the price. The man grinned and said the labor was "a bit higher" than expected in man-hours, supposing erroneously that Mrs. Vanderhorn would just pay the bill to avoid a hassle like most women for whom he had done work.

"Man-hours? Then next time hire a woman!" she had replied, while calmly handing him a check for the original amount.

"Well, Ma'am, the work is done and this is your bill. You can well afford it, so pay up!" he said with an arrogant have-not vs. have-everything sneer.

Never losing her cool or even cooler smile, Emily replied, "If this check doesn't suit, you can take your driveway and man-hours back. You know, the three business-day return?"

"You dumb broad, you can't take back a driveway!" he announced red-faced, hands on hips, refusing to accept the offered check. The man's major mistake was not noticing the change in Emily's eyes: cold steel blue, like the blade of a well-made knife.

Emily snatched the check back, instantly getting a better idea, saying, "Do you want this or not?" She was now holding the check under his sunburned nose, provokingly.

Face and ears turning fire engine red, he began to walk away. "You will be hearing from my attorney and your credit will take a big fat nose dive!" he managed as he turned back, perhaps deciding to get the check for partial payment after all.

"That scares me immensely, Sir, but if you refuse payment, I guess I'll have to return your product," said Emily with an eye-meeting stare.

"The driveway? You will return it? Ha!"

The frustrated concrete manager brusquely grabbed the check from Emily's hand, and stomped away holding the check in the air, waving it in his right hand. Finally he made a big display of shredding the pieces like confetti as he walked. He was mumbling something unintelligible under his breath as he climbed into the white Ford pickup and squealed out of the driveway, mashing two newly planted Sago palms on his way out.

The next morning the two plants were replaced and three small Bobcats with cute, tanned young operators were busy digging up the freshly laid cobblestones and loading them into a large dump truck. They were subsequently delivered across town and dumped unceremoniously in the manager's front yard on Palm Terrace. Outraged, the man immediately called his business attorney who had already heard of the hilarious caper. The lawyer knew it was useless and even scary to deal with Mrs. Emily Vanderhorn. Emily had the driveway replaced the following day by another contractor. End of story.

No, her Granny was not your typical grandmother. Yet, she seemed so helpless now. The surgery was one thing she couldn't control. She hoped there would be time before the operation to find out all of Granny's life secrets. There was so much to know, and now, maybe so little time to find the answers.

Mikki jumped with a reflexive jerk when the quiet of Granny Em's room was banged back to hospital reality. Dr. Waterson in blue scrubs stalked in, mask hanging loosely from his neck and surgical cap still in place. His manner and eyes softened when he saw Mikki sitting in the corner chair, her eyes suddenly round and huge like a cornered doe.

"You are the granddaughter?" he asked.

"Yes, I'm Michelle. How's my grandmother? Is she okay?" responded Mikki, rising from the chair as if to flee to Granny Em's side.

"Sorry. I came from another case in surgery this morning. The testing came out pretty much as expected. The tumor is large, but fairly well contained. We'll know more after the full written report by the radiologists, but Mrs. Carr is doing well, considering her age. She is in very good physical condition other than the cancer."

Relief flooding over Mikki, her shoulders and neck began relax from the initial fight or flight response. Closing her eyes, she tunneled her fingers through her soft wavy hair at the top of her scalp. Small tears welled in the inner corners of her eyes, but heavy lashes swept them quickly away.

"I come from good stock, you know. Granny is a tough little fighter. She will be fine."

Dr. Waterson took her hand briefly and squeezed it. As he turned to go, his appreciative eyes focused directly on Mikki's as he quietly said, "I can definitely see you come from good stock."

As he left the room, Mikki felt almost sick with relief. Seeing the doctor enter the room so unexpectedly had tossed her temporarily into a sea of worry. She sank back into the soft chair and tears of gratitude fell unhindered, dissolving onto her T-shirt, quickly absorbed in the designer cotton. Soon the time for tears was over and time for serious thinking began. She saw Darla in the hallway carrying her purse, apparently leaving for the day. Now would be a good time to go get a cup of coffee and a sandwich. Mikki headed for the nurses station to tell them she was going across the street to the sub shop and would be back soon. She gave her cell phone number to call if any immediate problem developed and headed for the stairway.

Chapter 14

When Emily returned to her room, Mikki was not there waiting for her. But Kate soon wandered in to make sure her patient was again comfortably back in her own bed. "Your granddaughter said to tell you she was going out for a sandwich. Guess she couldn't take any more hospital food!" said the nurse. "I'm sure she'll be right back."

"Unless she finds some place to shop!" chuckled Emily, looking at the nurse.

Kate was about to respond when Mikki entered the room carrying a large paper cup with a lid and straw and huge sack from Subway. Both women stared at the size of Mikki's bag.

"What? …A girl's got to eat, you know!" said Mikki defensively.

Kate and Emily looked at each other and said in unison, "Did we say anything?"

And Emily added, "We know you're a growing girl, and you need your strength."

"Anyway…how do you feel, Granny?" asked Mikki while looking more closely, brow knitted into furrows.

"Just wonderful, thank you very much," Emily answered abruptly. "Any more poking and prodding and I could double as a voodoo doll!"

"Well, hearing that makes me feel better! At least you have your same sweet and gentle nature!"

"Actually… I'm kinda hungry and kinda sleepy."

"Listen Granny, I'll feed you and then you can rest up." Then turning to the nurse she added, "It's okay, isn't it? The Subway sandwich?"

"Sure! It smells great!" Kate answered as she finished checking Emily's vital signs. "Well, blood pressure, pulse, and temperature are all normal."

"See! I do have some good working parts!" announced Emily victoriously.

Kate smiled at the two and left the room carrying her equipment. She was careful to close the door, winking as she left, knowing they wanted some private time.

"After your lunch and a little rest, we'll get back to the story at hand. This is the part where you talk and I listen. Remember?"

"You are certainly tenacious. Can't you give a poor old lady a break?"

"You are not poor, not old, and no more breaks. Seriously Granny, I'll let you rest now since I have to get back to the motel and sleep a little myself. We can't continue these all nighters, you know. We're both getting older now. Maybe Brigetta could do it, but not us.

"Please don't drag your sister into this, okay? Let's eat!" said Emily with a hungry grin. Both women grabbed up the subs and began gnawing at the thick bread and making sounds of happy delight as they chewed. Once Mikki finished her sandwich she went to the bathroom to wash her mouth and hands. Wiping her fingers on a paper towel, she was ready to talk to her Granny. But she heard soft snoring. Granny Em looked so white and fragile now. Who could guess about the tough little lady who lived inside that body?

Mikki returned to the Comfort Inn and was actually able to get some much-needed sleep. She made some phone calls so no one would be wondering or worrying about her. After a quick shower she bounced down on the bed, turned on the news, and fell asleep right away. She awakened about dinnertime and quickly scrubbed her face and brushed her hair. A quick slurp of mouthwash, clean clothes, and she drove back to the hospital.

Granny was awake and watching a *Golden Girls* rerun on the tube. Her cheeks were much pinker and she was already sitting up with her head raised and the channel selector in her right hand. Amazingly, after another day of grueling tests, Emily looked quite at home and back in control of her situation.

"Thought you would show up by meal time, Darling!" exclaimed Emily to her granddaughter, smiling happily to see her.

"You know me. I smell food, even hospital food, and I am there," said Mikki.

"We can order you a meal and you can join me, you know?"

"Okaaay…. And what's on the menu for tonight? Jell-O and broth? That's what Brigetta always says the pre-test cases always get for dinner. I would rather have some steak, if you wouldn't be offended."

"You always were a little cruel!"

"Okay, sorry. But, yeah, let's order me something and enjoy some fine dining together."

Soon a kitchen worker in a starched white waiter's uniform brought a tray with linen napkin, silver lid covered entrees, and a small pink rosebud in a tiny vase. Mikki's brows arched in surprise.

The young waiter removed the shiny lids and revealed the contents. For Emily, yellow Jell-O with a small slice of orange on the side. The main entrée was clear tan broth with a sprig of parsley floating like a life raft in the center of the lukewarm liquid. Emily's nose wrinkled as she stared at the concoction. Mikki fared much better. As lids were removed, well-seasoned and aromatic meatloaf with rich brown gravy was revealed. Mashed potatoes, a freshly baked bun, cooked carrots and a slice of banana cream pie were accompanying the delicious smelling meat. Mikki's beverage was steamy coffee and Emily's tray held a small pot of herbal tea. A nurse entered the room and checked the trays.

"Now, no sharing ladies. Seriously. NO sharing," the nurse warned threateningly as she helped Emily prepare her tray, unwrapping the silverware and placing the napkin on her chest. She was smiling, though, as she saw to her patient's comfort.

"They said after the surgery I'll have more of this same type of food?" inquired Emily. "But once I fart I can eat, …right?"

Mikki just shook her head. Such a class act!

The nurse seemed undaunted by farts in any language. She had probably heard and seen it all. "Yes, Mrs. Carr, once you can demonstrate some bowel sounds and flatulence, you will be ready for some gradual solids. We won't want any problems, right? Let's just worry about that after the surgery, okay?" the nurse questioned as she gave both of them a hard look that said she really meant it.

"She would be happier if she let a few fly, I think," said Emily, after the nurse left the room.

"Granny, try to behave and let's eat. I'm starved," countered Mikki, grabbing her fork and stabbing it into a huge chunk of meatloaf dripping gravy.

Emily's eyes followed the path of the fork to her grand-daughter's mouth with greedy jealousy. Resigned, Emily began to sip her tea, sighing audibly.

"I will tell you everything, you know. I guess I have to," announced Emily while peering cautiously over her teacup. The room was now quiet and the two were alone. An attitude of contemplation encompassed the room. The two women finished their trays and the waiter from the kitchen returned to gather the remains of their meal. As he stacked their dishes, Emily explained to Mikki that she had learned that a hotel service had taken over some of the hospital services. These included meals, and they would soon be adding actual, on premise hotel-style rooms for families of current patients. These rooms would also offer room service and other hotel amenities. Listening, the young man added, as he guided lids back into place on the empty bowls, that a few gratis rooms would be available if they could find a grant for funding them. These would be used mainly for families of children with cancer or other serious illnesses.

"Sorta like a Ronald McDonald house right here in the hospital. Guess they are looking for the extra dollars now. A few of the docs are going to make a big donation, I heard," he offered.

"Sounds like a great idea. Hope it all works out. Do you know the name of the foundation funding the rooms? I might know some contributors through my job," said Mikki.

The waiter handed Mikki a small, business-sized card that she slipped into her handbag and said she would see if she could find someone to help. As he exited the room, Mikki followed him to the door and pulled it shut behind him.

"A worthwhile cause, don't you think?" asked Emily.

"We'll do it?"

"For sure," said Emily with a thumbs up towards Mikki, and sighing with satisfaction.

Now the ladies would be alone and undisturbed for a while. Mikki knew there was much to know about Granny Em. She walked back to the chair and scooted it towards the bed. Granny Em's eyes were now closed.

"Are you really asleep?" she asked quietly.

"No, not yet. I am very tired. My chest is quite uncomfortable right now. Right at the biopsy place."

"Uncomfortable. Like pain? You are telling me you have some pain and want to sleep?"

"Well, some morphine or Demerol would be nice right now."

"Okay, let's buzz the nurse."

A few minutes later a nurse arrived with the pain medication and injected it swiftly into Emily's butt. She said she would be back later to check on her and left, closing the door behind her.

"Well, I know enough from Brigetta that you will not be coherent and talking to me for long now. So, just one little question, okay Grams?"

"Sure," answered Emily already a little groggy.

"Wow, I don't know how or what to say about this," Mikki said hesitantly, subconsciously knotting her hands into tight balls.

"Just spit it out. You were never all that quiet, Dear."

"Do you....did you or do you...hmmm. Well," she continued, taking a huge breath, "Do you make money 'eliminating' people or something? There, I can't believe I just asked my grandmother that question. Are you a 'hit-chick'? I am hoping you'll say no, but I think I know the answer if that makes it any easier, Granny," Mikki blurted out, words popping out like machinegun fire. "You seem to go places and then people end up dead."

Emily just looked at her granddaughter. Not horrified. Just calm. Then Emily turned her face slowly away from her and sighed heavily. The morphine giving a false sense of peace and security, she turned back to face her young beautiful grandchild. "You are partly right, Honey. That's what I want and need to tell you."

"What part is wrong? Please tell me," begged Mikki, now holding back stoic tears.

"I do *favors*, and sometimes I get paid very well," said Emily, eyelids heavy now.

"How did you ever get started in this, what was wrong with you!" Mikki now demanded, fists suddenly balled up in a fighting stance, jumping up and towering beside the bed. Mikki felt the pressure of the moment and wanted to strike out at someone. She did not want to feel like this, to really know these things, or to be put in this awful situation. It was her Granny's fault and there was no one else to blame. How could this have happened in her family?

Emily now lay quietly as her granddaughter's tears and admonishments stabbed her through the heart. But there was now no time to go back and undo it all. Mikki knew much more than she had envisioned.

"It began as a form of self-preservation, I guess. I had a perception of myself as judge, jury and who-knows-what. There are just so many injustices, so much unfairness in the world. I always knew it was wrong in the eyes of the law, but somehow it seemed like the right thing at the time. I am just an old fool, living a lie my whole life. But I never meant to hurt any of you. I would have died before my family would have been brought into all of this," said Emily cautiously but clearly.

Mikki looked at her Granny Em as if seeing her for the first time. The suspected was now the admitted, the unthinkable now a huge ballooning thought process. There was no hope of return to normalcy. Normal family life? Ha! *And what does your grandmother do in her spare time? Knitting, bridge, bingo? Oh, she offs people she doesn't like. But don't worry; she is well-paid for it!* These new revelations would have played well back in the first grade "Show and Tell" on Fridays. Of course, no one would have believed her. That would have been a little more than outrageous.

The grandmother lying quietly on the bed sheets was now perspiring, small dots of sweat forming on her forehead and chest. Eyes closed, she groaned slightly as she tried to turn in the small bed. Mikki rose to wipe her Granny's brow with a cool damp washcloth. Emily opened her eyes again and met her granddaughter's gaze. Mikki said nothing more.

"Thank you for being here with me. I am so sorry for everything. I hope you won't hate me," said Emily, almost in a whisper as the drugs were reaching full effect. At last Mikki bent over the old woman and gave her a hug. Standing up again quickly she reached for her purse.

"Granny, I know you are tired, but one more question, then I am out of here to let you get some sleep. Okay?"

"Anythwing," said Emily with a slight slur.

"When was the first time? I really want to know."

Emily mumbled something, not quite intelligible. Mikki moved closer to listen more closely to the drug-induced sentence.

"Ahhwanin," murmured the sleepy Emily, lids now at half-mast.

"What, Granny, say it again?"

"Ah wahss nine."

Mikki drew back from Granny Em's face in shock, standing straight up. She must have not heard right. She leaned closer again. "You were nine? Nine years old? You were a nine year old girl when you killed someone?"

The dozing patient just barely nodded her head, but it was enough to confirm the positive answer. Mikki at first refused to believe it was anything but the Demerol talking. None of this was really true after all. But in reality, more lost puzzle pieces were now being picked up off the playing floor and being placed back on the board... just within her grasp. All she needed now was to place the jagged edges together and soon the whole picture would be visible. It would not be the little girl's dream scene portrayed on the puzzle box, filled with fairies and angels. The completed puzzle would for sure more closely resemble a nightmare with dragons and swords and death.

"Good night, Granny," said Mikki as she placed a light kiss on the sleeping downy cheek. There was much more to know and now for sure much more to do. Mikki picked up her bag and slipped her feet back into kidskin loafers. As she left the building, no one would have suspected anything was different about the young beautiful woman heading towards the BMW convertible. She drove quickly out of the darkening parking lot, but was not headed in the direction of the motel by the bay. The little car and its occupant were soon out of sight.

Chapter 15

Mikki arrived early the next morning to check on Emily and found her talking to Dr. Waterson. His eyes brightened when he saw the approaching female figure. Smiling, he nodded a greeting. This morning he wore freshly pressed tan Dockers and a bright white polo shirt. He carried a stack of patient charts and a gold pen was stuck behind his left ear. Probably on his way to tee-off time, thought Mikki. Well, it certainly was a gorgeous morning for golf. She would pretty much rather be anywhere than at this hospital today. Mikki met his eyes with hers with raised brows and unspoken question.

"All's going as well as expected, Michelle. Your grand-mother's a real trooper for sure. Test results are pretty much as expected. We have done scans and x-rays and fortunately haven't found any other cancer sights so far. Brain, bones... all look great. We will take a good look at the colon today, just to be sure we have everything. Surgery is tomorrow around 10:00 if all goes as scheduled." he said to Mikki.

"That's great, Doctor," said Mikki as she then turned to Emily. "How are you feeling Granny? Are they being too mean to you?" She bent over the bed opposite the doctor and gave Emily a quick peck on the forehead.

"That's my little darling, Michelle. Always worried about her grandmother. Not worried enough to be in touch on a regular basis though," Emily said, quickly turning her attention back to Dr. Waterson. "The good surgeon says I'll soon be up and running around after the operation. Isn't that great news?"

"Well, let's qualify the running around. I think what I said was that you would soon be out of bed and able to walk down the hall. In fact, those were my exact words as I recall," Dr. Waterson said, grinning at the small elderly woman and then glancing back approvingly at Mikki. This morning her dark red hair was pulled back tightly in a knot with tortoiseshell picks holding it in place, smooth and shiny. A tasteful and simple rose-colored T-shirt and low-rise jeans emphasized her long slender figure. The doctor's gaze went sliding down to the hint of belly button showing above the wide leather belt....eyes glazed, as if he had never seen a naked female body. Straightening and returning to his professional manner, he tried to focus on the clipboard full of records, almost afraid to return his eyes to Mikki's. As he stammered through his getaway, he said he would be back tomorrow and tripped over an invisible obstacle on the way towards the door.

When the door shut, Granny Em announced with a grin, "Married and definitely not gay!"

As both women stifled their giggling, Mikki said, "So, back to reality, are you feeling better? How's the chest incision today, Gram?"

"Much better. The worst thing about the whole situation is no real food. They'll starve me for sure. How 'bout you stop at McDonalds and bring me a cheeseburger?"

"Right, and have some sort of dia-poopoo set in and they will come and find me and make me clean it up for spite. No way."

"What if I wrote you into my will? Gave you a bigger slice than your sister, you know, just between us?" she continued with a devious grin.

"Yeah, right. Sure. Right now, let's just see if the Jell-O gets any better; maybe they will add fruit cocktail or marshmallows. Only if you are a good girl. Think that will ever happen?"

Emily pulled the sheet up to her neck, sticking her lower lip out.

"All right. Maybe you can have a small shake or something like that after the tests this morning. But, I will ask first. You know me. I always follow the rules. Ms. Straight and Narrow."

"Well, that sounds pretty good. Maybe strawberry?"

"You are worse than a kid, Granny, I swear." Mikki then went to her grandmother and gave her a big but careful hug, wrapping her arms around her. "I love you, Granny. You remind me of when I was young and stupid. Now let's talk."

"That's pretty much you're asking for a mere milkshake."

"Granny, let's be serious. We have a big problem here. I need to know more. We need to get you outta here. But while you're here and a captive audience you will have to do what I want and tell me what I want. Okay?"

"When did you get so damned bossy? Been hanging around your mother too much again?"

Mikki just stared at her in her most serious look she could muster up at this time, trying not to smile and get off the track. Here in this bed was her sweet and beloved grandmother she had just confirmed was possibly an axe murderer. Just what we need in the family, thought Mikki. Everyone needs at least one serial killer just to keep the conversation interesting at Thanksgiving dinner.

"Let's get back to your innocent childhood Gran. I thought I heard you say something about being age nine," offered Mikki, trying to get the ball rolling.

"Everyone is age nine sometime, dear," Emily replied with a frown, and looking towards the closed door. "Go through the bathroom and lock the other door, please. Don't want any visitors on the other side of the door listening to my tales. I already have enough to worry about with nosy Darla skulking about."

"Don't think about her right now. Things will work out in time. Just get on with the story before more nurses, lab techs, or doctors descend upon us."

Emily sat up as straight as she could while Mikki fixed pillows behind her neck and back. The sound of rolling distant thunder seemed to be edging towards the hospital. Exhaling loudly, Emily began, as a little drizzle of rain began to tap on the window.

"When I was a little girl, we lived in a small rural town. Our house, if you want to call it that, was a dump with a capital 'D.' My father was dead and Mom took up with the first man who came around. When I think back about it now, she was probably just trying to save us from the poorhouse. My mother was really a nice looking woman, and could have done better.... but I guess she just felt lucky she didn't have to raise us on her own. The guy had a job, and that was the only plus. He was a fat mean slob and a pervert on top of that. He raped my older sister."

"You have a sister?" Mikki exclaimed.

"Please. Let me go on. This is the only way I can get this out."

"Sorry. I'm just surprised."

"Well, you will probably more surprised by the time you've drilled all of this out of me. Anyway, he came at his whim into the room I shared with my sister. I mean, I was this little kid and I could hear and see all this going on in the bed next to mine, same room! My mother did nothing. Nothing."

"Unbelievable."

"Well, this was backwoods and there were no official protective agencies for children back then. You were pretty much stuck with what you got. No child labor laws either. You just had your parents or whoever was taking care of you and you were glad for food to eat and clothes to wear."

"Go on."

"Soon, not to anyone's great shock, my teenaged sister ran off with a kid from across town. She told me about it and warned me I would be next with Frank. I never saw my sister again. I hope she made a life for herself somewhere, but I honestly don't know what happened to her after she left. I had a pony. A neighbor gave it to me. That pony was the most wonderful thing in my world. I think that's why sometimes I prefer animals to people. She was my friend and family and the only thing I really had that was mine. I became a princess when I was with the pony. She was so sweet and friendly. Frannie. That was her name. When the day came for swimming lessons and I said I wasn't going, my stepdad took the pony to the slaughterhouse where he worked."

"What! He took her to the slaughterhouse? No! Why? No one could be that cruel!" exclaimed Mikki, eyes bulging and mouth open with horror.

"Well, he was planning on starting me off to follow in the realm of my sister. Jessie warned me it all started as a 'swimming lesson.' There was no way I would be next. No way. When he took the pony down the road, he meant to make me pay for my disobedience. I can still see the little mare looking back at me. I was screaming and crying and my mother did nothing but tell me that life was not always fair. I can still remember those exact words. Suddenly it was like someone turned a knob in my head to another channel. Things were going to be fair. That was what I decided. My nine-year-old self would make the world more fair.

"I started that very afternoon. After he got back with the halter and lead rope, just whistling and singing as he came back down the driveway, I had a huge sense of hate that was displaced temporarily by a sense of calm and cunning. I said nothing during supper. Just minded my manners, cleaned up the kitchen, and slipped out the back screen door when he and Mother went to the porch to listen to the radio. I found the halter in the shed, stuck it under my dress and took off running the back way through the fields. Out of breath, I arrived at the slaughterhouse, praying and cussing alternately.

111

"Tears of relief streamed down my sweat and dust-covered face when I saw Frannie. Her carcass was not hanging from a meat hook, but there she stood, alone in a pen next to three calves. Her fuzzy ears turned towards me and she nickered exuberantly in recognition. She had no food or water, but seemed to be okay. I grabbed a handful of thick Bahia grass growing unattended by the pen and offered it to her. I had been right. The slaughterhouse was closed today. All the kill equipment was locked up. Frank had planned to return to work and do the job in a day or two. I quickly crawled thru the board fence and haltered the little mare. Once I had pushed open the heavy pipe gate, I left it open for the calves to also make their escape. I pulled Frannie along with the rope though she wanted to stop and pull up the long grass as we went. The pony and I both trotted down the back path to the woods back behind our house. She would be quiet here on familiar ground. I led her back into her enclosure and tied her with a long rope stolen from the shed. She was tethered to the far end of the pasture where there was a clean stream for drinking. I hoped the calves would not follow and give us away. Once Frannie was secure, I went to the house, washed away most of the grime, and went to bed unnoticed.

"In the morning the bastard was telling me to get my swimsuit, which was a hand-me-down from my sister and way too big. Frank soon ordered me into the old Ford truck and down the road we went for my 'swimming lesson.' I hated him at that moment more than anyone in my short nine years. My mother was a close second."

"So she knew all this was going on with your sister and then it was you? And you were nine years old? I still can't believe it. Poor Granny," said Mikki, almost in tears, her chin now on her pulled up knees on the old chair, green eyes filled with shock.

"Frank was now trying to be Mr. Nice. I said nothing. Finally my silence pissed him off and he said I would learn to swim today if it took all afternoon. I had my bathing suit on under my clothes, so as soon as we got to the little beach by the river, I scooted out of the truck. Without even closing the door, I ran to the cloudy green water and jumped in. It was warm and smelled fishy, but I was really too scared to notice at the time. I was hoping the big old alligator was there and I could call him over to eat Frank. He would be a nice juicy morsel for the twelve-foot gator we all had seen there on occasion. No alligator was seen, so I

112

splashed around in the shallows just beyond the marshy grass trying to attract him. Meanwhile, blubbery Frank was leaning on the truck and stripping down to his old torn blue-striped boxer shorts. As he picked his way through the rocks down toward the sandy beach, I swam quickly and quite well to the end of the old pier.

"'So Emmy, you can swim a little. Maybe you can teach your old man. Come here, little Darling, and show me how to do the breast stroke!' Frank ordered, chuckling out loud at his great humor.

"'Hahaha! Come here, you little twit!' he shouted through clenched teeth, as I headed past the pier and well out of his reach.

"Now, he was a pretty fair swimmer after all. I mean, let's face it, did you ever try to sink a pat of butter in a bowl of water? All lard floats pretty darn good. Well, by now he is mad and swimming fast towards me. I wait 'til he is pretty close and then duck underwater. I am swimming for my literal life now as I head toward the dock. Once I reached the wooden pier I pulled myself out of the water and onto the dock. There, I looked for the same nail that had cut my toe a few months ago. Sure enough, the wood plank was now bowed in the middle and the nails were completely pulled out of one side. Only one nail held the plank in place on the walkway. Working on pure nerve and a jolt of adrenaline, I suppose, I yanked the board with all my might. Frank was swimming closer and closer now. It was my 65 pounds versus that nail and I had to win. I pulled harder and harder, again and again! Finally it pulled free, almost tossing me backward into the dark water when it let loose. At the sound Frank turned from his watery path and saw I had climbed onto the dock. He yelled or cursed something unintelligible and turned to swim my way. Breathing hard, I held the board behind my back as Frank approached the wobbling pier.

"'You will pay for this, you little bitch! You come here when I call you! I will string you up right along side that damned good-for-nothing pony!' he puffed as his chubby fingers grabbed for the edge of the dock at the deep end.

"Now I will tell you, timing is everything in a lot of things. Especially when you are trying to stay alive. At the exact moment those flabby hairy arms pulled on the dock to raise Frank to the walkway, I whipped around fast, like a home run hitter, and slammed that board onto the top of his balding head as hard as any nine-year-old full of fury could hit. I think my feet left the ground, I hit him so hard. I still remember the sound. It was like when you accidentally dropped the watermelon off the deck at 'Pink Flamingo' and it hit the concrete lanai below. A muffled 'thwunk'! Amazingly, Frank appeared to be only stunned, but as he heaved his body upwards it seemed to stop midway in his assault on the dock. His dark eyes looked up, round with surprise, as a rivulet of blood began a slow descent from his scalp towards his left eye. As his mouth opened in a circle of question, I swung the board again, aiming for the hairline just above his left ear. Another solid hit. Thunk! This time Frank's body folded downward at the waist and hit the water face first. As he floated there, I hit him again and again, always aiming for the same spot. Panting like our beagle after chasing a rabbit, I finally squatted on the pier and watched the floating body, mesmerized by the scene before me. When I was sure there was no movement, no breathing, I rose. Then I stood to watch some more. He was surely quite dead. I felt nothing but a sense of accomplishment. I washed the blood traces off the board by splashing it in the water and pushed it back into place on the deck. I ran down the walkway and found a flat rock to pound the remaining nails back in place. Frank was still floating face down. No sign of the alligator, but then dead was dead. Even a nine-year-old knows that. I found the key to the truck in Frank's overalls he had left on the beach and jumped into the driver's seat. The swimming lesson had turned into my first driving lesson. Being the smart female I am, I had watched the action of the pedals often enough on the trips to town. Clutch, brake, gas! After a few jumpy tries, the old Ford lurched onto the dirt road with me behind the wheel. Now I was in charge! Though barely able to see through the steering wheel, I felt like a bomber pilot as I flew along the road towards home. *See me now, Daddy!* The wind was whipping through my wet curls; the warm air was drying my skin better than any towel. And I smiled. I smiled all the way back home, right to the end of the driveway. Seeing the tin-roofed shack, willed tears began to fall and the phrase "drama queen" was coined for me. I was a great actress as I hysterically explained how poor Frank had misjudged the distance to the dock while teaching me to swim underwater. He had somehow come up right under the support beams and knocked himself out. Of course, I told the sheriff, I had tried and tried to save my poor stepdaddy, but I was just too little to pull him out of the water. Finally he just floated away, I had demonstrated, as I threw myself on the grass in my best dead body impersonation. Everyone felt oh-so-sorry for me. Except Mama. She knew something was up. But then, she didn't really seem to care. There was no investigation, of course, even though Frank's head was battered to a pulp. By the time they got there, the old alligator had just shown up in time to bite off a foot. Too bad it didn't take his dick. That way Frank could be living in hell without his most precious possession. Good thing there was no "CSI" back then. Even our dumb sheriff could've probably figured it out if he had tried. But no one cared too much about Frank. And no one knew about Frannie's journey to the slaughterhouse and back except Mama and me. I would like to say we lived happily ever after but that wasn't quite the story. Should I go on?"

"Granny, I am both appalled and spellbound," whispered Mikki. She unfolded her knees and got up from the chair. This was just too much to absorb all at once. "I think its time to go to McDonald's. I need to stretch my legs. Plus, it's almost time for the tests. They'll be here soon."

As she picked up her bag, she seemed distant in her pensiveness. Emily watched as she left.

"Are you coming back?" said Emily tentatively, as she scrunched back down in the bed to a more prone position. She was worried she may have said too much, too quickly.

"Sure. Can't miss this, Granny. I'll be back right after your tests are over for today. Really!" said Mikki as she waved a little good-bye. As she stepped through the door, she did a quick reverse and blew a soft kiss toward her grandmother. Emily smiled and closed her eyes. She was very tired, almost exhausted, from the confession. It was easy to doze off although she knew it was important to be awake and thinking.

Soon another technician pushed in a wheelchair for Emily's journey to testing territory. She was just glad that all of this would soon be over, she thought as her feet were placed on the chair's supports and she was rolled off down the hall. The rain continued its dance on the window in the now vacant hospital room.

Chapter 16

About two hours later, Mikki was back, bearing a small strawberry shake that was approved by the nurses at the third floor station. There were a few drops of rain still clinging to the light red hairs on her forearms as she opened the bag of fast food. Having just returned minutes ago from the land of testing, Emily was starving. Her eyes stared with joyful surprise at the culinary delight presented by her granddaughter, complete with both spoon and large-bore straw.

"You are my lifesaver! This is fabulous and wonderful!" exclaimed Emily.

"Thought I would sweeten you up, Granny," said Mikki.

"Ha! I am so sweet even bees love me! But this is great!" said the slurping Granny Em, as she sucked heartily. The thick pink concoction rose so slowly through the white tunnel, that finally, exasperated, Emily flipped off the plastic lid and dug in with the spoon.

"I guess you like it?" asked Mikki.

"Well, it is a little thick, but soon it will melt to a lovely consistency."

"Okay, so now that you are comfortable we can talk some more? Is there anymore pain, Granny?"

"Well, it will hurt me to talk, but not so much physically as the emotional aspect."

"I know, but we need to get this all out in the open. I should at least know what I am dealing with here."

"I'm at your mercy."

"What happened after your stepdad was dead? What happened to your mother?"

"The cops went to find Frank's body and said he was dead. Big surprise. Then Mama went out to feed the chickens. Never said a word to me about what happened or anything. Just a little more than strange, wouldn't you say?"

"Right."

"So life went on. I went to school every day and Mama worked at home around the house. She baked pies for extra money and made chicken and dumpling soup to sell sometimes too. Then one day, I came home from school and she was gone. Just left me a note and was gone. I never saw her again. Not ever. I remember I didn't even cry. Went to the neighbors place and they called the sheriff. Within a few days, my uncle came and took me to his home in Georgia. My uncle, my real Daddy's brother, lived pretty high. He had married a Southern belle whose father owned some tobacco fields that were doing quite well. Uncle Robert McCracken was also a member of the Secret Service training staff. He worked at the nearby training facility. Auntie Clare stayed home and ran the huge plantation house. I thought I had died and gone to heaven for sure. I had my own room, complete with canopy bed. And my own bathroom with a genuine marble tub. They let me bring Frannie and she and I cantered through peach groves on the acreage behind the backyard all summer long. Colored ladies, Mamie and Bess, who were like my new grandmas, served the meals. I can remember sitting in the kitchen at the big wooden table in the center, just watching them work and smelling the best cooking in the world. When I think back, it was amazing I didn't end up weighing 300 pounds!

"They sent me to private schools and then to an all-girls' college close by. I learned manners, social skills, and proper English at home, being educated at the best schools. The little country bumpkin was transformed into a debutante. A smart and proper lady. I wasn't too bad looking, either. In fact, one of the boys from a nearby tobacco plantation often came to call. We would set out on Uncle Robert's Tennessee Walkers and ride the wooded horse trails for hours. Then he would take me to a secluded area where we would picnic by a little stream. We ate boiled peanuts, fresh peach jam on croissants, and ham sandwiches. I can still remember that. Sitting under a huge oak tree and lying on a big plaid blanket we had packed on one of the horses.

"'Hey, Jimmy, want more peanuts?'

"'Miss Emily, I would surely explode, or maybe break old Tom's back riding him home. But how 'bout I kiss you? Pretty please? We're both nearly grown!'

"'I will let you kiss me more than once, if you let me shoot your rifle?'

"Walking towards the tethered horses, he pulled the Winchester from his saddle strap and loaded it up. It was there, in those woods that I learned to shoot. I also learned about sex that same summer. It wasn't awful, as I had expected; it was fun and felt good. I was surprised about that, but quite happy to be in possession of that knowledge.

"When I told my uncle about the target shooting, not the sex, of course, he was relieved that was what we were doing out there. His mind now pictured Jimmy and me not rolling about in the grass, but in a scene more suitable to a Secret Service agent. His innocent little niece learning to fire a weapon was just right as far as he was concerned. In fact, when Jimmy told him I was a natural shot, he had to find out for himself. He took me to the training facility where he worked and we went to the firing range. Astounded by my accuracy, he was a man inspired! Nothing like the smell of gunpowder and targets blown to bits to raise a man's testosterone level. He was a man on a mission now. He got special permission to let me attend the firearms classes with the agency trainees. When I took the written tests with the guys and aced every one, he somehow arranged that I could train to become a Secret Service agent. This was, of course, very exciting to me, and I left the plantation. I took a sabbatical from college and began to work and train at their facility. My fellow trainees, who were all men, did not particularly like me, especially when they realized I was better than them in many fields. I became trained in undercover operations, emergency medicine, self-defense, arrest and control tactics, and protective and defensive driving techniques. Also, there is the element of law and criminal evidence. But it was common knowledge that I could handle and fire any weapon they gave me. I was good. In fact, I never missed my target... ever. You are supposed to be impressed at this point."

"Well, I must say, I always wondered about your driving and where that came from," laughed Mikki. "I can't believe you were a trained agent. My grandmother! Makes the little self-defense course I took seem too meek for our family. So what happened? You were Secret Service and you could shoot. Those are the good guys, right?"

"Oh yes, definitely the good guys. Although the agency started out as being a Treasury Department watchdog, looking out for counterfeiting, the agency's responsibility was expanded to protection of the President and his family, the Vice President and family, visiting heads of State and Governments, and Presidential candidates.

"In fact, that was my job. Protection of the President, mainly. Sometimes, other public figures where important issues were at stake. I was so good, I became a sniper for the Secret Service. Well, it was actually called the Countersniper Team. We were specially trained to neutralize any long-range threat to a protectee. We had specially manufactured rifles and other sophisticated equipment. They positioned us on rooftops and in windows, and other strategic sights for the purpose of protection."

"So you were the one who shot Dupris?" questioned Mikki, trying to put more pieces together. This person she was talking to no longer was even vaguely sounding like her grandmother, anyone's grandmother.

"No, the police had a shoot-out with Dupris. I was going to shoot him all right, but with a specially made dart. No noise, not much blood. He would have just gone down and before anyone could call for help or figure out what was wrong with him, it would have been too late. Then I could have just skedaddled out of there and been home to all of you"

"What went wrong? How did you end up here?"

"I pretty much knew Dupris's routine and how he would slink about like a snake at night. I was going to the roof with my weapon when I accidentally dropped the ampoule of toxin. I had put some planning into deciding what to use as the poison on the dart. First I considered Batrachotoxin…"

"Who?" interrupted Mikki.

"It's the substance secreted by the poison arrow frog that happens to be the most poisonous animal in the Animal Kingdom. Just for your lesson from Mother Nature today, did you know that the toxin from one frog is enough to poison sixteen people or twenty thousand mice….whichever you would like to die, I guess? And you can buy these frogs 'shipped live to your door, packed with great care, live arrival guaranteed' from website ads on the Internet. Pet supply places!"

"Well, let's see, how many did you order and are these running and hopping around loose at Pink Flamingo?" queried Mikki, thinking about the next time looking between the bed sheets when staying at Granny's house.

"No. I didn't buy any. First of all, I figured anything that poisonous wouldn't be good to handle or even have around, though they looked kinda cute in the pictures. All kinds of cool colors, blue, orange... Anyway, also I decided if I used that, there might be a homicide investigation after this Dupris dies of 'frog venom' poisoning here in little Citrus City. There are not a lot of those froggies just lurking about in Florida, you know. These little guys live in tropical jungles. The natives rub their arrows and darts on the frogs skin. The toxin kills the prey when it's hit with the arrow.

"But, I had been into the apartment a few days earlier where Dupris was holing up and saw something interesting. Now I already knew he was a highly allergic guy. I got that from my computer break-in to his medical records during his last incarceration. His body just went into fits over about anything he came in contact with. And I mean bad allergic reactions. So I am nosing around the living room and I saw a box on the end table marked 'EpiPen.' This is a syringe with premeasured epinephrine used to prevent anaphylactic shock, usually prescribed for bee stings. It made sense that he would also be allergic to bee stings, since that is fairly common in the general population. The next day I had ordered and received in overnight shipping some concentrated bee venom. It was delivered to my post office box. One drop would equal about three thousand stings; I think the brochure had read. In any event, I was sure just a small prick with the dart would be plenty to kill him almost immediately before there could be any attempt at resuscitation. His cold dead body would be found and if an autopsy was performed, pathology would come back as anaphylactic shock from bee stings. Nothing that would require any investigation or too much excitement. I was planning on trying to hit the neck, close to the jugular for quick absorption. The dart was so small that if I didn't have time to recover it after Dupris was down, it would probably not be found anyway.

"Anyway, I accidentally dropped and broke the first vial. Going back to my bag on the ground where I had one extra, my foot hit a rusty step on the fire ladder and down I went. Gashed up my knee big time and the landing knocked the wind out of me. I had been feeling a little dizzy that day. I was trying real hard to hold in the coughing and may have taken just a bit too much cough syrup. Anyway, someone apparently saw or heard me there as I fell and called 911. Just by accident, the cruiser that responded to the scene happened upon Dupris. The officers chased him into the apartment and Dupris decided he was not going quietly."

"So he died in the hospital? Did you have to do something or what?"

"It was like a God-given present. Here he was one floor below me. Poor Tyrone just happened to have some serious allergic issues. That's all."

"So that's what he died from? That's not what they said on the news."

"Just goes to show you, don't count on truth from the news. Actually, they don't know why he died. At least not yet. I am sure there will be an autopsy and inquiry, but for now, he died from surgical complications and a gunshot wound to the kidney."

"This is all quite amazing, Granny. If it weren't so unbelievably horrible, I would be in awe of you. Really!"

"Do you think you will ever forgive me for being such a wicked woman?"

"The jury is still out, but I want to hear more. Each defendant shall have his evidence brought forth....or something like that."

"Mikki, I am really sorry for all of this, but my life is not at all what you girls envisioned it to be. I just hope you can understand some day and forgive me. You will, of course, realize why I have to be so secretive. There is just so much to hide. So much that should remain hidden."

The big room door swung open and the waiter reappeared bringing some lunch for both of them. With a big smile he set up the trays and helped Emily with her napkin and silverware. As he left, the door remained open. Rising and stretching from the corner chair, Mikki moved towards the door.

"No, let's leave the door open for a while" said Emily. "We'll just have our lunch and then I have to take my nap. We don't want anyone to think we are recluses in here, you know. Don't want people wondering about our constantly closed door."

"Okay, Granny," said Mikki, returning to her seat and spreading out the large napkin across her khakis. "Maybe we both need a little break from this. I need to run to Walgreens for some makeup, shampoo, maybe some magazines. Although I can't imagine anything quite as interesting as spending the day talking to you! Can I bring you anything later, nail polish, a candy bar, shotgun shells, binoculars, new scope....you know, any of your ordinary items you might be running out of?"

"Once a smart ass, always a smart ass."

Sticking out her tongue and then throwing up her arms in mock dismay, Mikki then began to unwrap her roast beef sandwich from its cellophane. There would be more time for talking and thinking later. Right now thought waves were pulling her emotions in a million different directions.

Chapter 17

Darla, ever observant, saw Mildred's granddaughter leaving the floor. Watching her leave, she felt a surge of jealous envy. That girl was something much more beautiful than herself. She really needed to talk to Kate about the revelations from Helen. The blood spots on the stairs, coupled with the interest in Dupris added up to something. She was not sure yet what, but she would find out. Dupris was dead and no one really cared, but there were secrets that needed to be told. She knew that much and would soon know much more. Why the closed doors? Sure everyone needed privacy with his or her relatives, but something didn't add up. If these two were estranged, why did they care so much about who over heard their "small talk"? Darla could see the love on their faces and their feeble attempts to conceal it. Why?....That was the question. What was going on here? And most of all, how might this knowledge benefit her? Darla knew she had to look out for number one. Selfish? Maybe. But, a basic life strategy.

"Darla, what are you doing? Have you finished your bath rounds?" Kate suddenly demanded, walking up behind the staring girl.

Startled, Darla jumped from her thoughts back to the world of the third floor hospital wing. "Sorry, Ms. Bingham, I was just thinking about what to do next. You're right, I have to get busy. Nancy has given me a big assignment today."

"Only because you are a good worker and we know you can accomplish all of your goals, right?"

"Yes, Ma'am. I was just wondering about Mrs. Carr. How is she doing?"

"She seems fine, but we have to see how the surgery goes and get back the final cancer staging reports. She seems much more comfortable, though."

"Good. It just seems like she and her granddaughter are behind closed doors every since she arrived at the hospital. And doesn't it seem strange how she suddenly appeared?"

"Strange that a granddaughter would come to her cancer-stricken grandmother? No, that doesn't seem strange in the least."

"Not that. I mean how did she find out? Lots of things just don't add up."

"Your job isn't to 'add up' patients, Darla. Just take care of them. Michelle is here to be with Mrs. Carr and that actually makes my day. No one should be alone at a time like this, don't you think?"

"Of course, but..."

"Darla, please get back to work. We will talk another time when we are both not quite so busy."

At that, Darla scooted off to get a cart with fresh towels and bed sheets. But Kate Bingham couldn't stop her from thinking while she worked. And Darla's mind was always working on something. Tonight she would finish sorting the photos and continue to look for the connection to Brigetta. The more she saw of Mrs. Carr, the more she knew she had seen her at the freshman tea. Unless Mrs. Carr had a twin sister, that woman was there at the college. And why would she be hiding that fact?

Helen was pushing her cleaning cart from the other end of the corridor. Squeaking wheels and the smell of Lysol accompanied her as she rolled along the hallway. Gathering up some cloths and disinfectant spray, Helen seemed engrossed with her work. Mr. Foster had passed away during the night and his room needed cleaning and preparation for the next patient. Darla thought maybe she could rush down there and work on making that bed first, so she could talk some more to Helen. Glancing sideways she saw Kate watching her and decided against it.

"Good afternoon, Mrs. Clancy," she announced as she went to the next assignment. Reluctantly, but cheerily she expertly guided her cart full of clean sheets through the next room door. She would find Helen later during afternoon break. They could talk more. They would conspire to learn more.

Mikki arrived back from her shopping excursion in time to see Darla heading out of the hospital employee parking lot in her Honda. Mikki had planned her return to avoid any more annoying and potentially dangerous questioning from that little problem in the making. Since her Granny had given her these new revelations, Mikki had trouble getting much sleep. Her dear grandmother was not who she thought. And was, in fact, a premeditated killer? Now what? What if this got out? The whole family would pay. And pay dearly. Her standing at the firm would be damaged irreparably. Her mom, her kid sister.... what in the world would they do with this news? What was her grandmother thinking? Plus, this was not an isolated incident, this was a life style. A life style kept secret. Well, thank God for that. This would have made for an interesting term paper in Sophomore English Composition. Write a paper about your most interesting relative. Tell about their life and how it has affected you. Old Mr. Humphrey would have had a coronary over that one. Mikki would have preferred to perpetuate the old story about the sheik and Granny's sex life. Shocking, but not particularly incriminating.

Walking briskly through the mid afternoon heat, Mikki burst through the lobby, waving at the desk personnel and headed towards the elevator. Seeing the flash of color on her left, she noticed the busy gift shop really for the first time. Turning back she entered the fragrant room, full of cutsie things for new babies, new moms, and kids having surgery. There were racks of paperbacks and magazines, congratulation and get well cards. No condolence cards she noticed. No one wanted to advertise that people could die at hospitals. You just get well and go home. Seeing a pile of local newspapers, she grabbed one off the stack and dug into her bag for change. Then she saw what she was really looking for. The most adorable pink flamingo pen. Its feet were a pink suction cup and its long pen body was a mass of bright pink unruly feathers sticking out everywhere. Black wiggly eyes peered from beneath the feathered mass in a most comical expression. So, for $3.95 she would make Granny Em smile. She grabbed up the treasure and headed to the cash register, and paid the volunteer manning the check out, and was on her way back to the elevators.

"Oh! That is the cutest thing! How did you find that?" squeaked Emily. Her face was stretched into a wide mouthed grin. "I would hug you so hard, but it hurts too much!"

"Well, it was definitely you. And it was sitting there, perched in loneliness. It was calling out to me, so I snatched it up. Found it right downstairs, Granny. I knew you would love it, silly as it is."

Emily licked the bottom of the sucker feet and pressed it firmly onto her tray table. The ridiculous pink feather bird stared wildly back at them, jiggling eyes bobbing stupidly. They were both sure that "Pinky" was quite happy to have found a home in Room 311.

"Lookie what else I found. 'If you like Giorgio Ocean Dream, you will love George's Ocean Wave,' read the label. And it really isn't bad! You needed some body lotion, so I will give you a back rub and smooth you up."

"You know, I like shopping for bargains as much as you girls do, but really. You know the rule. No 'smell-alikes'!"

As Emily peeled off the cellophane wrapping and popped open the tube, she hesitantly drew the opening towards her nose. "Well, it's not bad!"

"I would never steer you wrong. I am a true shopping genius, am I not? Admit it! You may be older and wiser, but I definitely have the family's shopping gene! It's not just you and the Brig, you know!" laughed Mikki, exuberant and triumphant.

"You never fail to amaze me, dear grandchild. What will you come up with next?"

"Well, how 'bout some nonpareils, dark chocolate! And, a little cassette player and ear buds! I even got some 'Sounds of the Sea' for you. You can play it when you are taking your naps."

"I am amazed and overwhelmed. Truly. I love you."

Mikki went to the bed and carefully engulfed her grandmother into her arms and hugged. She held that hug until she felt tears begin to creep down her nose. When she pulled back, she turned away, unwilling to let Granny Em see her worried face. She quickly dabbed with a coarse hospital tissue and turned back smiling towards the bed.

"I know you are upset with all this, Honey. Please, everything will be okay," promised Emily. "And the family will be okay. I won't let anything happen to any of you. I cannot and will not let anything I've done harm our family. I will guarantee you that."

"Granny, right now, I just want you to get better. And I want to know all about you. Everything."

"Now that we have started down this road, there is, I suppose, no turning back. I am just so sorry I did not continue my retirement before this last job. None of this would have happened. Now what a big mess I have."

Mikki tenderly took Emily's small hand and squeezed gently. "We will all be all right. I know that too. Trust me to get all of us through this. We will stick together. We are family."

Emily was now tearing open the cellophane package containing the nonpareils and stuffing a few chocolate morsels into her mouth. "Think if I eat enough of these I will fart a lot after the surgery?"

"You are incorrigible."

"Yeah, but fun."

"Yeah, but fun. I admit it. Don't you ever think about anything but food?"

"Oh yeah, like you're one to talk. Oh well. I guess I had better tell you what happened with the Secret Service."

"Really. Can't wait, Gran."

"Well, I was with them for about 2 years. Really enjoyed it too. Still some of the guys didn't really care for me. Since I wouldn't jump into bed and also could outshoot them, I had no value in many eyes. Not everyone, but many."

"God, you mean men were even more shallow back then?"

"Honey, you don't know the half of it. But anyway, some were my friends and some weren't. No one dared mess with me though, since they knew my uncle was promoted and now a bigwig with the Agency. One day we were assigned a Countersniper project. The government was a little nervous because of the attempt a year or so earlier on President Harry Truman. Two Puerto Rican nationalists had tried an assassination and Officer Leslie Coffelt was shot and killed. We were all, in fact, a little nervous.

"The Puerto Ricans were named Collazo and Torresola. There was a big shoot-out at Blair House where the President was staying with the First Family. They had moved there due to some repairs that needed to be done at the White House. Security those days was nothing like it is now. But these guys Collazo and Torresola were terrorists and had planned the assassination of Truman. They had been inspired by events in their homeland that put the U.S. in a bad light. Another inspiration was a bad guy named Campos."

"I remember some history or political science course that discussed that situation. So we had terrorists even back then?"

"Yes, even back then. Well, the widow of the officer who was killed actually went to Puerto Rico just four days after her husband was shot. Still in shock and sick herself with kidney problems, she was persuaded by presidential aides to postpone upcoming surgery to remove her kidney. She did and traveled to Puerto Rico before the operation. Can you imagine?"

"You are kidding me."

"No, she went and was well received by the whole island. She gave a simple speech absolving the people of Puerto Rico of any blame. Many thought her visit helped calm tensions and build a better relationship with Puerto Rico. Later the U.S. gave Puerto Rico full political autonomy and eventually the island became a self-governing commonwealth."

"So what happened to the two terrorists? I don't remember much about that."

"Torresola was killed in the shoot out. Torresola had mortally wounded Officer Coffelt, but Coffelt maintained consciousness long enough to get off a head shot as Torresola was shooting at other officers. Officer Coffelt died less than four hours later, but many think he prevented the attack from reaching President Truman."

"So Coffelt's wife had at least the comfort of knowing her husband died a hero."

"Right. They both made sacrifices for the good of the country. But anyway, Collazo was wounded but not killed. He was convicted of murder, attempted assassination, and assault with intent to kill. He was sentenced to death, but his sentence was commuted to life imprisonment by President Truman."

"Why would Truman want to do that? He could have been killed!"

"I guess he didn't want to give Collazo martyrdom. In fact, he was released by President Carter after serving 30 years and went back to Puerto Rico. I think he died about 10 years ago."

"Amazing. So, where did you come in?"

"Well, as I said, the security was beefed up big time now and I got the Countersniper team. There was a Hispanic guy named Rafael Torres who did everything to get on that team. He was a good shot but an even bigger bullshitter. Had a foul mouth and quick, nasty temper. But he got on."

"Why?"

"Appeared to me it was because he was of Puerto Rican descent and no one wanted to stir up any more bad feelings with the island. They decided to give the guy a chance. I didn't like him and he didn't like me. Always would speak in Spanish when I was around. He even asked me right off if I could speak Espanola. I

said 'no' of course, but what he didn't know was that was my
minor in college. I could order tacos with the best of 'em."

"Gram, there was no Taco Bell back then!"

"You get the idea. He was always on the horn with someone jabbering away, and his manly macho brain could not even
ponder that I could understand everything he was saying. One day
I heard something that made me pay a little more attention. We
were in the break room, just Rafael and me. He dials up the phone
like I am not there, per usual. Then he begins to say stuff about
Mrs. Truman. Something about revenging a death and generally
some pretty condescending statements. I continued to look
uninterested, my nose in the newspaper. Then he tested me. Said
he heard my uncle was a huge fuck-up and he would love to burn
down his high and mighty house. Take the whole family down too.
I kept my breathing calm and regular, never even glancing away
from the paper. I casually went to pour another cup of coffee,
walking right past him, offering a little smile and a 'hey' like
usual. I know to this day he never knew I spoke his language."

Emily reached for some water and Micky jumped up to
help. The chunks of ice hit the water with a little splash and Emily
drank thirstily.

"Nothing like plain cold water when you are thirsty."

"Do you want anything else? Are you tired?" asked the
hovering Mikki, rubbing her own arms as she spoke as if she were
cold.

"No, I'm feeling pretty good. Actually there is a weight
being lifted off my chest as we talk. I just hope you are going to be
okay with this burden of knowledge."

"I'll be fine. Go on if you can."

"Of course, I didn't tell my uncle since this guy was a
class one fabricator with a big mouth. What I did do, was pay lots
of attention to where he went, who he saw, and what he did. I
started following him around after work hours. Something was up
and I felt obligated to find out what he had going on. There were
no computers to access and bring up lots of free information like
there are now. But I was in the investigative mode and found out
what a good little sneak I could be. When I accidentally turned up
the fact that his name, Torres, was shortened from Torresola, it
only took me a minute for my brain to start screaming warnings.
All alone, and digging deeper and deeper, I found out he was a
cousin to the infamous and now dead would-be assassin. At that

point I could have gone up the chain of command like we were supposed to, but you know me."

"Unfortunately. Let me guess. You decided rather than make this a national incident, little ol' country girl--you--would just handle it yourself. Am I right?"

"Mostly. I had seen him meeting with another sleaze at the El Rancho Grille. I dared not go in, since my fair complexion would be like a glow-in-the-dark bulletin. The clincher was that Mrs. Truman and some charity ladies were speaking to raise money for the Children's Hospital in Washington, D.C. When the roster for that assignment came up, Torres practically sold himself to be out of town for that occasion. He wanted vacation time and that initially surprised me. But from the phone tap I had illegally but discreetly set up on Torres' line--remember there were no cell phones--I was able to figure out their method and design. Mrs. Truman would be a brave but ignorant bull's-eye. This angered me, especially because I had the good fortune of meeting the First Lady, Elizabeth Virginia or Bess as she was called. Her daughter, Margaret, was a little older than me. Bess was one woman who seemed unchanged by the White House. She was really down to earth, I thought. Always would remember names, had a great sense of humor, and just enjoyed life in general. She was Honorary President of the Girl Scouts, the Washington Animal Protective League, and Honorary Chairman of the American Red Cross. I found out Manny Cordova was the name of Torres' partner in crime. He was to approach the First Lady's chair with his wife and ask her to stand in commemoration of an illness-stricken child she knew about. As she stood, somewhere the sharpshooter would fire and Mrs. Truman's death would serve as some sort of retaliation, according to his fanatical ideals. Now that I knew the plan, I needed to know where the kill shot would come from. When Torres said he needed to go to Chicago I knew he would be right there in D.C. with the rest of us, but hidden away. I went downtown to check out the sight. There was only one building feasible for a frontal shot and no one was home there. It was an abandoned office building. I knew that is where some of our team would be placed. Torres would be there in secret somewhere and set up to place the blame of the shooting on someone on our team. Terrorists only like to take the blame when they cannot be caught or incriminated. After they have escaped and their plan has succeeded, they are then willing to stand up and say, from a safe distance, 'Look at what I have done.'"

"So nothing has changed.... kill and run for cover."

Nodding and reaching for a little more water, Emily swallowed and continued, a little dampness forming on her brow. "Right. Anyway, when I checked my name on the roster, I was given the fourth floor in the building. There would be two agents above me and two below. I was the only one on the fourth floor. I was in the center of the building. I left that afternoon, taking the cross-town bus from our office near the government buildings. I arrived at the old Miller's Fabric Warehouse and went to the rear of the building, looking for open doors or windows. Sure enough, one of the basement windows, dusty and opaque with grime, had been pulled open. Torres was so arrogant he hadn't even bothered to cover up the fingerprints.

"Wearing a pair of cotton slacks and an old flannel shirt, I slid down through the opening. I had a small pack with a flashlight, a ring of keys, a screwdriver, and a fingerprint collection kit. Of course, my service revolver was strapped to my leg and fully loaded. I found the stairway through a previously made path, probably the way Torres had gone. Cobwebs and unknown insects stuck to my hair and arms as I made my way up. Floor number four. I wasn't even breathing hard by the time I hit the level I wanted. I wondered if the elevator would still work when the power was reconnected. Doubtful. I creaked open the stairwell door and stepped into the hall. Opening the door had put the stale air in motion. Gray particles spun through the rays of sun looking like bacteria I had seen swirling on a microscope slide. The corridor was actually pretty well lit. Most of the old office doors were gone. There were rooms only to my right; on the left was a large window that ended the hall and overlooked what used to be a parking lot. Advancing slowly and cautiously down the hall, I saw vague remnants of a shoe print with treads. Combat shoes or boots. The prints were hardly visible and not in any particular pattern.

"The room where I had been assigned for duty was probably the one on my left, I had decided, directly facing the pavilion across the street. The pavilion had been set up temporarily just yesterday for the upcoming address by the First Lady. The tarnished brass door plaque read, J.Haynes, 412. I crept silently along the hallway, looking carefully into each doorway on the left.

All had street-facing windows. The building would be cleared before we set up, to remove any transients and other overnight guests. How would Torres get in here? I was reasonably sure he would choose that floor, since I was the only one assigned at that position. But how would he get past security and get set up? Then there, I saw it! Looking at a room in the center section of the floor, there was a small office toilet and sink adjoining. The door was locked, but gave way easily when I found an old matching key from my jingling collection. Inside there was a hole where the toilet used to be. The actual plumbing fixtures were long gone. A large hole ran through the floor and down as far as I could see. The street side of the bathroom wall had received some recent carpenter work. An opening had been cut into the wood exterior and then replaced. A tiny knob allowed easy withdrawal and replacement of the wooden panel that was set carefully into exterior siding. A shooting window for an easy shot. And who would be the fall guy? Me."

"But Gran, how would the ballistics match? Wouldn't they able to do the imaging on the ammunition and see it was not your gun?"

"I think his plan was to do the shoot and in the confusion afterwards, run to my post, slip the weapon into a hidden area in my room and then run back to escape down the toilet hole. That would leave me with an extra gun, the one that would have fired the fatal shot. To him, I am sure it was the most perfect plan. Take down the First Lady and also get me removed from the Service in shame."

"Bastard."

"Yep. Also, there was more to the story. His partner in crime, Manny Cordova, was figuring this was a great way to knock off his wife at the same time. She was the hospital public relations figure and a real peach of a lady. I had also met Kitty once at a charity ball while I was on assignment. Just the most pleasant and charming woman.... I really liked her right away. She came from big family money. Her father had something to do with Firestone tires or something. She had met Manny at a party in college and fell in love with his Puerto Rican tough guy good looks. They married young, and her family did not approve. They supported her in her decision, though, and put up with Manny, who could be charming when he felt the need. So her darling Manny who ended up with a peon's job in the city auditor's office, was having an affair with a co-worker. He wanted Mrs. Cordova gone, but not at the risk of losing access to her money."

"So men and women both can be gold diggers if the situation demands."

"Oh yes, and both sexes will kill for cash, if the price is right."

"I see," said Mikki, eyes unable to meet Emily's at this point.

"Sometimes it's right. Intentions are nine-tenths of the law in my book. You may not understand it, but that is my own morality. I know you're judging me, but do you want me to continue?"

"Wouldn't miss this for the world," said Mikki with a small smile and gently running her fingers through her bangs as she exhaled.

"Anyway, I had recognized Manny Cordova when I saw him with Torres at the Spanish bar. It was easy after that to figure it all out. I just kept playing dumb and in all his arrogance, Torres practically served himself up on a turkey platter. I knew Cordova would be sitting with his wife, Kitty, behind the speaker's stand and that she would be the one introducing the main speaker, Bess Truman. That much was a given since we all learned that during our early briefings. I guessed that Cordova would give some sort of clue as to when the shots would be fired, and then leave the area of the podium. He was too much of a weasel not to be a coward, and I am sure he did not trust Torres to target his wife and not him too. He would be the only witness as to the real plot and he knew that. So when Cordova got up or moved away from Kitty, it would be too late to hit him. The shots would be fired quickly and look to the investigative team like a miss on Bess that hit Kitty, and then followed by a hit on the First Lady. Torres knew about my shooting ability since we were about evenly matched, but in the excitement of the attack he was figuring authorities would be able to believe I missed my first shot. I was never sure of my supposed motive. Maybe he just wanted to watch me squirm and insist I was not the shooter, while he laughed his ass off in the background.

"The day of the event arrived and I was nervous, but felt in charge of the situation. My plan was ready in my head and there would be no faltering, no margin for error. I went to my post and set up my tripod with the scoped rifle. The captain checked us all in by radio and I began to wait. The stagecoach arrived late and

Bess Truman stepped out to a big crowd who clapped politely in appreciation."

"The stagecoach? Gran, I know you are old, but really!" exclaimed Mikki in big-eyed mock surprise.

"The Presidential limo, child. Almost always a Cadillac. Now usually a Deville, with run-flat tires, reinforced frame, bullet-resistant glass, and about 2,000 pounds of extra weight. I hear it drives like a tank. It is used for 'special occasions.' Anyway, there were some motor driven vehicles back in my days, Dearie," said Emily patting Mikki's hand in satirical consolation.

"I suppose it was black, huh?"

"Back then, yes, but since then they have developed other colors of paint! So amazing, you young, inventive whippersnappers! Seriously, I think now the color of choice is sometimes a non-descript champagne."

"Not another boring beige car!"

"Well, you know I don't drive one."

"No, that would not be you, Grandma. Please, on with the saga."

"The car arrived, the important people were in their places. By then, I was not at my post, but I still had the radio. Carefully and quietly I went back to the room with the locked bathroom. I could hear him in there setting up and not even trying to be that quiet. Such self-assurance. I had my service revolver but with an added attraction. I had snapped on a sound suppressor, a silencer. The door to his bathroom was still unlocked. Sloppy work on his part not to recheck that. I glanced out the window of the office and could see the speakers were getting up and heading for the podium. I had to work quickly. My hands were clammy but I felt sure of myself. I grabbed the wobbly doorknob on the bathroom hiding place, pulled it open, and aimed quickly. The shock and instant recognition on Torres' face was, as they say today, priceless. I fired without hesitation. A small "poof," a sudden hole in his right forehead and Torres dropped like a clubbed steer at the slaughterhouse. I had to work fast now and yanked off the silencer and reholstered my weapon. Next, I took Torres' place at the shooting window. He had done most of the work for me. The scope was perfect and the long-range rifle was aimed directly at the unsuspecting Kitty Cordova. She would have been hit first, like I said, then Mrs. Truman. I only moved the tripod swivel a hair, carefully repositioning the crosshairs. I began to worry a little as I had never fired this particular weapon. But I was sure Torres would have only the best weapon and have it in perfect condition. The heavy gun felt light on the tripod as I gripped the trigger and prepared to squeeze. My fingers were damp, but moisture was not a problem. Soft, thin leather shooting gloves covered each and every digit. It was not really important that I kill Manny Cordova, since it would be interesting to see his reaction to being shot apparently by Torres. Wonder how he would explain that? Would he say that Torres was supposed to shoot my wife not me? As Mrs. Truman approached the podium, led by the Cordovas, the crowd began to applaud. Bess wore a beautiful navy blue suit and white silk blouse. There was a strand of small pearls around her neck. She looked happy and professional, truly glad to be there and doing her share. Those on the stage stood and clapped, too, as the beaming Kitty turned the microphone over to Bess. The two women briefly touched cheeks and Kitty and Manny returned towards their seats. At that moment, Manny took advantage of the standing crowd to edge his way away from his chair, excusing himself politely as he went. Manny began to move more quickly and then hesitated briefly as if waiting for something. I took my shot and he fell where he stood. He was dead before he hit the ground. The crowd gasped in unison and panicked screams were followed by Secret Service jumping to cover Bess. They looked up to the building as to the source of the shot. Meanwhile I radioed in to say that the shot was fired from close to my position. I can hear the others running on the stairwells towards me. I fired again quickly and the men ran to my position. When they saw me, they found the dead Torres with two bullet wounds and I was holding the kill weapon. Panting and excited, they took my gun and examined the quite dead body.

"'I heard the shot come from this floor and I ran over here. He was ready to shoot again and I fired twice!' I reported.

"There were several discrepancies regarding the number of shots the guys heard fired, but in the noise and confusion, there wasn't much credence given to that. There was, of course, a big investigation that followed. No one could figure out why Torres would shoot Manny Cordova, so I happened to mention that I had overheard some phone conversations in Spanish and that Torres was arguing with someone. Gee, it sounded like maybe it was over a woman or something. I just planted a tiny seed and let it grow.

"After the inquiry, I was cleared of any wrongdoing and in fact, given an 'atta girl' for taking down Torres so quickly. But things were not the same on my team. Once you shoot one of your own, the guys tend to see you a little differently. If they didn't like me before, they mostly avoided me now. Many were too wary to even eat a sandwich with me. Even my uncle looked at me with a strange eye. That was when I left the Secret Service. The President's family was ever grateful, though, and in fact has helped me out a few times when I needed some 'behind closed doors' answers and information. Kitty Cordova was upset at first, but I think she knew all about her husband's philandering. She soon had suitors lined up and didn't seem to be unhappy or lonely too long. Two years later she married a Senator from California who treated her like a queen. I don't think she ever knew that Manny wanted her murdered. That may have been too much for anyone to deal with. Anyway, I went back to college and finished up my degree, met Granddad and got married."

"Okaaay. Somehow, I get that is not the end of the story."

"Of course not," answered Emily, "but right now I am exhausted. Really."

"Sorry, Gran, I know I've been pushing you. I'm grilling you like a tube steak and you're having major surgery in the morning," said Mikki tenderly.

"Well, nothing would help right now like a little dinner. Oh, almost forgot! I get real food tonight. Kinda like the Last Supper or something." Emily's eyes were about half-mast now, and she looked drained from the effort of telling the truth after all these years. Her right hand gripped the stainless bedrail, fingers white. "Just have a bit of a headache again. Must be the stress."

"That would be easy to believe. While you have your dinner and take a little break, I am going to run some errands while I am here. I have to call the office with some sort of story and check in on things again. I need to touch base with Brig also. I am not sure exactly what to say about all this yet," said Mikki as she gathered her purse and keys. She wore a stoic and determined look that Emily was not sure she had seen before on Mikki. Her granddaughter quickly planted a kiss on the patient's forehead and swept out of the room. Within ten minutes, a waiter came with a tray, but Emily only picked at her food. Alone and worried, she began to think more about the surgery. Maybe it would be best if she did not survive the operation. It wouldn't be so bad, you just don't wake up. That would solve Mikki's dilemma also. She could make up some story of how she found her in Citrus City. She could arrange a private ambulance to take her body back home. She hoped she would not have to tell her granddaughter to let her die to save the family from destruction. But she would, of course, if necessary. In fact, she suddenly had a brilliant idea! She rang the call bell for the nurse. She had an up-to-date will, but now she wanted a DNR order signed by her doctor. Also, she wanted the woman from Social Services to come back and help her fill out a Living Will. She would make sure there were no extraordinary measures taken to prolong her life. *No resuscitation and no life as a carrot in a vegetable bin for me! Now I know what they mean by death with dignity. That means grace for the whole family..*

Chapter 18

Emily sat morosely staring at her food and watching Jeopardy until Mikki arrived back at the door.

"I'm back!" Mikki announced, Arnold-like. She looked and smelled great. She was freshly showered and shampooed, and was wearing a crisp white cotton camp shirt. It was open just enough to show some cleavage. Olive green silk cargo pants hung just right on her long, slim legs. Mikki looked like the girl next door who just happened to step off the Glamour magazine cover.

"Hi to you too! Such a sight for sore eyes, as they say. Glad you're back!" said Emily.

"What's wrong? You look a little down," asked Mikki.

"Just thinking about the surgery and tomorrow and my life in general, I guess," answered Emily. "Do you think we could just talk about normal things for a while? I think I am about all stressed out for the time being."

"Sure. In fact, I talked to Brigetta and Mom just before I came back. Everything is fine at the store. Mitchell Brothers Company is having a grand opening for their new building …over on Palmetto Drive?"

"Oh, yeah, the men's clothing outfit. Very exclusive, I hear. Only carries the high-end stuff in men's wear and especially suits. I heard they even had a small jewelry department with everything from earrings to tie tacks. They had an ad in GQ last month, I think.

"Anyway, Mom went to the champagne opening and got Dad some shirts, not much else. Didn't even have a glass of bubbly, I suppose."

"Well, I have seen your mother a little loose once or twice, Mikki. She's not always the stodgy, practical one you think she is."

"No one in our family seems to be what I believed, Gran," said Mikki with an accusatory glance and roll of her eyes. "Anyway, tomorrow you'll have the surgery, you'll get better enough to go home, and off we roll to Palm Beach. Badger is missing you, you know. Brig says he has been slinking all around the house searching for you. He finally gave up and Brig found him curled up in your closet right beside that crazy pair of hot pink fuzzy slippers, those dumb ones that look like bird heads."

"Actually, believe it or not, your mother gave me those, and I treasure them," answered Emily. "And to set the record straight, they are flamingos, not just 'birds', my dear child."

"Oh, excuse me. Well, one of the wings is now missing, thanks to Badger. Chewed it right off to spite you, I am sure."

"I'm shocked. Not that he chewed off the fuzz, but that he has that many teeth left to do the job. I have been thinking about getting another cat, a kitten actually, to keep him company. Or do you think he would get all bent out of shape?"

"After he got over the surprise, I am sure he would love it. Such a friendly old beast. Built for comfort, not for speed. Fat and friendly, that's him. How old is he anyway, Gran?"

"Not sure. Picked him up from the pound. Got him neutered and a flea bath and he just moved right in liked he owned the place. Such good company. A good book and a good cat is all a woman needs at this stage of life. Well, of course, her family too."

"Gee, I am glad we are at least in the ranking with old Badger. Makes me feel better already." Actually Mikki was feeling better to see her Granny acting more like herself.

"Mikki, there's something we need to talk about. Tomorrow there will be a DNR order on my door. I talked to the nurses and they sent in a social worker to help me with it. I signed it, and as soon as the doctor okays the whole thing and signs, we are all set."

Now Mikki was the one who was distressed. "What? You did all that without even talking to me about it? I realize the rest of the family isn't here to argue with you, but now you're getting me upset."

"As you said, I'll be fine. It's just a precaution. I don't want to be a burden, and the more I thought about it, it seemed it might work out if I would just die on the table. Then there would be no need for any explanations. You always were a good storyteller, Mikki. So, you could just figure out a story about how you found me here, and the whole family would be spared."

Mikki just sat there staring at Emily, still reeling from the implications and the shock. Her mouth hung open dumbly and as she attempted to speak, no words would form.

Emily continued, "I know all of this is just too much to bear. And I began thinking, what if there is an investigation and some of this shit starts coming out? I refuse to be the ruination of the family name. I promise you, that is something that will never happen. I guarantee it."

Finally Mikki was able to make her lips form sounds. "Gran, nothing will happen. Between the two of us, we will make things work out." But she knew as she said it, her face was giving her fear and doubt away, as easy to read as a first grade primer. She was horrified to realize that her Granny was right. The thought had actually crossed her mind that if Granny died, there would be no family crisis except for the funeral. No murders to explain, no investigations to suffer, no lawyers to hire, no odd looks from others at the Palm Beach Country Club. What is wrong with me for thinking like this? This is my grandmother!

For a pro like Emily, she saw the truth on her granddaughter's face. She was the one who had caused the commotion and deserved whatever happened to her. Yet, when she saw that look in those green eyes, and the veil that fell as an attempt to hide those honest emotions, she felt pity for Mikki. She was very glad she had already asked for and signed the DNR order. Everything tomorrow would be out of her hands, out of her control.

"Mikki, please promise me, no tubes, no CPR, no force feeding. I don't want any of that. If things don't go right, then that is what was meant to be. Promise me. You know what to do, …please."

Eyes now moist, but not crying, Mikki rose and took her Granny's hand. "You know you can always count on me, Gran. I love you. I will do what's right, I promise."

"Thank you. I knew I could trust you," said the now teary-eyed woman, suddenly feeling very old and submissive.

Soon a nurse came in with a tray full of I.V. tubes and needles, and a bag of fluid bouncing along on a stainless steel rolling hook on wheels. She gave Mikki a look that said it was time for her to go. Mikki got up, straightened her shirt and kissed Emily good-bye. "Seeya in the morning, okay?" Turning to the nurse, she asked, "What time is the operation? Still 8 A.M.?"

"That's what the schedule says, but you know how that is," the nurse replied, checking a folded paper that was in her pocket. "The early ones usually are pretty much on time. It's the later ones that get delayed if there is an emergency or complication that takes longer. Mildred Carr...hmm...should be real close to on time, I would bet. I'd be here about an hour earlier, just in case. Sometimes the docs get anxious to get going, or else there might be a cancel and then, *voila*! You are first in line!"

"Okay, I'll be here bright and early," said Mikki. She gave Granny Em another hug good-bye and went out the door.

After a quick stick with the needle and deft taping of the tubing into place, the I.V. fluids were again dripping silently into Emily's left arm. The nurse wrote with a pen onto the tape, noting the time and date at the insertion sight. She gave her patient a smile and a wink of reassurance and, after gathering up her tray of supplies, left for the corridor.

Chapter 19

Though actually early morning, it seemed that Emily was just beginning to doze off when the heavy door was banged open by a surgical gurney. "Things are moving quickly downstairs, so I am here to take you away, Darlin'," said a pleasant young man with a green surgical cap and matching scrub top and pants. Just as Emily was about to complain that her granddaughter was not yet here, Mikki rushed breathlessly into the room. It was exactly 7 A.M. A nurse soon followed and gave Emily an injection. It gave her an almost immediate false sense of peace and calm. As the surgical transport tech checked and rechecked Emily's paperwork and ID wristband, Mikki held her other hand. The young woman seemed to have been changed overnight somehow. She smelled like gardenias and her hair was still damp. Refreshed and stronger, she offered a dose of morning optimism to the fragile-looking grandmother under the green surgical blanket.

"Try to behave down there, now," Mikki admonished with a smile.

"I'll try not to say anything crazy, Dear, while under the influence," answered Emily.

"Are you ready to go with me now, Mrs. Carr? Young lady, you can come with us as far as the elevators if you wish," said the orderly, carefully placing a blue paper cap over the patient's hair.

"Let's roll," said Emily with a courageous effort.

And the cart did roll with teetering but sturdy wheels down the hospital hallway towards the elevator doors. Kate came from the nurse's station to sign papers and gave Emily the "V" for victory sign as a well wish. Mikki saw Darla skulking about in the break room doorway. Mikki was already wondering what she could be up to next. Quickly Granny Em was gone and Kate told her where she could wait for news. Mikki gave her a cell phone number in case she was outside or off the floor. For now, Mikki headed towards the visitor's lounge with a Danielle Steele novel and a *USA Today* she had purchased in the gift shop. This was going to be a long, stressful day, and Mikki just wanted to get it over with as soon as possible. Today there was a mission of importance to accomplish, loose ends to tie up, so to speak. From the lounge area she could see most of the coming and going in the corridor. Mostly she wanted to watch Darla from that viewing point. Soon she saw Darla taking a cart with soiled linens to the laundry room. Darla then looked at her watch and went to the nurse's station. Mikki could see her say something to one of the nurses and head for the stairway carrying a small lunch cooler. Mikki knew she would be on her way to the cafeteria.

Darla, now on her lunchbreak, was eating yogurt and a salad she had packed at home this morning. As she ate she watched for Helen, and when she saw the round Polish woman she motioned her over to her table. Helen sat down with her tray full of potato chips, BBQ chicken, cookies and 2 puddings. Darla stared in amazement, but said nothing. She wanted to use and abuse the woman just long enough to ask her some questions. After she got the information she needed, she didn't care if the fat old lady's cholesterol when through the roof. A walking heart attack for sure. Probably swishing that mop was all the exercise she could ever handle.

"Hey, Helen. Nice to finally have lunch with you."

"Yeah," said Helen, more interested in getting the bag of chips open with her yellow, crooked teeth. They snapped open suddenly and chips went flying onto the tray and onto the floor. Helen quickly reached down and grabbed up the kettle-cooked spuds from the floor. She grinned widely, showing her dentally challenged mouth. "Five second rule!"

Darla could only look away in disgust for a second and then determinedly continued, "Well, what do you think? I mean about what we were talking about before? The blood on the stairs that you traced all the way to Mrs. Carr's bathroom?"

Crunching noisily on chips and licking BBQ sauce from her fingers, Helen said with her mouth full, "I only know what I saw. Mopped it up. Done with it far as I'm concerned. None of my business 'cept the cleaning it up part. I done my job. That's it."

"But don't you, too, feel that was weird? What if the old lady had been downstairs to visit Dupris? I mean he died that same night!" pursued Darla.

"Girl, don't be stupid. That old lady can hardly get around. I heard she has lung cancer and she is old as dirt. Think about it. That's plain dumb."

Darla watched as Helen now attacked the pudding cups, one chocolate, and one tapioca. She peeled off the lids, slurped them clean with her tongue and set them on her tray. Her plastic spoon almost daintily dug into one cup, then the other, carefully mixing the brown and lumpy yellow globs. As she spooned them into her eager mouth, she seemed to pause and think, chewing and smacking her lips. "Of course, strange things happen every day. When I get home I watch Dr. Phil and Jerry Springer. All kinds of wackos and strange ones on those shows. Think they're real or actors?"

"Probably real. But that's what I mean. What if Mrs. Carr did something to Dupris? It sounds crazy, but what if she killed him? What if she snuck in there and did something?"

"Now you're back to the stupid part. Why would she? And how would she?" responded Helen with her mouth full again with oatmeal cookie.

"I don't know. But something is really fishy with her granddaughter showing up suddenly and all these closed doors and secrecy. Inquiring minds want to know!" said Darla.

"Far as I'm concerned, I'm done with it. Too farfetched even for me to believe," countered Helen.

"Well, I think I have an instinct for this and it says to tell someone anyway. Will you back me up with telling what you know about the blood drops?" asked Darla.

"I suppose, but it still sounds stupid to me, so don't ask me to do or say anything else. Are you going to finish your salad? The doc told me to eat salad every day," said Helen.

"I think he may have meant *instead of,* not *in addition to,* your regular lunch, Helen," responded Darla. "Anyway, I'm going to tell Kate and if she doesn't do anything, I'll call the police and talk to Lt. Sanderfield. I think he's the one who brought in Dupris."

"Why would he care? I heard he was the one who shot him. I thought the cops would be glad to be rid of that guy. Dupris was nothin' but a creepy drug dealer and probably a killer too," questioned Helen.

"Cops always want to know everything. Then they can sort it all out, put everything in its place. You know, law and *order*!" answered Darla. "They always want a full investigation and all the clues. Just like on TV. Besides, those two women have just shut me out. Almost like too high and mighty. And Mrs. Carr supposedly a poor homeless woman. I just don't believe their little story, and I'm going to get to the bottom of it soon."

"Whatever. I am going to get a diet Coke to take back to the floor. Want anything?" asked Helen.

"No. No, thanks." God, how could that woman put anything else into her stomach? That was the clincher, diet drink. What a joke, she laughed to herself.

As Helen got up and moved back to the cafeteria line, Darla gathered up her lunch remains and took the tray to the trash bin. Dumping most of her lunch in the receptacle, she was lost in her thoughts. On her way out, she failed to see the pretty auburn haired woman studying *USA Today* who was seated two tables away. The woman who was wearing designer Oakley tinted glasses and had ear buds in each ear. She had her back to the table where Darla and Helen had sat. She was apparently listening to music on her MP3 player. Or maybe she was just listening.

Chapter 20

At about 2 P.M. Mikki felt the vibration of the pager to her cell phone and grabbed for it wildly from her belt. She raced from the lounge to the third floor nurses' area and saw Kate. Her smiling face meant instant relief for Mikki. She knew Granny Em was okay.

"Hi Michelle! Your grandmother did great! In fact, Dr. Waterson will be here soon to talk to you about the surgery. I think he has pretty good news, though," said Kate, giving Mikki a hug upon seeing the tears begin to fall.

"Oh, thank God!" sobbed Mikki, unable to hold back any longer. "I was so worried, just terrified, actually!"

Patting Mikki's back, Kate continued, "Any kind of surgery or illness is scary. The whole hospital scene is downright Stephen King for some people, if you know what I mean. Just a real nightmare. But now the healing can begin and you can both get your lives back on the road to normalcy."

"With my Granny, things will never be 'normal,' but I appreciate all your help and reassurances, Nurse Bingham."

"Please call me Kate, Michelle. We're such a small hospital and we try to form close bonds with all our patients and patient families."

"Everyone has been great, and we really appreciate the extra efforts, believe me. And don't worry, we will be paying our bill in full. I went down to the billing department and worked out a way to take care of everything and also a little donation to your new project. Seems like such a worthwhile idea."

"Wow! That's great, Michelle. If there's anything at all either of you need...! Well, I have to get back to work. They will be bringing Mrs. Carr up from recovery soon. In fact, here they are!"

Kate went to the hospital service elevator and helped wheel the groggy patient back to her room. Emily opened her eyes long enough to see Mikki standing there, still teary.

"I lived," mumbled the patient.

"No doubt in my mind, Granny. How do you feel?" asked Mikki.

"Happy to be back on planet Earth, all in one piece. Pretty sleepy though. And some pain," whispered Emily.

Kate said, "Don't worry, we'll be bringing you some nice pain meds in a few minutes. Just have to assess you first, get some vital signs."

"I don't feel so vital right now," responded Emily, awakening a little more.

"I mean, we have to check your blood pressure, pulse, and all that stuff. Get you all settled and hooked up to your oxygen," responded Kate taking the old woman's hand in hers and giving it a little pat. Turning to Mikki, she said, "If you wouldn't mind just stepping out for a few minutes, we will get her all set up, get her shot for her, and then you can sit with her if you want. She won't be much company for a while. Usually takes several hours, sometimes days, for the anesthetic to wear off."

"Okay, I'll just wait outside the door. Oh, there's Dr. Waterson. I'll go talk to him in the hall while you do your thing in here, Kate. Thanks so much!" said Mikki as she headed to the corridor.

"Ms. Smythe! I am very glad to inform you that all went very well. Surprisingly, the tumor was partially encapsulated and I don't think there was much, if any, spreading. We got all of it out and should follow up with some chemotherapy to get any stray cancer cells. Overall, a pretty good report," said the handsome doctor, still wearing surgical scrubs covered by a white lab coat. He was smiling widely at Mikki, as his eyes involuntarily began a slow trip over her features.

"Then when do you think she can be discharged? I would like to take her home as soon as she is able to go," asked Mikki, flashing those emerald green eyes with mile-long lashes.

"Let's see how things go. We have to watch for possible complications from the surgery. Make sure the healing process is proceeding properly," said Dr. Waterson.

"Well, how 'bout just a time frame, then?"

"A few days, maybe a week at the outside. She seems to be a strong woman for her age. She kinda surprised us all. She really is doing well. No need for a ventilator or intensive care."

"Yeah, she is certainly full of surprises," said Mikki, her mind whirling with things she now knew about her Granny. She took Dr. Waterson's hand and thanked him for all his help. Then she tossed her shiny auburn locks back over her shoulder as he gazed in appreciation. She purposely wanted to leave an impression on the man. You never knew when you might need someone's help.

Kate called Mikki back into the room as Dr. Waterson went towards the surgery department. Married or not, there were some things a man just had to look at. That girl was like a work of art, a sculpture, a masterpiece, Dr. Waterson thought to himself. He would never touch, just ogle and stare. He loved his wife and besides, he had seen the emotional and financial damages caused by divorce. It just wasn't worth it.

Emily was back in her own bed. She looked pale and her eyes were closed. She was breathing quietly and actually snoring a little. Clumps of damp hair spidered down her forehead. Right now Mikki thought it was hard to think of her as a hardened killer. She looked fragile and quite vulnerable; not exactly a sleeping angel, but not the devil in disguise, either. Mikki was really not sure what to think at this point, but it appeared that Granny would soon be able to go back home. They needed to get out of here as quickly as possible, leaving a cold trail of false identity. Mikki went to the bedrail and leaned over to kiss the soft cheek of her Granny Em. Running quick fingers through her hair, she gathered up her purse and tucked in her shirt, preparing to leave for a while.

"Kate, I'll be back later when she is more awake. Feel free to page me or just call the cell if you need me, okay?"

Kate responded, "She will be fine now. She just needs to rest and get through the next couple of days." Kate was checking the white Thrombo-Embolism Deterrent stockings on Emily's legs. "As we discussed, these are to help prevent clots after the surgery. Once she is up and moving around again, we'll take them off. Too much sitting or lying around isn't good. Pneumonia, blood clots, weak muscles. All kinds of things happen when we're immobile too long. We'll be getting her up and moving probably this evening."

"Already? Can she do it?"

"Oh yeah, there is pain and a lot of complaining, but the patients who move do the best."

"Well, she never was one to sit around and do nothing. You'll probably have to tie her down to keep her from overdoing

it," said Mikki. "She loves her food, so when will she get back to her regular diet?"

"We'll see how soon she can get some bowel sounds. Everything shuts down in there for a while after the anesthetics. The pain medicine slows things down, too. That is another thing that moving around will help."

"Okay, I'll be back soon," said Mikki as she departed, leaving Emily in the good hands of Nurse Bingham. She felt quite comfortable with Kate and felt that under other circumstances, they could have become friends. Right now she needed a break and also some lunch, maybe a martini lunch, and then a little nap back at the motel.

The nap turned into a three-hour marathon and Mikki awoke with a start. She quickly showered and put on some denim low-waisted shorts with a wide web belt. A flowered camp shirt covered a blue tube top. She tied her freshly shampooed hair back into a ponytail and stuck some small gold hoops into her earlobes. She decided to quickly refresh her pink nail polish, both fingers and toes. She still had time to run to the grocery and grab some cat food and litter. Maybe a scratching post and cat toys, too. Badger was going to love this! Soon they would be going home.

When Mikki returned to Emily's room, she found Nurse Kate Bingham talking to her Granny at the bedside once again. Kate's twelve-hour shift was nearly over. Emily was still a little groggy from the pain shot, but her eyes widened immediately when she saw Micky come towards her. She quickly tried to sit up like she had something important to tell. Words began to spill out in rapid fire.

"I felt a little woozy and Nurse Kate had to help me get back out of the bathroom. For a moment I thought she was my cousin Bridget. You remember Bridget, don't you?"

Kate said, "Yes, she said 'Brig, what are you doing here? Aren't you supposed to be watching Badger?' "

Mikki was horrified at this revelation, but remained cool and calm on the exterior. She replied evenly, "Yes, Grandmother, I certainly remember seeing photos of your *cousin* Bridget. She's dead now though, right? Why would you be talking about her?"

"Guess no more Demerol for me, huh? I see dead people," she whispered harshly in mock secrecy. "Well, admit it, Nurse Bingham does resemble her!"

"Okay, Grandmother. Sure, whatever you say." Turning to Kate, Mikki said, "Think this is bad, you should see her when she's drunk!"

"Michelle! You said you would never give up any family confidences!" Emily scolded.

Kate just laughed and said, "Don't worry, everyone gets a little tipsy from the Demerol or morphine. I gotta get back to my rounds. Call me if you need anything later, Mrs. Carr."

Both women were silent, almost afraid to say a word or move until the heavy door again swung closed.

Finally Mikki was first to speak. "I feel there is a big hole being dug and we are both trying to fall in."

"Sorry."

"I know you didn't screw up on purpose, but this could all fall apart in an instant. We are closer than you think to being blown apart here, Gran," stated Mikki as she paced the floor anxiously, thumbs hooked in her short's pockets.

"Please sit down! You are making me nervous. Nothing else will happen."

Mikki said, "I am making you nervous? But what if the nurse mentions what you said to the dear little Darla? That would really put her over the edge. She would go nuts with that information. She would put 'Bridget' together with her fellow student Brigetta in an instant. She may be a pain in the ass, but she is not dumb."

"Why in the world would she mention that to Darla? At least I don't think it would be anything that would need to be in a patient report, anyway. It's not like I insisted she was my cousin and then became violent and tried to beat her up for stealing my husband or something. Now that would have been newsworthy!" Emily said haughtily, but wincing with pain as she made the effort to talk.

"In any case, it's time we fly this chicken coop as you always say, Granny. We need to get out of here before loose lips sink our battleship. Ever since I got your lips flapping you can't seem to know when to stop!" admonished Mikki.

"Okay. No more info for you, Babe."

"You know what I mean, and don't start that! You could sink the whole family here... Mom, Brig, Dad, my job, your shop, everything! This is important, Gram!"

Now sullen and depressed, Emily looked away out the window, fiddling with her I.V. line, wrapping it round and round her finger. "Maybe I should die and solve everyone's problems. I sure don't want to be a burden to the family," she said quietly, her face now serious.

Mikki's face filled with emotion and tears swelled in the softening green eyes. She took her grandmother's small hand and stroked it gently. She saw the pale brown age spots and the bluish discolorations from needle sticks on her hand and arm, and felt a great sense of protectiveness. The family must remain intact at all costs. She would be the strong one as always and somehow pull this off without losing her love and compassion.

"You are not scheduled to die. Too belligerent. Too bossy. Too smart and too funny. We are fine. We just need to be more careful. I will take care of everything. Don't worry about anything anymore. It's my turn to be the tough old cookie. No more soft chocolate chip either, more like two week old peanut butter oatmeal," announced Mikki.

"Don't mention peanut butter."

"Huh?"

"Never mind, darling. TMI."

"In this little story, there is never too much information and you know it."

"Trust me on this one, darling. I love you."

Emily held up her arms, inviting the young woman to hug her. The two women remained entwined for a full minute. When they came apart, it was as if their souls were meshed as one.

Chapter 21

Dinner on Emily's first day after surgery was being served to patients at Citrus City Hospital. Having proved that she could flatulate with the best of them, Mrs. Mildred Carr, Bed 2, Room 311, was now permitted a regular diet as per the notice on the end of her bed. Mikki did bring in some smuggled extras for the evening meal. Artichoke heart salad with vinaigrette dressing and some favorite Pepperidge Farm cookies were a good start. Mikki had ordered an extra hospital meal so they could eat together. The waiter brought in an extra tray table and Mikki sat in the corner chair, her usual haunt.

"Now all we need is a little blackberry Merlot. What ya say, Mikki dear?" Emily suggested with a grin, as she held up her empty water glass.

Mikki leered back at her and said, "Right. That is exactly what we need, Miss Loose Lips!"

"Well, just one glass wouldn't hurt!"

"You are getting more like a little kid again each hour. Settle down and eat your dinner.... or no dessert for you!"

"Well, it's not like you can send me to my room, you know," Emily answered, as she stirred her cup of coffee.

Both women giggled like something hilarious had been said, and finished their meals. Emily only ate a few bites of everything. "I think my stomach shrank," she stated. Actually she felt a little nauseated from the food. The incision was feeling much better and there hadn't been much coughing lately. Emily began to think it was possible to get out of this alive after all.

After coffee and several orange Milano cookies, both admitted being tired and stressed out. Mikki got up to leave, kissed Granny good-bye, and waved as she left for the night. Although she had been forceful in gaining the full disclosures from her Granny, she hadn't been entirely forthcoming on her own part. A brief walk took her to the parking lot and her hot black car. As she started up the BMW and quickly turned the air conditioning knob to A/C Max, she began thinking as the car began to cool. The steering wheel was still hot from the day's heat as she turned onto the main road and headed towards the motel. Her best thinking time was always in the car, riding to work or on a trip, or even running to McDonald's for a quick burger. As the cold air hit her cheeks, she remembered back to the time she had accidentally stumbled on Granny's workout room. All of the family knew Gran liked to keep in great shape. Her lithe, strong body could rival women's bodies at any gym. Except for a few sags and wrinkles, some age spots and graying hair, she could easily pass for much, much younger. Brigetta and Mikki always wondered how the old-fashioned Nordic Track in her Granny's bedroom could possibly reap the benefit of all those firm muscles. Not only that, it was usually covered with a sheet and encrusted with dust. They thought that maybe all the gardening she did around her home had built those hard biceps and razor sharp reflexes. For sure, they both had often seen her in shorts, halter-top, straw visor, and pink garden gloves. She would be digging, carrying buckets and pots, raking and pruning. She had a little red wagon she used to pull along all her equipment as she patrolled the tropical pathways around the grounds at Pink Flamingo. Granny Em surely did love that house on the beach, Mikki had thought. She cared for it like part of the family circle. Touching, mending, beautifying, Gran made sure the house looked and felt like a happy and healthy homestead.

The girls also had both always loved the huge pink beach-front mansion with its massive white Corinthian columns, the wide balconies, and the wide welcoming stairway to the front door. The windows were many; Gran wanted all the rooms to be sunlit and airy. The interior décor could be called Southwest/beachy, Mikki guessed. Watercolors of painted ponies by Griggs and Dolittle were intermingled with Caribbean-style ocean and beach scenes. Granny's two loves--horses and the beach--held equal rights to the home. One day when Mikki was about 17 years old, she had been designated as the official house sitter while Granny took Brigetta and a couple of friends to Disney for a few days. One night she was looking for a good movie to watch and fumbling through the case of VCR tapes when she found blueprints in the drawer of the entertainment center. Faded blue ink on a huge folded paper, but you could still see what it was. Mikki was curious and excited to see the layout of the house and wanted to imagine the planning and building. The Pink Flamingo with all its nooks and crannies.

And that was the big surprise. She took the prints into the media room and switched on the overhead lights and unfolded them out on the floor. She had known long before that she wanted to be an engineer. Looking at the blueprints seemed like a great idea to her. It was just fun at first to find the "you are here" spot where she was in the media center and then follow the hallways and doors throughout the big house. It was like the mazes she used to do with pencil as a kid. Then Wow! Pow! There it was! She thought at first she had discovered the Flamingo's "panic room." She had heard of these rooms being constructed and used in the remote possibility of a home invasion.

Certainly, Granny did have a lot of security issues. Obsessed would be a better word, actually. She seemed to be always worried about the girls and their privacy and safety. Mikki had pretended not to notice the security guards discreetly milling about the perimeter of their parties. For her high school graduation party, she guessed there were nearly as many armed security as there were graduates. She had never let on to Granny that she knew they were all being protected. Even though she was shocked at first to see a glimpse of a holstered weapon beneath a gentleman's dinner jacket, she just thought it was part of every girl's growing up. She knew the extra security precautions were not to protect the valuables in the house from her friends, though. Granny was not like that. She had thought she was just a very overly protective grandparent. When she saw the perceived panic room, she thought she had just confirmed all her ideas about her grandmother.

Walking and carrying the blueprint as a guide, she arrived in the upstairs office. She had been there before and hadn't noticed anything unusual. She pushed open the French doors leading to the large room and looked around. Opposite the computer area and locked file cabinets was supposed to be the panic room and according to the printout, it was big. She saw nothing. No secret push buttons, no hidden doors behind picture frames, no way to open the room she now knew was there. She tried pushing and pulling along the edges of the wall. This always seemed to work in the movies! She even tried tapping with her knuckles like she had seen her dad do when looking for wall studs. Nothing special was found. Then she had an idea. It was a pretty simple thought, but just maybe she could figure it out. Logging on the computer she searched the desktop icons. She did notice the quick link to Granny's website for the store, "Favors.com." What was unusual was that there was another icon for "Extremefavors.com." She briefly wondered about that, but was more interested right then in finding and solving the panic room mystery. Nothing else on the desktop screen seemed of any special interest.

Logging onto Programs, she saw "Home Security," clicked the mouse and quickly a screen appeared showing the Pink Flamingo in living color. A beautiful photograph, but now what? As she moved the mouse around the screen, she soon realized she could click on areas of the house and get more information. Clicking on the gate, a schematic of the perimeter fencing appeared, complete with motion detectors, in-wall video monitor systems, and an alarm system. Advancing through the video system, several live cam shots appeared along the fence lines. There was no area of the landscapes that could not be viewed. A click on each view brought up the chosen full screen. Pretty cool, she was thinking. Returning to the house photo, she found if she right-clicked, she could enter several more areas. One was called "Blueprint." She clicked the mouse once more. Now the same blueprints she had unfolded appeared in miniature in front of her. These, though smaller, were more readable thanks to the bright monitor screen. She found the area of the panic room and then hesitated. Maybe I am treading on hallowed ground, she thought. Granny would be mad if she knew about this. But curiosity won over the seventeen year old. She tapped the mouse quickly, as if it would bite her, over the panic room area. Instead of a blow up of the room as she expected, a small box appeared. It asked "Enter?" Mikki, thinking this would show the room on the screen, clicked once again over the word. Mikki jumped back, grabbing the chair arms for support, eyes wide in complete terror! The wall opposite her chair had begun to move... straight up! The whole wall was being drawn up into the next floor of the house! Mikki, now completely terrified and in great need of a panic room herself, almost passed out from fear! Now what? She thought, *I am dead, Granny is going to kill me, disinherit me, disown me, and worst of all, hate me for being so nosy!*

Soon the amazingly quiet rolling sound of a wall being moved stopped. An instrumental serenade coming from within the room replaced it. Granny's damned Yanni tapes! Mikki forced herself up off the chair and hesitantly went to the huge opening. She gaped open-mouthed at what she saw. The music came from a giant screen entertainment center, with a digital projector. There were walls of VCR tapes and DVD's, but she found they were not your typical Academy Award winners. Mikki read the titles in quiet astonishment: "Fugitive Recovery - Agent Training." "The Modern Identity Changer." "Survival Expert." "Anti-Terrorism Security Risk Analysis." "Unarmed Combat." *What was up with this?* There was just one chair for viewing the tapes. A straight-backed wooden chair with a flat, hard seat with no padding. This was one very serious chair, like one would use for military interrogations or classes or something. The rear of the room was full of every type of exercise equipment known to man. As she walked, she saw a spinner, stair master, weight benches, mats, medicine ball, punching bag. A complete home gym. It all looked well used. A quick finger swipe showed no dust covers needed here.

The biggest shock to the teenager's short life came when she opened the cabinets. Rows and rows of weapons. Small handguns to machine guns, laser and night vision scopes, everything was there. Looking closer, Mikki tentatively reached out to touch a Russian M-38 carbine, a Ruger single action revolver, and several Walther style semi-automatics. She ran her fingers along the polished wood and steel as if actually touching the guns would make this more believable. Boxes of various caliber ammunition were stacked in cases everywhere in the cupboards. In addition, there were knives, daggers, swords, badges, gas masks, listening devices, tiny cameras, various wires, goggles, and binoculars. Circling the room, looking but not daring to touch anything else, she found wigs and make-up, various passports, credit cards, and driver's licenses. At this point Mikki imagined Grandpa being a spy or something. After all, he did work out of the country in finance and was gone most of the time. The little bubble was broken when the passport photo was a barely recognizable Granny. But on this one her name was Rose Anne Gingrich. Another card, another name! Long hair, short hair, blond, brunette, pale skin, dark skin, all amazingly still her Granny. Now the young voyeur was completely dumbfounded, but knew she had better figure out how to close the room back up before Granny reappeared with her sister. She now knew more than she had ever bargained for. Maybe Grandpa Joe had been an international spy and had figured out how to get Granny Em out of the country in case he was suddenly discovered! She didn't dare touch anything else, except to pick up a box with a device called the "Bionic Ear.... This ain't your Grandma's listening device," the box top read. Well, it apparently is *my* grandma's listening device. The equipment looked like an IPOD or maybe a micro cassette player for listening to music. There was a wire that plugged into the black plastic and two ear buds. She pushed the ear buds into place and pushed "play". Instead of the expected "Yanni at the Acropolis" she expected, she found she could hear everything in the room with great precision. It was weird, the sound was not so much louder, but so much more clear. All the sounds seemed to separate when the plastic case was aimed in a different direction. She wandered over to the office's large picture window that overlooked the driveway. When the case was aimed out the glass, she could hear the traffic on the North Beach Road easily. She thought she could even make out the sounds of the garbage collection truck and the raising and lowering of its loading equipment as it approached Pink Flamingo. She was listening in full attention as she adjusted the volume control knobs. Soon the lumbering green truck appeared outside their gate. A sweating man in gray coveralls threw the contents of the black rubber trashcan into the back of the truck. She could hear every word the driver and helper were saying. She could even hear the cracking of the driver's gum as he chewed. The truck was still swallowing and digesting its meal as the man hopped on the back bumper, holding on until the next stop. Mikki placed the device back on the shelf where she had found it.

After the initial shock was over, Mikki managed to use the computer to close the wall in the same fashion it had opened. As the huge rollers brought the wall back to position, Mikki sighed with relief. *I think I'll go back to playing with Barbie dolls*, she thought as she crept out of the office. Her mind was still spinning with the excitement of her new-found knowledge. But she knew better than to tell anyone about the discovery. Brigetta would probably rat her out and her mother would die from the shock for sure. Dad wasn't home that much to tell him anything. No way she could confess to Granny, so she resigned herself to the fact that she was a sneak and not only that, she was good at it. Of course, if Granny got home and knew immediately that someone had been in the room, she was doomed. She would sweat out the next few weeks in limbo as punishment for her indiscretion. Ever since that day, Brigetta would be wondering why she and her sister didn't talk about sex and boys like they used to while at Grandma's house. Mikki could hardly explain to her why they needed to make their lives less than an open book. A few days later, trying to appear as casual and nonchalant as possible with a heart racing a hundred miles an hour, Mikki ventured, "Granny, was Grandpa ever in the military?"

"Why no, Darling, with his vision? They would have had to give him a GI Joe Seeing Eye dog!"

Well, that was just a ruse, Mikki thought at the time. *Appear incapable of being James Bond, but in actuality, one could carry on undetected. The joke was that now, here in Citrus City, she really knew the truth. It was not Grandpa after all, but her very own grandmother.* After that day, Granny never said or did anything to let on that she knew about Mikki's secret invasion and nothing was never mentioned again.

Approaching the motel parking lot, Mikki reflected back on that discovery. How ironic that the one thing she had picked up in that room was the one thing she had needed today. It was a simple matter to retrieve and bring the spy ware along on her trip to Citrus City. She had heard every word said between Helen and Darla. At this time she didn't want to worry Gran any more than she was already. She needed to heal and fight cancer. This was not the time to reflect on the past, unless there was something there that would help her with the future.

Chapter 22

The next morning, Emily was feeling well rested and the pain seemed to be minimal. This was good since more Demerol was not going to be an option. She had a slight headache, but now wary, decided not to ask even for a Tylenol. Soon Mikki would be here and they would figure out when and how to get out of here gracefully.

As if on cue, Mikki, wearing a yellow silk sleeveless blouse, white Capris pants, and yellow-strapped sandals, breezed in the door, looking happy and relaxed. Her long auburn hair was hanging loose and wavy, and had a sheen like the models on Pantene commercials. That was how Emily knew that kind of hair actually existed off the screen. Her granddaughter had been blessed with shiny tresses that glowed and shimmered. Every time she saw her granddaughter she marveled at her beauty. Of course, the family came by the good looks quite honestly, having made generations of donations from their gene bank.

Flipping back her flowing hair, Mikki announced her arrival by raising a bag triumphantly and squealing, "I found Krispy Kreme!"

"You're already in my will, you know! You don't need to ply me with such forbidden treasure!"

"Okay, then. I will eat them all myself," said Mikki with devilish glee. She began digging into the bag and removed a fantastic looking glazed donut, making a big scene about slowing drawing it towards her overly open mouth. "Ummmm!"

"Don't you dare!" said Emily loudly, then mouthing something about a hit list and pointing a cocked finger towards Mikki.

"You win. You're scaring me. Here you go," Mikki said, as she handed the gooey treat to her Gran. She smiled as she licked her fingers and reached for a jelly-filled pastry for herself. Both now ate greedily, moaning in delighted exaggeration and lip smacking. There was a brief period of silence as Mikki bagged up the trash, got wet paper towels from the bathroom, and they wiped off sugary mouths.

"Well?" asked Mikki.

"Thanks. That was great!" answered Emily.

"You're welcome. But that's not what I meant. I am now waiting for more information. I have bribed my informant and now I want the payoff. I have lots of questions about how you got a 'business' started and how this works. You have lots of money, but apparently it's not all from your little party shop. How much money have you made, Granny, from doing these 'favors'?"

"You make it sound so unsavory. Besides, what are you now, my accountant?"

"Even worse! IRS! Seriously, please tell me."

"What to say here, hmmm? I guess we shall continue with the truth. Could you please lower the bed just a little? My head has been bothering me this morning."

"No Demerol!"

"Did I say anything about any medication? Just a little position change, okay?"

Mikki found the bed control box that had slipped between the mattress and rail and pulled it up by the cord. "Here you go. You are in charge of your destiny," she said, as she handed the controls to her grandmother.

"I forgot I had that!" Emily replied as she pushed the buttons until she found the position of comfort.

"Are you okay, really, Gran? You usually don't forget something that simple."

"Probably the after effects of all the medications. Brig says it takes almost two weeks to recover from all the stuff they give you for anesthesia."

"Probably true. For a normal person. But you, being Super Woman and all..." mused Mikki.

"I'm fine, or will be soon. Got to get rid of the cancer, though. That's the bad bugger."

"Right, for sure. We'll get you out of here soon and home where we can all take care of you and you can see the best specialists we can find."

As if on cue, the door swung open and Dr. Waterson tentatively peeked through the opening. "Hey, you ladies having a private party in here?"

"No, come right in, Doctor," answered Emily quickly.

Mikki rose politely and extended her hand, "Thank you for all you've done. My Granny is doing so well now, I think. Is she?"

Ed Waterson could not help to be again rendered almost speechless by the sight of this gorgeous young woman. He had always been surrounded and, in fact hounded, by lovely young women, but this one was stunning. His wife was quite beautiful, too, but testosterone forced him to stare like a schoolboy as much as he tried to control that impulse. "She seems to be doing quite well, considering. We'll soon be ready to move towards the next steps. Radiation possibly, and chemotherapy."

Emily frowned but said nothing. Nurse Kate arrived with a tray full of bandage supplies. Dr. Waterson was again bending over the bed and examining the chest incision. "Incision looks very good. I tried to leave a small scar so you can continue wearing your bikini, Mrs. Carr."

"How do you know I wear any suit, Doctor? I prefer *au naturel!*"

Mikki grinned as she saw the doctor actually blush! But he was quick with a reply, "Uh Uh. I see tan all over but some hint of tan lines, young lady!"

"Phooey. I do have to wear my suit when we go to the country club. But I was hoping you would join me in a midnight swim," continued Emily.

"Patients are not allowed to seduce their doctors, Granny," reprimanded Mikki.

"Okay," said Emily, "maybe another time, another place."

"But I'll be in to see you tomorrow for a morning date, okay? Any problems? Are you feeling okay? Let me listen to your heart and lungs," said Dr. Waterson as he pulled the stethoscope from his jacket pocket. Listening carefully, he stood up and said he was going to order a little more Lasix, but things were going as expected.

"When can I get unhooked from all these tubes, Doc?" asked Emily.

"How is she eating, Kate? Oral fluid intake looks good on the chart," he asked the nurse.

"From the look of the donut, candy and cookie bags in the trash, she is eating all right. Just not the prescribed diet," said Kate, hands on hips and trying to look stern.

"Whoops," said both Mikki and Emily in unison.

"It's okay, we just don't want her vomiting and then ripping up her stitches or worse, anything on the inside," replied Dr. Waterson, smiling but serious.

"I promise I won't puke. I haven't thrown up since I was ten. My stomach is tough," replied Emily in defense.

"Moderation, my dear," said the doctor.

"Okay, we promise," said Mikki.

Dr. Waterson gave them the thumbs up, gathered up his charts and exited the room with a little wink.

Kate began to rebandage the incision carefully. Emily touched her shoulder and drew her closer, whispering accusingly in her ear, "Rat!"

All three women then began to chuckle as the wound was redressed. Kate was soon finished and restated how glad she was that Mrs. Carr now had Michelle to comfort her. And feed her! Knowing the women liked privacy, Kate pulled the door shut as she went back to the hallway and her duties.

"So. Back to the subject at hand. Now that we are already food-sneaking criminals, please continue to fill me in on how you embarked on this life of crime," said Mikki, plopping back down on the soft corner chair. She crossed her legs and leaned back, looking like she planned to be there for some time.

"Uncle Robert was not well. He had a mild heart attack and back then they didn't have the knowledge to help him much. No cholesterol lowering medications, no routine heart caths, no open heart bypass surgery. I felt it was partly my fault at the time, so that was one reason I resigned from the Service. I wanted to finish my college, so I changed my major from English with a Spanish minor, to Business Administration. At least I could type and was pretty good at math. I had some minor science courses like zoology, biology, and bacteriology for fun. I really enjoyed those. It was time to break away from the plantation in Georgia and be my own person after graduation. With the two years in the Secret Service, I was older than most of my classmates and felt I had to get my life moving. There was not much money around in those days. When I met Grandpa Joe, he was tending bar in Atlanta. There was an instant attraction and we got married a few months later. He was my one and only love for this life. He had also been a Business major and was very much achievement oriented. He was working for his dad, who owned the bar, but he had much bigger dreams than that. Eventually he landed a job in

New York City as a gofer in the stock trade. He was very smart and soon became a financial advisor. He was promoted to overseas work and for a while I traveled with him.

"When your mother was born, I stayed home in the U.S. and maintained our household. We had money, but weren't really wealthy. Ever since she was a little girl, I took Susan everywhere with me. We went to the library, the ballet, concerts, and cartoons at the movies, just everywhere. I don't know how she turned out so reserved. She certainly had enough of me around her. Must have got a lot of Grandpa's genetic code. He was a very fun guy, but work always came first. He could be very serious and he was definitely ambitious. We were always in love until the end. I'm sure he never cheated and certainly I never would have done that to him. I think I'm still in love with him and always will be. He was the first person in my whole life to love me unconditionally no matter what. I hung on to him like to life itself. He was my sanity, my connection to the real world. After my aunt and uncle died, I inherited a lot of property. I sold it and had the Pink Flamingo built. Joe always let me have my way regarding where we lived since he was not home a lot. He let me have free rein about the house. He found out about the beach acreage during one of his business trips. It belonged to a Saudi royal of some sort who wanted to dump it and buy oil wells in Texas. It was a dream come true for me. As you know, I had always loved and been totally fascinated by the ocean and all marine life."

"But you were already in the 'favor' business before you built the house," stated Mikki tentatively.

"Now how would you know about that, child?" asked Emily with raised brows.

"The panic room. Or whatever you call it."

"And? We would know about that because...?" asked Emily.

"I am nosy?" responded Mikki sheepishly.

"Yes. Yes to both. You are nosy, and I was already set up doing favors and making lots of money doing it. So I incorporated the addition to the house, telling the builder it was a safe room, or panic room as they now call it. It was not really all that unusual to find those in the more affluent homes. It's just that mine was so huge with lots of cupboards, shelves and electrical hookups. The builder never questioned it, of course. The only thing he ever said was that someone could live in there for weeks unknown. He just wanted the job."

"Did you know I had been in the room?"

"Of course. That was easy to know. It was figuring out what to do with the fact that was a bit of a puzzle. I had concocted a real good story in case you ever asked, but you were apparently too spooked to even mention it."

"Well, I was spooked enough to wonder whether all our conversations were being recorded and relayed to mom!"

"I would never invade your privacy. That just isn't right. And I certainly would not be running to Susan with any hot scoop about you girls. I trusted you to grow up with only the normal parental interventions, and you did."

"So when did you get more 'jobs' or whatever you want to call them?"

"Joe and I were married for five years before I got pregnant. During those five years, I had plenty of free time and we were already accepted in a social circle of business, politics, and industry. Just as I was getting bored with Joe being across the Atlantic, someone found out I had been Secret Service and arranged a meeting with a friend of his. My first job was actually an illegal government action. One of those deals where if I am caught, I am on my own?" Seeing Mikki's eyes widen, she added, "Now don't tell me you are so naïve as to believe the government doesn't do stuff like that?"

"Well, you do hear things on the news that make you wonder," replied Mikki, still reclining on the chair.

"Since I knew Spanish, and had already killed a fellow agent, I guess they figured I was ripe for the job. I was almost killed doing it, but I pulled it off. I think to the surprise of those hiring me, they had to pay me and pay big. Don't ask me the particulars about that one. I will just say it was a high-ranking foreign official that needed to go. I made sure he went."

"Someday you will tell me all the story, Granny. I know you will."

"Well, I can tell you about my second job, because it was during the Korean War and all that is mostly history. Anybody can look it up in a sixth grade history book. Do you actually know anything much about that war?"

"Not really."

"That's what everyone says, unless they were unlucky enough to have been there. Well, the really lucky ones came back home, I guess you could say. Many believe there are still GI's there who are still alive that never came home. One of the POW's who finally came home was quoted as saying, 'I was prepared to fight, to be wounded, to be captured and even prepared to die, but I was not prepared to be abandoned.' There are still organizations focusing on not only Viet Nam missing, but also Korean War missing."

"Now that I did not know," said Mikki, now sitting up attentively.

"When the Americans entered the war, it was an invasion into Inchon. It was a total surprise and shock to the North Koreans, and why? They had been told it was impossible to launch a full-scale amphibious attack at Inchon. It was my duty to make sure that message was the one that got through to the North Korean general. That faulty intelligence got the Americans off to a great start as enemy soldiers had heavy casualties. Knowing that I would stick out like a sore thumb, being white and female, I was totally undercover. More like invisible. I was unceremoniously dumped offshore like the participants of the "Survivor" series. I was in a sea blue floating raft, similar to today's Zodiac boats, and rowed my way at nightfall to a muddy shore below a hilly terrain. It was raining at the time and this provided a little more cover for me. From there, with limited rations and water in sweltering summertime heat, I made my way through forests to the target area. It was practically inch-by-inch through the trees and you know how I like spiders! Yuck! I think that was the worst part. There were huge snakes, too, but I was not really afraid of them. Once I had to tie a bandana tight over my mouth, like a self-made gag. There were so many spiders dropping down on my hair, arms, neck....It creeps me out even now to talk about it. I was afraid I would scream and even a tiny noise would have been my end. There was no way to explain my way out of this one if I was caught. To be captured would mean torture, rape and death. And those guys were good at that; I had heard all about it in my training. The message about the Americans never being able to attack Inchon was being brought to the General via motorcar and I had to make sure that message somehow arrived.

"I located the vehicle to be used, parked in a field near a farmhouse, and followed on foot when they left. This meant when they stopped, I had to run to catch up. There were three men in the Jeep, the oldest probably not even twenty. I dared not set out on the road itself or even steal a motor scooter to keep up. It was quite a test of endurance. Luckily for me, they were not in the great hurry they were supposed to be. These guys stopped frequently for pee breaks, smokes, and then even a swim in a stream that I was sure was infested by leeches. Therefore I had to squat hidden with my silenced rifle in the vegetation, while mosquitoes ate my face off, so they could take a dip. I had seen huge paw prints when I was running through the spruce trees. Therefore, I was really nervous watching for a tiger to approach one of these three idiots and pull him away. Back then there were still some tigers in Korea. And this was a perfect area to find a tiger, if there was one around. I could afford to lose two of these guys, but not all three. If the waters were a drinking hole for tigers, the sound of the men splashing would surely attract a hungry one. All at once, like a nightmare come true, there was movement by the water, and I saw a huge form heading unseen towards the men who were splashing stupidly in the murky stream. I raised my weapon and prepared to fire, perspiration now running like Niagara Falls from my face and armpits. The bra area between my tits was now like a small lake, a reservoir of gathered sweat. By my right toe, I saw a good-sized river rock. Not even hesitating, I picked it up and heaved it from the underbrush toward the area of the tiger. It landed with a nice loud splash!

"All eyes went towards the animal's direction, and immediately all of the men saw the orange beast and started yelling and screaming in Korean. Now I did not know any Korean at all, not even hello, good-bye, screw you. Nothing. I guess the brass figured if I was captured, speaking the language was not going to do me even a tiny bit of good. The tiger was fast and swam towards the man nearest him. The guy kicked and screamed and tried to move as quickly as possible to the riverbank. Just when he made it out of the water, the beast leaped on to the rocky shore, mouth open in a snarling roar and grabbed the hapless man by the neck. Now, this thing was about ten feet long, no baby. As the others ran for guns in their Jeep, the man was dragged fighting and kicking and hollering into the grassy edge of the woods. Since the usual neck bite had not been fatal, the tiger must have decided to shut the guy up by drowning and pulled him toward the water. Soon the two were a rolling underwater tornado of blood, churning mud and uprooted river plants. Reminded me of alligator feeding in Alabama. Then, just as quickly, the tiger resurfaced, and swam with his heavy load away from us. Reaching the far bank he jumped out, pulling the now quiet and bloody mass with him. With a flick of his tail, he was gone, easily pulling his quarry with him. The other two men reappeared, heaving for breath and slick with sweat, to complete silence. The water was still rolling in little waves, but there was no sign of their comrade or the tiger. Even the birds and frogs had stopped their calling and croaking. With hardly a glance at each other, they took off running for the vehicle, prepared to zoom on outta there, leaving their dead associate to become tiger buffet.

"As I mentioned, I spoke no Korean, but I had no doubt as to what four letter words they were using once in their vehicle. They couldn't start the Jeep. They thought 'Tiger Bait' had taken the keys and put them on his neck with his ID tags for safekeeping. Yeah, like their Jeep would have been hijacked out here! Especially with good ol' me, watching it and them like a hawk.

"As they kicked the tires and pushed and shoved each other, ranting and raving, I realized idiots are the same in all cultures. They blamed everything regarding their circumstance of idiocy on anyone else but themselves. The only thing was, I knew where the keys were. The tiger hadn't swallowed them like they thought. I had them grasped tightly in my sweaty little palm. During the confusion I had raced to the Jeep, grabbed the keys from the ignition, and taken off back towards my hiding spot. I could hardly hold back my giggles as I listened to them trying to figure out what to do. One was gesturing in a way that I knew one of their brilliantly daring ideas was to hunt down the tiger with their guns ...highly unlikely... and cut him up, finding their pal and the keys inside. If a huge black spider were not at that point bringing me back to reality, I would have burst out laughing as they now proceeded to push each other towards the water. The Two Stooges in person. I was afraid both would now be killed by another tiger, and was more afraid I would be screaming if this giant furry black thing crawled any closer to my arm. The spider seemed to be staring with all those eyes at my field watch. At that point he could have it, if he liked it that much. Maybe the watch's roundness had some sex appeal to it. Suddenly he must have caught the scent or sight of something more appealing and he ambled off on those stilted fuzzy legs. Argh! Then the two men apparently and thankfully decided just to head off on foot. It was another 23 kilometers to our destination. This would make my journey easier, tracking these bozos on foot, but I would have to be extremely quiet now with no motor noise to cover me. I thought briefly of following them with their own Jeep, but I didn't think they would find it as funny as I did, when I caught up to them.

"Anyway, they gathered up the documents and some supplies and set off down the dusty road, throwing backpacks over their shoulders and still cursing in Korean. It was relatively easy to keep up with them now. Eventually they arrived at the town that was their goal and the message was given. Pretty easy job for me, no hidden agendas or ambushes. General Eisenhower had been urging Truman to intervene militarily and now the invasion went on as planned. At that point I had no problem deciding who would win this one.

"Getting back to Seoul was quite difficult and arranging a clandestine meeting was nearly impossible. I needed to remain invisible but they needed more from me. I was on an adrenaline rush and besides, you can't just say no. There were spies everywhere. A lot of students from South Korea were going North while merchants and intellectual types stayed with the South. There were political and military personnel who mysteriously disappeared in strange circumstances. Covert paramilitary actions or guerilla warfare were commonplace."

"Gran, these weren't government okayed actions?"

"The National Security Council Resolution 10/2, Section 5 authorizes covert operations that are secret and small enough to be deniable by the CIA. The CIA Plans Division runs spies, guerillas, and other covert operations and often does not report the whole truth. Something we Americans find hard to believe at times. We often don't get the truth, but a distorted reality that we're eager to clasp as truth. People like me were used to run U-2 spy plan operations, obtain and publish Khrushchev's secret speech in 1956 or overthrow leftist governments. We are a rather busy lot, you see?"

"I think I see."

"I came home after being held back in secret for General Clark's 'Operation EverReady.' There was a plan to arrest or assassinate Rhee, who was stirring up anti-American demonstrations and had ordered martial law. He was then re-elected through a rigged election. I came home shortly after the war ended in 1953. I was completely and totally worn out, stressed out and needing some love and comfort."

"So that's where Grandpa Joe came in, right?"

"Yep, I had made a lot of money anyhow, but it was time for a break.... and a baby."

"I see. Killing can be stressful and trying not to be killed is even worse, huh?"

"You make it sound so cold and calculating," Emily continued. "But anyway, it wasn't for the money, always. It was the adventure, the adrenaline, the sense of justice, mainly."

"Like Dupris?"

"Like Dupris. No plea bargains, deals or whatever for that bad dude. He's dead, that's it!"

"Brigetta said you were talking to Yolanda Grimes a few weeks ago in the shop. Did you get paid well for this one?"

"I took the money, but it was like a 'blue light special,' a real bargain, because I really believed in the cause. Sometimes I work for free, you know? Or even do charity work."

Chapter 23

"Charity work? Now isn't that stretching it a little, Granny?"

"Remember a few years ago, when those show horses were injected in their legs by a caustic substance? Right in their own stalls, by persons unknown? All I could think about was those trusting beautiful animals just standing there... for someone to cripple them with pain. Several had to be euthanized. Do you remember?"

"Yes, that was terrible. Big horse farm in Kentucky, right? Didn't the farm put up a big reward though?"

"A huge reward. $500,000, to be exact. Remember, it was donated to the American Humane Society? The reason it was donated was that the perpetrator was caught."

"I don't remember anything about how the bad guy got caught," replied Mikki as she now sat forward and straight up at the edge of the chair. Emily now was sitting up and leaning toward the railing, getting closer to Mikki.

"I got him," stated Emily in a low voice. "And he won't be messing with any more horses, trust me. Turned out he was pissed off about a reprimand at the farm. He was a groom's assistant. Mostly did stall cleaning. While the owners were away at a big show, he took a few days off from his duties and when they came back, the brood mare stalls were a mucky mess. I guess the newborn foals were lying in urine-soaked wood shavings and even their ears and eyelids were caked with manure. Well, the shit hit the fan, so to speak! Little John, as he was called, was not even fired, but told this was his last chance. Somehow he thought the world owed him this job and so he came back with some kind of cleaning solution and damaged those horses. I can't believe they even let him back on the farm in the first place. He was still working there when I arrived. The owners didn't know me from the pile of poop in back of the barn. I had simply called them anonymously on one of my cell phones using a voice synthesizer. I told them the bad guy would go down and the reward should be sent to some sort of animal charity, their choice. I told them I guaranteed they would know beyond a doubt when the job was done. They were quite skeptical, but willing to agree to anything to get justice for their animals.

"They were still grieving for the lost and foundered horses when I arrived at the farm. I came with reference papers from a big show farm in Ocala and I was hired as office help. I said I had some experience in accounting and answering phones and filing, and that was what they needed. I had live-in quarters in an apartment over the barn. My name at the time for this venture was Beth Johnson, office clerk extraordinaire. My hair was brunette with a few silver streaks left in. You know I am pretty vain about my gorgeous silver locks, but I made the sacrifice. I worked my way around the farm, saying how pretty the horses were, but how I was so afraid of them....blah, blah, blah. Everyone tolerated the old lady wandering around the barns.

"It didn't take long to narrow the list of suspects. Little John had a nasty way about him when he thought he was not being observed. At night I had set up about half a dozen small cameras in various sections of the barn areas. I had my wireless monitor right there in my little apartment that was over Barn A. Most of the mare and foal stalls were already equipped with video equipment and it was simple to just go down one night and turn them all back on. I even put a piece of black electrical tape over the red light. No one knew the cameras were still recording. They were usually turned off once the foals were born, unless there was an injury or illness that needed to be monitored. Not only did I reactivate the cameras, I directed the images to my own monitor in my room. I almost lost it myself when I watched John punch a ten day old foal in the muzzle. He, out of curiosity, got too close to John's load of manure. I truly believe that if the colt had knocked over the wheelbarrow, John would've killed him with the pitchfork and blamed it on the mare kicking her foal. My blood was boiling now, and I had a plan to see if I could get Little John to confess. I had enough information to have a gut instinct that told me he was the bad guy we were all looking for."

Emily's story was suddenly interrupted by the door flopping open unceremoniously. A mop swishing back and forth preceded Helen, who grunted some sort of greeting and worked her way to the bathroom. She dragged along a bucket on wheels full of antiseptic-smelling water. To Mikki she demanded, "Legs

171

up!" And Mikki obliged, too shocked to speak, drawing her legs up quickly to avoid the slopping mop from splashing her white pants. Mikki and Emily just stared, first at the obstinate Helen and then at each other. Neither spoke until Helen swished her way back out the door, leaving it ajar. At this point, some fresh air was vastly needed in the room, so Mikki let the door remain open. After all, they didn't want to appear as complete hermits, or worse, as conspirators.

Finally, Emily spoke, "Any more donuts?"

Both women broke into smiles and decided to talk about the weather. It had finally stopped raining after a downpour of several days. And sure enough, Helen was back. This time she brought with her a cleaning cart with various sprays, rags, and brushes. She gave the women barely a glance as she went to work on the bathroom. They could hear water running, and flushing and mumbling. Another happy worker. Emily decided to turn on the TV so they could stare at something else. Helen was soon finished with the toilet duties and began running her rags on the bed rails. Emily pulled back her hands quickly since she felt Helen would run the rag right over her fingers if she were in the way.

Emily finally chanced, "Good morning, Helen. You are doing a great job. Excellent cleaning, I must say."

Helen did not even look up when she answered, "Yep, I always do a good job." And soon she had dusted and wiped her way right out of the room. This time Mikki got up and shut the door behind her.

"Quite the personality, wouldn't you say?" queried Emily, rolling her eyes.

"Any hospital would be glad to have her. Are they desperate or what?" asked Mikki, shaking her head and folding her legs back under her on the chair. "Okay, back to the story. You apparently got him to confess?"

"Little John was a little man with a big ego. Probably came from a real lack of self-esteem and he felt that acting big and bad would make him a real man. If I hadn't hated him and all he meant to me I might have felt pity. But he reminded me of Frank."

"So what did you do?"

"Are you sure you want to hear this? This is probably R-rated, maybe X."

"Go on. I am a big girl."

"I had planned on seducing John with alcohol, but the thought of that seduction almost made me choke. I mean getting that close to this little turd was enough to gag a maggot. The guy was about forty, a lot younger than me, but then I am the mistress of Shahid and know all the ways of love and lust."

"Gran, somehow I believe you."

"I decided the straight-up approach would work with the arrogant bastard. I just walked up to him and said, 'I know what you did to the horses. Unless you want me to tell the boss, you will meet me at the Trackside Bar and Grill." Then I just walked away. I imagine he was too surprised to respond, because he said nothing. I am sure what few brain cells he had were working overtime, though.

"The crowd was rough and noisy at the tavern. Patrons were mostly farm workers and exercise riders and it was payday. Friday night on the town for all the people that lived and breathed horses. A live country band was playing, not exactly Nashville, but I remember they weren't that bad. A few women were doing a line dance or at least trying. I think they had been there awhile. Their 'Boot Scootin' Boogie' looked more like the 'try to balance and not fall down shuffle.' But they were having fun and didn't really care what anyone else thought. There was a disco ball for some reason in this country style bar, maybe left over from another era. It was spinning patterns of light off the ceilings, walls, and faces of the dancers in an almost eerie fashion. I was seated at a small dark table at the back, sipping on a Corona with a lime twist when I saw Little John slink through the side entrance by the parking lot. He just stood at the doorway, seeming to be uncertain as to what to do next. As his eyes adjusted to the light, I quickly went to his side.

"Let's go," the new office clerk had demanded and grabbed his arm, with unfamiliar pinch and amazing strength, and pulled him toward a small table. He complied, mostly not wanting to make a scene. He didn't want to draw attention to his current predicament. They sat and stared at each other. Venomous looks were pointed in both directions.

"What do you want?" John demanded huffily.

"I want to kill you," said Beth Johnson. "But I might not. What did you use on the horses? I already know you did it, and I already know pretty much why."

"Bullshit!" he said, as he pushed back the chair preparing to get up. He stopped suddenly when he felt a grip on his knee that was like being held in a vise. A very strong squeezing vise. Pain shot through his left knee that was already scarred from previous surgery. Surgery required because one of his past horse victims had dared to fight back. John went pale and sank back in his seat. "Who are you?" he whispered, voice croaking. Sweat was visible even through the absorbent flannel of his old work shirt. He glanced around, wondering if anyone else had seen him become the captive of this petite but aggressive woman.

"What did you use on the horses? Where did you get it?" Beth demanded, ice-cold blue eyes piercing like a dagger. She now sat so close to him, it would appear they were lovers. "Talk now or maybe you will be shut up forever!" Little John looked away and quickly looked around for an exit. "Don't even think about making my day a little brighter. There is nothing else I would like better right now than to castrate you here and now. Such a brave, brave man, picking on innocent tame animals. Animals that trusted you to care for them. I really hate that. In fact, I hate that a lot, Little John. I came a long way to even the score. How I do it depends a lot on your fucking attitude. So you might say, you could possibly save yourself."

Suddenly John reflexively jumped and then froze. The flash of metal he saw between his legs caused a tiny, short, and pig-like squeal to leave his tightly closed lips. No one would hear this little scream since everyone else was having a great time. Dancing to the loud music and talking and yelling to each other in fun. The sharp blade rested on the inseam of his crotch, forcing him to push his butt back against the chair as far as he could go.

"Okay, okay, okay. Please. Relax, lady. I'll talk. I'll tell ya everything you want. Just calm down," he mustered, forehead now sweating profusely. "Can we get outta here?"

"No. No, we are going to stay right here. In fact, you will soon be at the microphone singing a little song for all of our entertainment."

"Look, lady, I don't sing. I don't do karaoke either."

"Oh, you will learn to sing tonight, my dear. And the name is Beth Johnson, not 'lady'. You may call me Ms. Johnson."

This bitch was serious, he thought, and maybe worse, probably a psycho bitch. The knife was real though, and looked sharp. Probably military issue. He was having a lot of trouble sorting all this out. He was in deep shit, deeper than the loads of manure he had shoveled today. He could try to make a run for it. She might cut him, but it would be a big scene in front of all these people. She would get arrested and go away. But she might also accomplish her deed, or slash the femoral artery so he could bleed to death before help arrived. Maybe he could just humor her along and see what she had in mind.

"Ms. Johnson. I didn't do nothing," tried John, instantly sorry as he felt a warm liquid running down his pant leg. The blade was so sharp he had felt nothing. Now a burning sensation began in the area of his groin. With complete and total fear, he realized she meant to do some serious harm.

"Please, stop! I got some cleaning fluid for use on toilet stains. I don't remember the name. Honest!"

"Where did you get it?" demanded Beth.

"Home Supply, I think."

"You think? You think!"

"No, I know. I got it there. Still have the receipt in my wallet, I think...I mean, I have it for sure."

"Let's have it. Reach behind you slowly to your left rear pocket. I saw your wallet there before you sat down. Don't move too quickly as I might get nervous and have some sort of jerk reflex. Know what I mean, Johnnie Boy?"

"Got it, just relax, I'm doing it," he said quietly as he reached delicately behind him, withdrawing the scraped up leather trifold. He carefully withdrew a faded receipt and handed it tentatively across the table. Beth had a mini mag light in her khaki safari shirt pocket and had already pulled it out. The receipt was still legible. She stuffed it carefully into her bra's hidden pouch. John moved as if he were finished and ready to leave.

"Sit!" Beth insisted, and deftly grabbed his arm, squeezing the nerve center at the elbow.

"Christ! Easy, lay off! I am not going anywhere!" cried John, trying to be as inconspicuous as possible. His eyes darted left and right trying to evaluate all his options at this point. He couldn't believe he had put himself in this position. A woman his mother's age was holding him hostage in a bar room full of people. Not that any of them would come to his aid. They all cared more about the stupid horses than they would about rescuing him. And the embarrassment! He felt the blood from the initial cut on his leg, warm and sticky, and began to feel a little faint. An involuntary whine slowly escaped his pursed lips.

The band was now on a break and a disc jockey was playing tapes and passing out cards for karaoke hopefuls. As he came by their table, Beth took a request card and wrote, 'Little John has something to sing. It is original. No music will be necessary. This will be newsworthy!' and underneath she drew a little smiley face. "Now, Butt Face, this is how it will work. You will get up and tell everyone what you did. If you don't, I will kill you. It's pretty simple. I have killed before and I am a professional, if that makes you feel any better. You will only get one chance. If you don't do as I say, I will walk out the door." At that statement, John's face brightened slightly. "You will never make it home. Trust me. You will never be seen alive again. The coroner will not find a pretty sight. They might even make a story about your death for some unsolved mystery show! You do watch television, don't you?"

Little John thought he would pass out. His hands shook badly. He whimpered, "But this crowd will kill me!"

"They probably would, but when I hear you finish saying what you need to say, I will use my cell phone to call 911. The police will come and rescue your sorry ass from the maddened crowd and take you to jail. There you will give a written confession and be arrested and locked up. If I were you, I wouldn't try to get out on bail and take off. If you can find a lawyer around here that will actually defend you, you might get light time. When you get out, if no one kills you in prison, I will be keeping tabs on you. I will know where you live, where you eat, and who you sleep with. Everything. You will never have another job anywhere around any animals. If there is any kind of a problem with your behavior, I will be back. You won't see me. The last sound you ever hear will be the click of my 45 Magnum. Are we clear?"

"Yes."

"How clear?"

"Perfectly clear…Ms. Johnson," he added, almost crying. Whoever this woman was, he was now willing to do most anything to be rid of her. Mr. Disc was now center stage and calling for him. "Can I get up? They're calling me."

"Oh sure, and I will be sitting right here. Don't worry, you are the star attraction of the night!" said Beth, putting her cell phone on the table and relaxing backwards into her chair, arms crossed in determination.

The crowd was noisy and laughing as Little John was introduced. To his credit he stammered through the whole confession without falling down from fear. The stunned patrons stopped drinking and flirting once the basis of his words were realized. Anger and shock began with muted murmurs and quickly progressed to shouted bursts of temper.

"Sully Boy was my personal charge and you killed him? The horse was so gentle my two-year-old daughter could feed him sugar cubes and sit on his back! She cried for days about 'her horse'!" an enraged young woman with curly brown hair screamed from the crowd. As the loud frenzied mass surrounded the stage, an older woman in the back at a table for two dialed for emergency services. Both police and medical, please.

Chapter 24

Early the next day, Kate Bingham arrived with a bandage tray. "I'm going to take out the staples for you this morning. Okay? One less thing to worry about," she said, noting that Mrs. Carr looked like she had been up and running around all night. She recalled that the night nurse had found her bed unoccupied, went in to check, and found the light shining under the bathroom door. She had completed her rounds, but when she checked back later she found Mrs. Carr's blood pressure elevated. In fact, she reported that she found her a little short of breath also. Kate thought she looked tired this morning, but not really sick. She thought maybe she would keep a closer eye on her patient today.

Emily could see by Kate's examining look, something was on her mind. Emily questioned, "What's wrong, more bad test results?"

"No, no. Nothing like that. I was just wondering why Lt. Sanderfield was here on this floor. When I asked why he was walking around he said he wanted to talk to a few people. Apparently Darla had requested that he come by the hospital. Told him she had some 'evidence' he should know about. Wanted to see him here for some reason. I have no idea what she would have wanted with him, would you?"

"Now why would I know, dear?" responded Emily, feigning disinterest but both hands were making and unmaking fists below the sheets. "What would that have to do with me?"

"I guess its something about Dupris' death. Darla said something about that to me. Did she say anything to you? I know she is always talking to the patients, telling her life story."

"No, not a word to me. We never discussed that," Emily lied.

"Well, she couldn't have been too concerned because she didn't even bother to show up for work today. She lives only two blocks from the hospital, so she can't claim her car had a breakdown. So much for that. I told the police officer that when she came in, I would notify him. Darla is sometimes late, but usually she calls. Probably boyfriend problems or something. Guess I won't worry about it now," said Kate as she tossed the surgical staple remover into the disposable plastic tray and finished applying the sterile gauze pad with tape. "There, that should be more comfortable for you."

"Thank you. And let me know if Darla comes in, okay? I hate to have another stranger helping me with my bath, you know," said Emily, while she rubbed her temples.

"I don't really have a replacement today, so I'll be back in a bit with your bath supplies. I'll help you myself," said Kate as she left the room carrying the bandage tray with her.

Emily exhaled a huge sigh of exasperation. She must get out of here soon. Never had she been so close to being discovered. Not that they could figure out she had done anything to Dupris, she just didn't want any investigation as to who she was and why she was here. I must protect the family, she thought, as she suddenly felt quite woozy. The headache was back in full force and a sense of nausea was overwhelming. Pain shot bullet-like through her right temple and towards her forehead unlike any pain she had known before. Showers of lights were spinning in a long black starlit tunnel as she tried to reach for the call button. The buzzer never went off at the nurse's station. When Kate returned and cheerily announced that the bath spa was now open, there was no response. Mrs. Carr, arm draping over the bed rail, was blue and not breathing.

"CODE BLUE. CODE BLUE. Third floor, Dr. Belmont, Dr. Waterson," was being announced over the hospital paging system when Mikki arrived on the main floor. She had opened the door with her butt while carrying two black coffees in Styrofoam containers with lids. Hearing the page, she immediately knew. She had a sense all morning that something was not quite right. She quickly set the fast food fare on the lobby reception counter and ran full speed towards the stairs. Taking the steps two at a time, she arrived on the third floor in twenty seconds. Chest heaving and hardly able to speak, she saw the cluster of white coats and blue hospital scrubs scurrying in and out of Granny's room.

"Oh no. Shit! Graaannyy!" she yelled as she raced the rest of the way to the room.

She was stopped at the doorway by a man in blue scrubs who grabbed her shoulders, and said, "They'll be finished in a minute and you can go in. Just hold up for now, let them have a chance to do something for her."

"A chance to do something? What happened?" Mikki asked hurriedly, still trying to push her way through the door.

"I think she may have had a stroke. It's always a possibility after surgery. The immobility combined with the surgical procedure can cause a clot to break lose. They're giving her some clot-busting drugs and we'll she how she does," said the male nurse with compassion.

"When can I get in there? She needs me by her side. I can't let her be in there alone!"

"Soon, but they'll be transferring her to ICU to keep a closer watch once they get her more stabilized."

"Then can I see her there?"

"Yes, but the visits in that unit are restricted. The patients there need lots of care and lots of rest. We need to let her try to heal after this insult to the brain."

"What will be the outcome? Will she be able to walk, to talk?"

"I'm sorry. No one knows the outcome of a stroke. They'll take her for a scan and see the what and where of things. Until we know that, we can't predict the outcome. She'll definitely have some left-sided weakness, perhaps a permanent paralysis. Prognosis could be anywhere from completely normal to never regaining consciousness."

"Oh, my God," said Mikki quietly, hanging her head. She was thinking that this could not be happening. She had just seen her Granny Em last night and she was pretty much her usual self and seemed quite well. At least no one would be questioning her for a while, but how would she explain all this to the rest of the family? Granny is in the hospital in Citrus City and how did I know about it?

"You can go in now," a soft voice said as a motherly gray-haired nurse touched her shoulder. "She is more stable, but not responsive as yet. We'll be moving her to the ICU in a few minutes."

Dabbing at tears, Mikki walked bravely to the room prepared for the worst scenario. Gran was resting quietly, but oxygen and fluid-filled tubes were now in place. Her eyes were closed and her face was Wonder Bread white. "Gran? Can you hear me, Gran?" asked Mikki. "You'll be all right. I'm here," she said as tears welled in the corners of her dark green eyes. She wiped them away as to present a stronger countenance and took Gran's hand in hers. She raised the small hand and kissed it gently before placing it back onto the damp bed sheets.

"We will be taking her downstairs now," said the nurse.

Kate Bingham was behind her. "They'll provide excellent round-the-clock care for her in ICU. Feel free to find me here upstairs if you need me for anything," she added. "I'm so sorry."

"Okay, thanks a lot for everything. I think I'll walk down with her now," said the watery-eyed Mikki. She followed the rolling bed as it was pushed into the awaiting elevator and the attendant pressed "Floor 2."

As she walked with the cart and emergency personnel towards the ICU, her mind was full. All these constant revolutions and now this, just when she thought she had everything worked out. Mikki was stopped at the glass exterior doors of the Intensive Care Unit when a supervisor pulled her aside. She explained the visiting rules and everything that could be expected. Dr. Waterson had just arrived, too, and after speaking briefly to Mikki, rushed inside to check on his patient.

Finally Mikki was allowed inside and found Emily appearing small and brittle, enveloped by tendrils of life support. At the head of the bed, in tall red letters, was written DNR...Do Not Resuscitate. Was this how it was all supposed to work out? She had seen Lt. Sanderfield in the hall, waiting to talk to Emily and probably herself, too. The stroke was now the only thing that had put the investigation on hold. And he would be back. She had seen him talking to Helen just a few minutes earlier back on the third floor and they were looking towards the room of the Code Blue. The stroke had stopped the lieutenant, but had it wiped out the life of Granny Em? Was this what Emily had wanted after all? Spare the family by dying? Now what should she do?

After a few minutes, Mikki was ushered back out to the hallway and family waiting area and told when her next time to visit might be. Now that Granny Em was stable, she decided she had better return to the motel and think. Digging in her bag for the BMW keys, she nearly crashed head-on into Lt. George Sanderfield.

"I know this is a bad time, but may I ask you a few questions, Ms. Smythe?" he queried. His large body was effectively blocking her exit but she was not ready for this.

"Whatever it is, could it wait? I am really stressed out right now, as you can tell," she stammered, fussing with her hair with a free hand. "I'm on my way out right now. Could we talk later?"

"Let me be brief. There are two women in the hospital who believe your grandmother is not who she says she is. Also they believe we should look into Mr. Tyrone Dupris's death more closely."

"How would I know anything about this Dupris's death, Lieutenant?" said Mikki, now cold-eyed as the self-preservation mode was switched on.

"Perhaps you don't. Perhaps your grandmother, Mrs. Carr does," he stated bluntly, eyes narrowing on Mikki's face. He watched her closely, not appraising her beauty, but surveying her as a subject in his investigation. "But...more than likely, a little old lady did not do anything untoward to Dupris. Unless, of course, she had an accomplice. Where did you get that bruise on your chin?"

"What? What are you saying? An accomplice in what? What in the world are you talking about?" said Mikki, hands on her hips now and going on the offensive, and automatically feeling the sore area on her face. "I must have banged my chin on the stairway door trying to race up here. What are you insinuating?"

"The man died in his hospital bed under more than strange circumstances."

"So? What does that have to do with Mrs. Carr and myself?"

"Seems two employees can vouch for the fact that there was blood found on the stairway that morning after Mr. Dupris's death. Secondly, that same morning, your grandmother had a blood soaked bandage and torn stitches. Something just isn't right, Little Miss, and we plan to open a full investigation. Another thing is that a Ms. Darla Simmons thinks your grandmother is actually someone else. Now why would a person have a false identity? All this seems pretty strange to me."

As Mikki watched the police officer with his dark brooding eyes, dark hair and mustache, she realized he would not be so easily thrown off the track by her mere good looks. In response, she narrowed her green eyes and just said simply, "What a bunch of crap. That doesn't even make sense. Let me know when you figure it all out, because I have no idea what you are getting at, sir."

The policeman just scratched the stubble on his cheek and looked at her, eyes wandering up and down her lithe body, as if he had just noticed she was female and beautiful. Then amazingly, he just turned and walked away wordlessly. Mikki suddenly realized she must not be linked to the BMW with license plates registered to Mikelle Walsh. The car that sat obtrusively in the parking lot awaiting her return was no longer an asset, but a burden. Mikki walked to the end of the hallway back on the second floor where she had gone to retrieve Emily's personal belongings. Bagging Emily's items in a plastic drawstring sack, and carrying the cane over her arm, she stood at the window overlooking the parking lot. She watched as Lt. Sanderfield went to his squad car parked in the emergency zone, got in and drove away. He didn't seem to be observing the BMW or link her to the car as yet. Grabbing up all the items from Room 311, Mikki rushed down the stairs to the parking lot. Quickly unlocking the door via remote keyless entry, she tossed everything into the back seat, jumped into the driver's seat, and turned the ignition key. The engine revved up and she exited the parking lot wearing dark sunglasses, trying to become as invisible as possible. Once out onto Magnolia Boulevard, she headed straight toward the motel and parked. Grabbing the plastic bags, she slipped the key card into the lock and flung the bag and cane onto the bed. Digging furiously in her own purse, she found the ATM card and headed back out to the bank to get more cash.

Finally back in the cool comfort of the BMW, Mikki watched for police cruisers like she was a common criminal. Now not only was Granny Em under suspicion, but she was too. Although it maddened her that Granny had put her in this situation, she got a real push of adrenaline that moved her body and mind to complete her plan. She had to take the chance that Granny wouldn't need her for a few hours. She pushed the gas pedal to the floor as she entered the Florida Turnpike access towards Orlando. She needed to take this car back home as soon as she could. She quickly arrived at the Orlando Southern Comfort Suites, a gated condominium building. She punched in the numbers to the keypad without even thinking. Parked in her underground space beneath her condo, the car was secure and back where it belonged, out of view and above question. Now to find something a little more discreet and anonymous. Boarding the uptown bus, she found herself at Ugly Goose Cars and Rentals. She saw just what she needed. An old white van that was guaranteed serviceable, though not cosmetically appealing. As she drove back to Citrus City, she tried to get something on the radio. It didn't work, but the engine hummed proudly, like it powered a brand new Caddie. She had paid cash for the van and got a temporary tag under the name of Michelle Smythe. She had quickly made up an address somewhere in Georgia, saying she had engine problems. She explained to the salesman that she would rather buy instead of trying to rent something just for a few days. The salesman was all too eager to sell a vehicle any way he could, but to this striking young woman, he would have given it away.

Arriving back in Citrus City, Mikki speed dialed the hospital from her cell phone. No changes. Mrs. Mildred Carr was in stable but critical condition, per the report. At Granny's rooming house she found the keys to the Taurus rental car and to the storage garage among Emily's belongings. She called the Hertz number to have it picked up next week at the Jackson Street address. She would leave the keys under the mat for them and leave the car in front of the building. She was pretty sure that the rental agreement would not be questioned. She remembered when the agent named Cruz called last week, leaving the message that a Mrs. Kensington had rented the car. She had only asked him to call if any elderly woman even close to Emily's description came in to pick up a car in the specified time frame. It had taken Granny Em only five minutes from the time the girls dropped her at the airport until she signed for the car with another name. By then, Mikki was already putting things together, not quite sure of the whole story, but knowing something was not right. She had planned on questioning her grandmother when she returned, but when the phone call came from Darla, Mikki was called into more immediate action.

Now feeling a great need to get back to her Granny, she quickly showered at the motel and changed into a flowered sundress, letting her hair hang long and loose. A quick spray with an oriental ginger cologne and she was ready to face the world once more. Driving the white panel van, she felt safe within its large space and listening to its purring engine. It was like driving a dinosaur since it was so much bigger than her BMW. The cargo van reminded her of long summer days of helping Granny Em make deliveries for parties. They would cart and haul large boxes of table decorations…everything from the placemats, matching napkins, name holders, to the individually made favors…. that had to be carried to the event. Usually, the kitchen help or hired valets would help with unloading the cartons. Last year Granny had bought a pair of PT Cruisers, which looked like old surfer "woodies." They were used to pick up and deliver especially fragile items and had the FAVORS logo emblazoned on their sides. Ice sculptures were delivered via refrigerated trucks right from the artist's business, but it was always Emily's job to be sure everything arrived safe and sound. Though the girls had thought it was great fun to help out, Granny always paid them something or let them have an extra pajama party at Pink Flamingo. Mikki again thought about the security at those pajama parties. She hadn't given it much thought back then. Now it was all starting to make sense. Stopping for a red light, she took time to glance around the little town. Still hot and humid, and since it had just rained again, there was steam rising from the damp sidewalks and streets. The lumbering white van had air conditioning that worked like a refrigerator and that was a big plus. Forgetting, Mikki tried to tune the radio again, but there was no response.

At the hospital parking lot once again, Mikki climbed down out of the van, rearranging her dress to smooth out the wrinkles. The moist air had a loamy smell that reminded her of the wet dirt and sand found in gardens and greenhouses. It was a smell that reminded her of rural Florida no matter where she was when she smelled it. There was no better place to grow up, she thought.

As she approached the building entrance she made special note of the opening and closing times, and the sections with other exits and entrances. She would make it to ICU just before the fifteen minutes allowed for visitors. Since it was only one flight up, Mikki chose to walk the stairs. She was glad she had purchased a pair of soft canvas sandals at an outlet mall. Very comfortable and Granny would be proud. She would prove that Brigetta was not the only one with the shopping gene in this family.

Arriving at ICU, Mikki introduced herself as Michelle Smythe and quietly asked the nurse by the door closest to Emily's room how her grandmother was doing.

"Not much change, I'm afraid. I have to tell you, it doesn't look real good. Dr. Waterson was just in to see her a few minutes ago. You can still catch him. Want me to page him?"

"No, I think I'll just talk to him later. Can I go in now?'

"Well, I guess we can allow two visitors at a time, but only for the fifteen minutes," said the nurse.

Mikki's voice wavered in bewilderment. "There's ...someone in there... to see her?" she stammered.

Chapter 25

"Oh yes, your sister, Becki. She said you were expecting her," explained the nurse. If she saw the shock in Mikki's eyes as those heavy lashes flew up, clearly astonished, she didn't let on, but kept writing on a patient chart. Mikki's face was now clouded in uneasiness, but she moved into the room where her grandmother lay comatose.

"What the hell are you doing here, Brig? Or should I say, Becki?" Mikki managed to spit out, while quickly pulling closed the privacy curtain. She dared not talk in more than a loud whisper, but wanted to scream as her nostrils flared with fury and confusion.

"You didn't think I would let Granny die here and me not be able to see her, did you? You can't keep the whole family out of your little secret forever, you know!" Brigetta whispered in response as she flipped her blond tresses back over her shoulder in defiance. She was sitting on a hard chair near Emily, still holding her Granny's hand as she spoke. Suddenly Mikki saw the familiar kid sister in jeans and a T-shirt, wide blue eyes misting over in sadness. Her own sorrow was suddenly a huge, painful knot in the center of her belly. She rushed to her sister and the two entwined, holding on for dear life, afraid to let each other go.

Brigetta murmured, "I'm sorry, I know I said I would stay put, but I needed to come. Mom even knows I am here."

"Oh great, just great!" said Mikki, standing up and beginning to pace the floor. "You just don't understand the danger of what's going on here."

"Well, I had to tell Mom, since she is now babysitting the house, the store, and the cat. I could hardly just drive away from all of that, could I?"

"No, but you could have stayed put. I was keeping you informed."

"Oh yeah, like 'Well, I will explain all this later, little Brig, when you are older,' just doesn't cut it. This is my grandmother too, you know. Mom is worried sick, but agreed to stay there until I called with some answers."

"I am just telling you, this is not the time for a family reunion. I can't tell you everything right now, but I will."

"Promise?"

"Yep, promise."

Then the two girls turned their attention to the patient. She was now breathing with a ventilator that moved hissing air in a steady, mechanical rhythm. This was just what Emily did not want, thought Mikki. Tubes entered and exited almost every orifice to the steady beat of beeping and whirring machines. Almost simultaneously, the two young women began talking to Granny Em, soothing her with words of comfort.

"We're here for you, Gran. We love you and we're here," said Brigetta, fully believing that the comatose patient can still hear, if not respond. At least that possibility was what she was taught in nursing school.

The girls asked for a wash basin and washcloths and began massaging Emily with warm wet compresses, speaking quietly and positively, as they rubbed her with the moist towels. Brigetta said she saw some movement in her left hand and said, "Did you see that? Maybe she was trying to reach us and squeeze my hand!"

Mikki was more cautious and certainly had a lot more on her mind right now. Abruptly, a man who was a night nursing supervisor pulled back the curtain, and said, "Oh, hi girls. I hate to break up the party, but I need to check Mrs. Carr's incision and start a new bag of fluid. I really have to ask you to come back in the morning."

"Okay, we were just leaving anyway," said Mikki, as both girls gave the old lady, captured in the wrappings of the cocoon of bedding, a careful hug. They emptied the basin of warm water and tossed the washcloths into the hamper by the doorway.

As the two left the ICU area, Mikki glanced around restlessly, suddenly anxious to escape the disturbing surroundings. "Brig, bring your car and follow me. I have that white van." Mikki pointed quickly to the vehicle as she walked towards it.

"Van? Where's your car?" asked Brigetta suspiciously, as she followed Mikki to the parking lot.

"There's a time for talking and it isn't right now, Brig," said Mikki, still nervous and moving towards the van. "Just follow me. We'll go to my motel and spend the night talking."

The two sisters pulled out of the darkening lot and drove slowly in tandem to the blinking neon sign announcing "Vacancy." Mikki parked and walked towards Room 145 on ground level by the pool. Brigetta, sensing the stealth and mystery, parked several vehicles away and followed inconspicuously to Mikki's motel room. Once inside, they pulled the window curtains closed and bounced flat-backed onto the beds.

"Well?" queried Brigetta.

"Well what, sister Becki?"

"At least I knew to ask for Mrs. Carr and I knew to give another name, didn't I?" said Brigetta, now fiddling with the phone book.

"Who in the world do you think you are calling?" asked Mikki.

"Don't worry, just looking up pizza delivery," answered Brigetta, now thumbing madly through the yellow pages.

"In that respect, you and Granny are just alike. Nothing stops your appetites!" said Mikki, now undressing and putting on a pair of cotton drawstring pants and t-shirt. "I have a feeling this will be a long night, so I'm getting comfortable. Be sure you have something suitable on to go to the door for the pizza guy, 'cause I am now undressed for the night."

"Okay, is there a soda machine? I could get some Cokes before he gets here," asked Brigetta, already digging in her handbag for change. Soon she had made her call for delivery and left to get two sodas. Mikki was again alone in her room. She briefly considered just locking the door to avoid all the interrogation that she knew would follow. But her stubborn sister would throw one of her tantrums if she didn't get some sort of story. Plus, she wanted her here in case the phone rang during the night with bad news.

By 9 P.M. the girls were nibbling pepperoni with double cheese and mushrooms and slurping down the Cokes. The TV was off and both were in pajamas and under the covers. The air conditioner ran cool and quiet, the fan on low speed so they could talk. They had rolled to face each other, elbows on the bed, hands holding up heads, time for talk and thought. They were smart girls and could figure this all out. There were many decisions and calls to make. Brigetta had decided this was harder than all the tests in college so far. Mikki gave her sister a disclosure of sorts to some of the information she had to this point. Mikki stressed her concerns and they discussed the DNR order, the probability that she would ever be okay after the stroke, and the hard choices that they must make together. The repercussions to their parents and their own lives must be taken into account. Granny had lived her life fully, more fully than either one of them was ever aware.

"Mikk, you're right. We just can't let the family go down the tubes because our Granny has a secret life. A secret career! Boy, does that sound weird. If she dies, will Lt. Sanderfield go away? We know Darla can't see me or know I'm here. But what to do and when?"

"Forget about Darla for now. Let's see how Granny is by tomorrow morning. If no improvement, we have to make a move. There is just too much at risk for everyone."

"I understand. I'm just not sure I can do it. We could get caught and that might be worse than letting her wake up. I think it's my nursing background that's pulling me in another direction."

"Do you think that she'll actually wake up?"

"I don't know. With strokes, anything can happen. She might be even be awake when we get back in the morning."

"She can't. We just can't let that happen. Sanderfield would be there in an instant."

"I know. There's just a lot of risk."

Mikki pulled off the covers and sat on the edge of the bed. She was still glamorous--even sexy--with bed-head hair, thought her sister, as she watched Brigetta set the alarm and plump her pillows one more time.

"This has to be a decision we make together, Brig. Do we do it or not? Your nursing experience from class will be a big asset to us. We do it together or not at all. We cannot risk her coming out of this comatose state and to start talking. Who knows what she would say!"

"I agree that it's too risky to leave to chance. I'm sure the cops will be swarming all over tomorrow, so we have to be low profile," said Brigetta, now also sitting up and raking fingers through her own tousled blond hair. "Once Granny Em is gone, there will be no further investigation. I mean, they don't have her real name or address, right?" asked Brigetta, getting up to brush her teeth and get a glass of ice water for the bedside table.

"So it's agreed? We'll have to take Granny Em out?"

Mikki studied her sister once again, seeing the familiar half-squished toothpaste on the sink and the tan blond with fabulous figure standing in pink shortie pajamas, toothbrush in hand.

"Yes... I don't see any other choices. Granny would have really wanted it this way, I think."

Mikki replied, climbing back under the sheet, "She told me she didn't want to ruin the family. Ruin our lives. And I'm sure she really meant it."

Brigetta walked back to her own bed, and then suddenly went to her sister and held her. "Tomorrow then, unless she is a lot better, we do it. I am pretty sure I know how."

Brigetta reached for the light and switched it off. No more words were spoken as each young woman lay silently, unable to go right to sleep. Eventually the plan settled in their minds, like torn pieces of a photograph painstakingly pieced back together with love, forming a perfect picture. As a sudden thunderstorm began to fling yard debris and rain with a staccato beat on their window, they finally both drifted off to sleep wondering what they had become and what would become of them.

Chapter 26

As the girls awoke and readied for the day, taking turns in the small motel bathroom, neither said much. Mikki volunteered to make the run to the front office for coffee, since she was the first one up and dressed. The day was somewhat cooler and the sky was a brilliant blue. As Mikki breathed in the air cleaned by last night's showers, she said a little prayer. *Dear God, I hope we're not going in the wrong direction with this. Please forgive us, if we are screwing up.* Just as she reached the motel's front office she saw a small rainbow forming in the misty garden adjoining the building. Rays of early sunshine shone through the steamy plants as they dried, replenished from the rain, and a myriad of color arched above them. Mikki stared in awe at the simple natural beauty for a moment, and then pulled open the door to greet the manager.

"Hey!" she said to the man at the desk.

"Hi, Babe, what's new this morning?" he answered, while wiping pastry goo from his fingers.

"Not much, but I'll be checking out today. Guess I'll settle up my bill now and then I'll just leave my key in the room. That okay?"

"Sure. Cash, check or credit card?" he answered, while slurping a large coffee and wiping his mouth.

"I'll be paying cash," said Mikki. "What time is check out?"

"For you, Ms. Smythe, it can be any time you want. It's not often we get a beautiful young lady to grace us with her presence, you know!" said the manager, while his computer calculated her total and printed out a receipt.

After the cash exchange, Mikki grabbed the two coffees and headed for the door. "Real thirsty this morning?" he said with a sly grin.

"No, its just my sister came to see me and now we're leaving. Nothing more exciting than that, Mr. Johnson," explained

Mikki with a fling of her hair. "If I had a man in there, I would definitely be sending him to get the coffee, now, wouldn't I?"

Mr. Johnson just threw his head back laughing and said, "You're right! What was I thinking?"

"Well, I would like a late check out if possible and I need one other favor, please?"

Mr. Johnson laughed some more, agreed, and waved good-bye, getting back to the cherry turnover and coffee as she left. When Mikki got back to the room, Brigetta was dressed in her usual outfit of jeans and T-shirt, hair freshly washed and minimal make up. She looked great as always. Should have been a California surfer chick. Straight sun-streaked blonde hair that cascaded over her back like a living, golden waterfall. Tall, tan and sure of herself, she was ready to go.

"I called the hospital and there is no change in Granny's condition. I'm anxious to get over there and see for myself though. We're allowed in at ten, they said," said Brigetta.

"Okay, let's just have our coffee and stop for some break-fast sandwiches somewhere before we go over there," said Mikki.

"Oh goodie, you're going to let me eat!"

"We have a big day ahead of us. You'll need your strength."

Arriving at the hospital about 9:45 A.M., they chose the stairway again to go to the second floor. They both felt they knew their way around the hospital now and could get anywhere without getting lost. The ICU supervisor for today was standing by the medication cart when they arrived. Smiling and cheerful, the pleasant woman allowed them to go in to the cubicle to see Granny Em a little early.

"Her doctor already saw her and she had her sponge bath, her bed was changed, and she was given all her morning medications. You might as well go in now," she had said to the visitors.

The curtain was still pulled and Emily looked no better than the day before when they peeked around the edge. The bleeping monitors and I.V. infusion equipment were still doing their duties. Emily's eyes were still closed and her breathing continued mechanically. She didn't even look like the same person they knew and loved.

"Does she still need the ventilator?" asked Brigetta of the nurse, as they went to Emily's side.

"Dr. Waterson said he may pull it tomorrow, especially with the DNR order. But she may do fine on her own without it. Right now it's an extra precaution since we are not sure of the full damage from the clot and stroke," answered the nurse, while checking all the equipment. "Anything else you have questions about?"

"No, not right now. Please, go ahead with your work. We'll just stay and keep an eye on her for a while. Maybe we can get some sort of response," said Mikki.

The girls began to talk to Emily and each held a hand as they tried to comfort the elderly patient. They were just sitting quietly with their grandmother when they heard a low cough behind them.

Lt. Sanderfield was standing at the foot of the bed, making his presence known. Mikki shot him a cold dismissive look. Brigetta chose to just ignore his presence.

"'Morning, ladies. May I speak with you out in the hallway, please?" said the police officer.

"This is our only time to visit with our Granny all morning, sir. What could possibly be this important?" said Mikki, so furious that she could hardly speak. Her face pale with anger and fear, she said, "If you wouldn't mind giving us a few minutes, we could talk to you later."

"All right. I'll be outside the unit's door, waiting for you."

Brigetta and Mikki looked at each other in silence, afraid to say another word. Finally Mikki said, "I'll go talk to him. You stay here. Don't say anything to anyone, okay?"

Nervously biting her lip, Brigetta just nodded affirmatively. "What about Darla? What if she shows up and sees me?" asked Brigetta, as she saw Mikki disappearing around the corner of the curtain.

Not answering, but giving a warning look, Mikki went into the hall to meet her adversary. She stood tall and swallowed hard, as if to choke back the fear and uncertainty. "Yes, what is it today, Officer?"

"Well, it seems there was a reason Darla Simmons didn't come to work yesterday. She's dead." Giving just a moment for a response from Mikki, he continued, "They found her last night after a neighbor couldn't get anyone to come to the door."

"Oh, no! I had met her and she took such good care of my grandmother. They really got along well. She was so helpful to her. What happened?"

"They're not sure yet."

"The neighbor found her?"

"Yep, and called 911. Mrs. Katonik had been looking for Simmon's cat. Had heard it meowing late at night and had been feeding it all week. She couldn't find it last night, so she went to look for it. She went to Simmon's house, found the door unlocked, and couldn't get an answer. She went in finally and found the girl on the kitchen floor."

"Oh, that's terrible! My Granny so loved that girl. Granny said she had some wild ideas, but was always so sweet and nice," said Mikki. "Oh my gosh, I just don't believe she's dead!"

"Well, she is. Right now, the cause is undetermined, but the coroner's first suspicion is hypoglycemia. That means low blood sugar," he added, as if Mikki would need a prompt.

"Oh, it does? I did not know that," said Mikki, trying to keep the sarcasm at a minimum.

"Yes, ma'am, the coroner filled me in on his first impressions."

"I feel bad, but what does all this have to do with me or my family, Officer?" said Mikki tentatively. "Surely you didn't come all the way over here to tell me about Ms. Simmons, did you? She must have had diabetes or something, right?"

"Well, no one remembers Ms. Simmons being a diabetic or having any kind of sugar problem in the past. They pulled her hospital physical and history and there was nothing red-checked on the forms anywhere. Everything normal. Supposedly the picture of health."

"So? Maybe she lied to get the job. People do that all the time, I hear. She told my grandmother she was a nursing student. Maybe she had health problems she felt she needed to hide."

"Well, they did find some evidence in her home though."

"What kind of evidence, Officer?"

"Evidence about her health. That's all you need to know."

"Anyway, why are you here? You never explained yourself about that."

"Well, it seems a little suspicious that we are called in to investigate evidence to be given in a suspicious death, and then the witness with the evidence suddenly dies before she gets to state her case."

"What evidence, what suspicious death? What are you getting at?" said Mikki, the tone of her voice now rising and her eyes turning dark sea green. "You are a very suspicious person, it seems to me!"

"I think you know what I'm talking about, Ms. Smythe. We're back to the trail of blood leading to or from Tyrone Dupris' room where he died. The deceased Ms. Simmons had reported that to me. Originally we thought Dupris died of his wounds, and trust me, no one really cared that much. But a murder is a different story. All crimes must be solved and the perpetrators punished, no matter who the victim is and how much you like or don't like him. We're still waiting for the written results of the autopsy. The County Coroner ordered the investigation. Second of all, Ms. Simmons said she had photos linking your grandmother, Mrs. Carr, to another identity. What she said was, if I remember, that Mrs. Carr was not really her name, but an alias of some sort. We're still looking for the photos."

"Well, that is beyond ridiculous. Do you know how strange that sounds, Lieutenant? You are still saying that my 77-year-old grandmother really goes by another name and with a body riddled with cancer and pneumonia ran down and then up the stairs with a cut-up knee to somehow eliminate this Dupris? We've been through this before! Come on, you seem to be a smarter man than that!" Mikki said, with a wry smile and her arms folded in front of her protectively.

The lieutenant's mouth took on an unpleasant twist as he jutted his thumbs into his gun belt and said, "That's exactly what we think. Sounds outlandish, of course, but then the autopsy findings were a little off the wall too. Seems the pathologist found remnants of peanut butter in his...umm... rectum."

Now it was time for genuine surprise. Mikki had not expected this. Peanut butter? And they really cut into your butt hole when you died? Who would know? Wonder if it was chunky or creamy peanut butter?

"Peanut butter?" Mikki asked with amusement barely hidden in her grin. "Now you are getting downright weird," continued Mikki with hands on hips, meeting his arrogance with defiance. "This is getting more outlandish as you go on."

"Yes, it is. And trust me, we aim to get to the bottom of all of this. As soon as your grandmother is awake and functioning, we'll be back to talk to her."

"Oh, I really can't wait to hear how peanut butter in your butt means you have been murdered! This is so very exciting!"

"He had an allergic reaction, young lady. A very bad allergic reaction! There was some other stuff too. And I must confess, it is a little hard to figure out. But I will. I promise you that!"

"So do you know how the murderer managed to get him to eat the peanut butter? I mean he must have known he was allergic to it."

"Of course he knew. In fact, he had lots of allergies. They're not sure he swallowed it. But none of this is your business. It's mine. That and finding out why we have two dead bodies in refrigerators downstairs. We are still looking at your grandmother. I told the nurse to call us as soon as she is able to talk to us."

"And I suppose she had something to do with Darla's death while she was here in a coma? Some sort of an attempt to save herself from investigation?" quipped Mikki still meeting his stare eyeball to eyeball.

"If, in fact, Ms. Simmons died of anything but natural causes," he started to answer, eyes cool and authoritative. "Good day, Ms Smythe." As he turned abruptly and walked away, Mikki let out a huge pent-up sigh. She felt like she had been holding her breath for an hour. She realized her nails had left indentations in her palms from fists squeezed tight in nervousness. She rubbed her hands on her pants and brought back the circulation as she turned and reentered Granny's room.

A raw and primitive grief almost completely overwhelmed Mikki just temporarily as she went back to the curtained cubicle. "We're screwed. Tonight for sure. We do it. And we're out of here," she whispered to Brigetta, as she reached for her arm for support.

Kissing Emily good-bye and telling the nurses they would see them later, they exited the hospital. Soon they would proceed with their plans and be back in Palm Beach by early morning.

Chapter 27

The latest visiting hours for the ICU were from 8 to 8:15 P.M. At about 7:45, Dr. Waterson was making some late night rounds. Stopping at the nurse's station, he picked up Mildred Carr's chart and began to pull out some forms. "Please make some copies for her granddaughters. They wanted to know all the medications she is taking right now. The blond-haired one, Becki, seemed to know something about nursing, going to school, I think. They seemed real concerned about pain medications for some reason. I told them she was not experiencing pain. They were also asking about the DNR orders, and if there would be pain if all life support would be withdrawn."

"Maybe they're thinking about letting her go?" offered one of the nurses.

"I do know that Mrs. Carr had expressed the definite desire to not become a burden or live the way she is right now."

"But she could still recover, couldn't she?"

"Possibly, with time and patience and rehab, I guess she could. She certainly has a lot of problems to deal with right now. Pretty tough little bird, that one," answered the doctor.

"Maybe they don't want her to recover, maybe collect some inheritance or something?" said the ICU night supervisor.

"No, I don't think that's it at all. Both those girls look like they have plenty of money. Much more than Mrs. Carr, I would guess. Did you see those Prada shoes and Gucci bags?" said one of the staff nurses.

"Yeah, and did you see the Louis Vuitton watch the blond was wearing?" offered another nurse.

Dr. Waterson was trying to appear nonchalant as he answered while continuing to write, "I don't really notice all that, but yes, you could tell they were from money. Not exactly street urchins. On the other hand, they seem to be truly concerned about her. Wanting the best for her. Who knows what motivates people? That's why I am a surgeon and not a psychiatrist, ladies. And with that, I am back to work. Would like to get home tonight sometime.

I think my lovely wife has prepared some Beef Wellington for her mother's birthday and I don't want it to be all dried out. She would kill me."

Just a few minutes after the doctor had left, the girls arrived as usual via the stairway. After waving hello and getting the paperwork they wanted, they went in to see Emily. She lay still as death. Her pale, cool skin was moist and clammy. Eyes closed, she looked so fragile and weak, that she was almost unrecognizable as their grandmother. She lay flat on her back with arms and legs splayed out grotesquely, as if she were a fallen paper doll. Machinery was pumping, hissing, and bleeping, reminding Mikki of a movie where an alien creature was being kept alive in a secret science laboratory. Granny Em did not appear to be a human being with a beating heart and inflating lungs, and family who needed her.

The girls approached the bed, one on each side, and lowered the rails to be close to the patient. Mikki spoke as she leaned her elbows on the mattress, putting her mouth close to Emily's face, "Granny, we are here, can you hear us? We've made some decisions and we hope this is what you wanted. Things are crashing in on all of us. We think we know what you would want, so we'll be back later to say our good-byes to this whole ordeal. Remember we love you." Mikki's voice was just a whisper as Brigetta held Granny Em's flaccid hand in hers.

The girls lingered a few minutes making notes about the equipment in the room. There were I.V. pumps, heart monitors, the ventilator, and various access lines and tubes for fluids, feedings, and urine. Soon they looked at each other and Brigetta said, "I think I've got it. Ready to go?"

They went down the same stairs, and headed for the parking lot and the white van. They decided to grab a couple of sandwiches before they made a few extra stops. They decided on the Black Angus Burgers drive-through. "Did you know that Black Angus meat is just meat from a black cow?" asked Mikki.

"What? Is that my trivia thought for the day?" said Brigetta.

"Yep."

"Well, are you saying it is any cow that happens to have black hair or what?"

"Yep."

"You mean there is no breed of cow called Black Angus? And how do you know all this?"

"If a cow is mostly black they can call it Angus beef when it is processed. I saw it on TV one day, maybe on RFD TV. But yes, there is a breed called that."

"Now I'm supposed to believe you watch RFD TV while you are cozied in on your couch in big-city Orlando? Oh, please!"

"I'm serious. I like to watch the horse programs they have. They're usually on several times a day. But then sometimes I just like to further round out my very well-rounded personality by watching something new and different. Besides, someday I might run into a cattle baron at one of the company cocktail parties. I would be able to speak intelligently about agriculture!"

"Well, I've heard of the 'Cattlemen's Ball,' but I never pictured you there as one of the guests." Brigetta just shrugged and looked out the window. She learned something new about her sister everyday. Maybe she got her eccentrics from Grandma.

"Guess you forgot about how I used to sling manure at the polo grounds just wanting to be around the horses."

"Gee, all that while I thought it was that exercise rider, Greg Devonshire."

"Well, maybe he had something to do with it."

"Where are we going now? We can't go back to the motel; aren't we already checked out?" asked Brigetta as she munched on her super-sized burger meal and licked French fry salt off her fingers.

"We've got a couple of errands to run. You know, things to do, people to see, places to go."

Brigetta just continued eating, as she slipped her sandals off and put her feet up on the dashboard. It was fine with her if Mikki was in control of this operation. She was nervous enough as it was, she was thinking, as she picked up the French fries one by one and poked them into her mouth.

Chapter 28

Four or five hours later that night, entering through the hospital's rear delivery door, the two sisters walked the dimly lit basement passageway towards the morgue.

"I have to tell you, I'm getting creeped out down here!" said Mikki to her sister in a quiet voice. There, in the hallway, they saw what they were looking for. Thank God for Kate. Then the girls took the service elevator up from the basement to the first floor. The main floor was nearly empty since the lobby, gift shop and florist were closed. All the information desks were empty and no volunteers or Candy Stripers would be working the midnight shift. The two security men sat at the front desk half asleep, crossword puzzle books on their laps, and a small TV showing Lucille Ball running amuck in black and white. The girls crept to the stairs and began the familiar climb to the second floor. They climbed in unison one step at a time. Left, right, left, right. Peeking through the glass-topped door at the top of the stairway, they could see the nurses. Since it was close to 1 A.M., they knew the patient rounds were complete and soon several of them would go on a break. Luckily, Emily's room was the second closest to the stairs, and they could see that the curtains were pulled around the bed for privacy.

"I don't see any feet in there," said Brigetta in a whisper, peering at the areas below the cubicle's curtain. "Seems safe."

"Okay, let's go then," answered Mikki.

Both girls ran in their rubber-soled tennis shoes to the room and jumped up quickly onto the chairs by the bed, making sure their feet would not give them away. One of the nurses glanced up, thinking she saw something in her peripheral vision. But as she turned, nothing could be seen under the curtain except the bottom of the bed legs, an almost full urine bag, and draped cords and equipment lines.

Mikki whispered to Brigetta, as she grabbed her elbow, "Are you sure you can do this?"

Responding in a low voice, Brigetta said, "Now is a great time to ask!" Slowly Brigetta's eyes roamed around the cubicle and surveyed the set-up of equipment.

"First, we turn off the alarms!" she ordered in a hushed but determined tone. "Let me do everything. You just keep watch!

As she flipped the alarm systems off as she had learned in nursing school training, they both held their breath and were as still as ice sculptures. No telltale buzzers went off. They both breathed a little easier when those blaring alarms did not scream for help. Now it was time for the serious stuff.

"Granny, we are sorry, but we can't let all this happen, not just to you, but to the whole family. I know this is what you would want. At least I hope so. Forgive us if we are wrong. We love you," said Mikki, as she watched Brigetta at work.

Starting with the ventilator, Brigetta, with the accuracy of a surgeon, began to release Emily from the encumbering tentacles of life support equipment. She cautiously removed the plastic airway and intubation equipment. Emily did not even cough reflexively as the tube was pulled from her throat, but was still and quiet. Gradually Brigetta began to discontinue more support systems, unplugging one after the other from their life-sustaining terminals. At last all was quiet and still; no one was there to hear the sisters' tears fall onto the crisp white sheets.

Emily felt almost nothing. The vague sensations that seemed to be buried in an opaque fog seemed distant and so subtle that her nervous system could not decipher them. Voices and an almost musical beat blended into a whirring, almost whistling sound. She felt some jarring and then a not quite perceptible vibration, constant and bringing a sense of comfort. Her throat felt thick and scratchy and filled with phlegm she couldn't swallow. Suddenly she couldn't hear herself breathe anymore. Was her heart still beating? She could no longer hear the melodious rhythm that counted her pulse like a metronome. Perhaps dying was not so bad. She felt strangely safe, as if wrapped in a warmed blanket to rest. She wanted to speak, to cry out, but could not. Therefore, she let herself sail wordlessly through the haze, hoping for a glimpse of what was to be.

Brigetta felt a strange sense of relief as she climbed down from the bed and looked around the curtain. "Now we just have to get out of here," she said hoarsely to her sister. "It's done."

"I'm ready, let's go!" exclaimed Mikki, also climbing down from her perch on the chair.

Brigetta ran quickly to the cubical across the circular ICU and darted into the curtained area. She grabbed one of the electrode pads from the comatose patient's shaved chest and yanked it off. "Sorry, sir!" she whispered into the man's ear whose eyes remained closed. She sprang like an antelope out of the room just as his heart monitor alarm began to ring excitedly at the nurse's station. The remaining nurses all jumped up in surprise and ran to the man's cubical. During the commotion, the siblings made their exit, pushing the button for the service elevator. The door opened and they carried the body inside, stabbing quickly at the lit button for the basement. It seemed like the slowest closing door in the world, but finally the elevator hummed its way down. They were careful and maneuvered their prize now on a cart, past the morgue and through the lower level corridors. They found the Econoline where they had left it. They loaded up the van and drove off slowly and quietly, so not to bring attention to themselves. There were two more stops to make and they were on their way to leaving Citrus City for good.

Chapter 29

Three months later, the girls were together again on a Saturday morning. A week or two after their experiences in Citrus City, Brigetta had gone back to school in Tampa and Mikki was still clawing her way to the top at the engineering firm. But this weekend they were both home and helping their mother clean up the Pink Flamingo.

"Let's make some iced tea, Mom," said Brigetta. "I have some of that good peach flavor that we use at the store, Gran's old favorite."

"Okay, I've got some Macadamia nut cookies that are almost finished in the oven. We'll take them out to the oceanfront deck and have us a little bit of a girl party!" said Susan. Soon there was a large glass tray with icy mugs of tea, bearing mint sprigs and a peach slice hooked on each frosty rim. A violet-trimmed plate was filled with still warm and gooey cookies. Brigetta opened the French doors that led to the marble-floored balcony, circled by pink sturdy concrete railings and banisters. Blue sky and bright sun provoked a dazzling display of dancing sparkles on the aqua-colored rolling waves. White foam rolled lazily on the sand, pushed towards the beach by the rising tide. After placing the tray on the round-planked table, Susan retreated momentarily to get some extra napkins.

Mikki and Brigetta sat in the cushioned seats and looked at each other conspiratorially. Finally Mikki spoke, "Shall we wake her?"

"I don't know," said Brigetta, using her napkin as a fan to direct the steamy aroma of fresh baked cookies toward the resting form. The elderly woman sat in a wheelchair with her eyes closed and an afghan draped over her shoulders. She appeared to be sleeping, her chin drifting towards her collarbone. At once, one eye came open as her nostrils opened and closed... sniffing.

"Do you think I can't smell those cookies? Do you really think I would let you eat them all right in front of me?" said the frail woman. As she became more erect, a purple sweat suit came into view. The afghan was pushed from her shoulders with her right hand, the left remained clutching a hand-sized rubber ball.

"Granny, we knew you were awake. We were just messing with your mind!" said Mikki.

"Don't you think my mind has been messed with enough?" asked Emily, grinning as she tried to reach for a cookie.

"Let me help you, for once. You are the worst patient I ever had, Granny," announced Brigetta. She then proceeded to move a small plate near Emily and place her mug of tea at the edge of the table after placing a straw in the glass.

"I'm just trying to keep you in training for the hard to handle dudes that might come your way at the hospital, dear," said Emily with lips now covered with cookie crumbs.

"I think more than likely you're preparing me for the psych ward! Not only that, I'm not sure if I'll be the nurse or the crazy patient, thanks to you, Granny dearest," said Brigetta now rolling her eyes and curling her fingers into claw hands, trying to do her best monster imitation. With her normally angelic face, baby blue eyes and fantastic blond hair, she did not much resemble a killer freak. That made it even more hilarious and all three began to giggle. At that time, Susan arrived with napkins and some fresh-from-the-oven chocolate chip cookies to add to the variety of goodies.

"Okay, let me in on the joke, please. I have been left out of a whole lot of crap lately, I notice," said Susan.

"Ohhhh, Mommy said crap!" chided Mikki, now breaking into serious gales of uncontrolled laughter. "Really Mom, don't you think Brig makes a great looking psycho freak?"

"I'm beginning to think you're all psycho freaks. Now let's just eat the cookies and stare at the water like semi-normal people," said Susan.

"Yeah, Granny, do your great dolphin call. You know, where you call for Flipper!" requested Brigetta still giggling and wanting to enjoy this good time with her family.

"Okay. EeEeEeEecEec!" squeaked Emily high in her throat. "Here Flipper, here Flipper!"

"You are all so weird I can hardly believe I am related to the whole bunch of you," said Susan, holding her head in her hands now, but giggling along with the rest.

"Loook! There they are!" screamed Mikki. And sure enough, a whole pod of dolphins was right in front of the mansion, slowing rolling over and over through the water, searching for fish. Or maybe they had answered the call of the one who loved them. Mikki began to wave outrageously at the dolphins. Meanwhile, Brigetta began making the noises of her own dolphin call as they stood at the railing being silly and watching the porpoises. Emily had pushed her wheelchair to face the sea and peered between the banisters to watch the show. All at once a large, dark gray body flung itself high into the air in a show of acrobatics presented just for them, as they all applauded his effort.

"That's Maximum. He loves to show off, you know," announced Emily as she guided her chair back to the table.

Susan said, "You always were like the ringmaster of a circus, Mother. You always had your own show."

"Is that a bad thing?" said Emily, now almost serious and pouting, hands folded onto her lap.

"No, that's not what I meant. But it's true. However, I'm sure glad you're back here, thanks to these girls who managed to track you down," replied Susan with truthful clarity. She sat back in her chair and ran fingers through her own gray-streaked, reddish-blond hair. The short cut suited her and the practical way she managed her life. "When the girls told me the whole story about your trip, where you were, and your 'career,' shall we call it, I was shocked beyond any sense of reality. Then, the more I thought about it, I became less shocked and really not as surprised as I thought I would be. I'm not saying I approve at all, especially the risks you took that could have involved all of us. I'm just glad all of that is behind us. Please, tell me again that you are 'retired?' I really don't want to be explaining this to Michael, or worse yet, to the women at the Club."

"Well, this wheelchair would make a nice accessory, wouldn't it? Just kidding, Susan. It's really the end of an era. I'm going to be perfectly happy to stay here, and when I'm a little better I'll go back to the store full time. I really miss that, you know."

"Okay, let's just not talk about it any more, okay?" requested Susan. "This was an awakening experience that has left me reeling. My own mother...a private eye!" Then she rose to carry away the plate of cookies and bring more ice and tea. As she left, Badger managed to squeeze through the door and immediately leapt onto Emily's lap.

"He really missed you. While you were in rehab at the Palm Coast Center, he kept climbing on your bed and slept on the pillow," said Brigetta.

"Well, that explains the cat hairs in my nose and all over my face each morning, doesn't it?" said Emily, now stroking the cat as he reached up to rub his head against her chin. "Such a sweet old curmudgeon. Kinda reminds me of me, don't you think?" She then held the cat's face up next to hers and grinned a Cheshire cat grin for the girls. "We have both lost some hair in our old age. Makes us bonded somehow."

"It didn't take long after the chemo for yours to grow back, Gran. You are looking like a foxy lady once again!" said Brigetta.

"Yep, you and that cat are just alike. Along that line, Granny, what would you think about another cat?" asked Mikki. "We brought her over a few times while you were at the nursing home…"

"Please! It was an assisted care and rehabilitation center, not a 'nursing home,'" interrupted Emily. "Let's just get that straight right now for the record."

"Yeah, okay. Whatever. Anywaay…Gran, Badger seemed to enjoy her company. She is box-trained and really cute. An orange tabby with white socks and a tip on her tail. I took her to Orlando, but I really got her for you. She's a rescue and I couldn't resist. But I'm gone so much it isn't fair to keep her in the apartment alone. What do you think?" asked Mikki, green eyes dancing with determination.

"Guess I can't say I don't have enough room, so, okay. As long as Badger is not jealous or feels put out. He's an old guy, you know. And we old folks can get our noses bent out of place if we are ever shoved aside," said Emily.

A squeal of relief from Mikki and the deal was sealed. Her mood was now even more buoyant. "Granny, you know we all love Badger to death and you have enough love for twenty pets, if you could take care of all of them. We know that for sure."

"When do you bring her over? Did you get her spayed? I don't want old Badger to think he's got a live one, you know. He's neutered and fat, but he needs a companion, not a girlfriend!"

"I'll bring her over tomorrow, she's at Mom's house right now. I had her spayed in Orlando and she's had her shots and has been microchipped. Of course, I listed you as the owner!

She even likes to ride in the car, just like Badger," said Mikki. "You can take both of them back to FAVORS to guard you at the store.

"Hmmm. Two attack cats instead of just one. How could I possibly resist such an offer?"

"In fact, I have to get back to Mom's to work on some drawings for the office, but I'll be back later. Maybe I'll even bring her along tonight, okay?"

"Sure, that works for me. You sure were confident I would take another cat. Are you leaving too, Brig?" asked Emily, turning towards the twenty-year-old.

"Nope, staying here with Mom for awhile. She said she had more stuff to do around the house. Then she and I will go home for a bit so I can study, you can nap, and we'll all come back and have dinner together. Mom is going to a fund raiser at the club later on, so it will be you, me and Mikki," answered Brigetta.

"Perfect. Never thought I'd be taking a daily nap. It's like I'm back in kindergarten! I want to ask you girls some questions. Things are not really clear about how you got me out of there. Maybe you can fill me in on all the gory details tonight, please?" pleaded Emily, still petting the purring cat, planted on her lap.

"Guess we can. Specially since you were so upfront with us," Brigetta said sarcastically, squinting and staring at her grandmother.

"There were reasons. I thought I explained all that. I'm sorry, but it was for your own protection."

"I know. You'll get your answers. In fact, Mikki and I have talked about it. You know, filling you in on the rest of the story," said Brigetta, rising to go help her mother.

"I'm going to sit out here for a while, if you don't mind. Might take a little nap right here in this comfy chair. See ya later, dear," said Emily, eyes drooping just a little. As she dozed, the ocean breezes wrapped her in soft, salty warmth, like a caress from a long-lost lover.

Chapter 30

Later the family of four women gathered in the screened porch area adjoining the formal dining room. They feasted on BBQ'd pork chops, homemade applesauce and pierogies with sour cream. A small salad with fresh homegrown tomatoes and banana peppers completed their main course. Granny Em was beginning to use her walker and after dinner insisted on making her own way to the ocean-front portico. There they had cappuccinos and carrot cake for dessert. Grabbing up her napkin and plate, Susan announced she had to get going or she would be late. She had to run home to change to evening wear and refresh her make up. The remaining three bid her good-bye for now, but she would return later that evening as they were all planning to spend the night together in the giant beach mansion. As Susan's Bentley pulled out of the circular drive and through the wrought iron gate, Emily began to usher the two girls back to the south deck where a fabulous sunset was forming. No one wanted to miss the spectacular colors created especially for them by Mother Nature. They watched and sipped the coffee until the sun blinked its good-bye and the water became a moonlit mirror. Emily put down her cup and faced the two sisters, resting her elbows on the arms of the wheelchair.

"Time for talk, and I don't mean to Flipper this time. Now that I am healing, I want to thank you again for saving me from certain disaster and, most importantly, Lt. Sanderfield. He was getting a little too close to reality for comfort. Do you think he's out of the picture forever?" asked Emily with a hopeful but cautious expression.

Mikki was first to respond, saying, "Once you were gone—mysteriously disappeared--they tried to follow up on Mildred Carr, but to no avail per the local newspaper report. We were careful to wipe all the bed rails clean of prints before we left, so there is no way they could match you with that crazy old lady."

"Just how did you get me out of the hospital? And from Intensive Care? That should have been a problem, I would think," asked Emily, her eyebrows forming a furrow as she concentrated on listening for the answer.

"We were sneaky, just like our grandmother. You see, once I knew what medications you were on, and how to take care of you, we knew we had to try to get you out of there," continued Brigetta. "I knew we could handle your care once we got you home with Dr. Getts to take on the responsibility. We were just so scared. We just had to take the chance."

"Remember Kate Bingham, the nursing supervisor on the third floor? She really liked you and, for some reason, she was ready to get me away from her boyfriend, Dr. Belmont," Mikki said with a wide grin and batting her eyes in silliness. "She was willing to help us get you out of there. She didn't agree with your DNR order when she found out about it. Also, she thought Darla was a little loony with all of her accusations, so when we told her we wanted to take you to a nursing home without the police following us and asking dumb questions, she agreed readily. She was one of many who did not care a bit what had happened to Dupris. The night we took you out of the hospital we asked her to place a gurney near the service elevator in the basement. That was up to her. She got one from the morgue and put some clean sheets on it and a blanket, even a pillow. She even helped Brigetta with some instruction about the monitoring equipment, so it could be disconnected without an accidental alarm going off. Our other helper was your Dr. Waterson. He was unaware of his compliance in your escape. He thought he was just giving family members some information. I had told him we planned to eventually take you to a nursing home if you survived and we needed some information, just in case."

"How did you know I would survive?" asked Emily, now very attentive and sitting straight up in her wheelchair.

Inhaling a huge breath of fresh, salty sea air, Brigetta exhaled loudly. "We didn't. That was the scariest part. We were terrified you would die en route or right in the hospital bed, once I extubated you from the ventilator. After you kept breathing, I knew you would make it. And probably kill us for not letting you go peacefully with your stupid DNR order."

"You do understand why I wrote and signed that and the living will, don't you? It was to protect you, all of you, my family. I already knew Mikki had figured out most of everything, and I had confessed a lot of the rest. She was already carrying a huge burden, just having that knowledge and not knowing what to do about it."

Mikki quickly interrupted, "After you were 'unplugged,' so to speak, we caused a minor disturbance to distract the staff and pushed the elevator button, hoping it was still one floor below where we had left it. We then carried you to the gurney waiting in the elevator. That was a tense moment, wondering if the cart would still be there when we reopened the service elevator door. We were counting on the fact that most of the maintenance and support employees would be off shift or not too busy during the night. Not running up and down on the elevator to the floors. Sure enough, it was still there. You're not that heavy, but we were sure glad to see that thing ready to roll you out of there. It was only two floors to the basement, and we prayed the whole way down that no one would try to get on at the first floor or be waiting at the bottom. We breathed a huge sigh of relief when the basement was empty and the huge garage door was open. We had concocted a story about being from a funeral home and picking up a body from the morgue. Also we had pulled the sheet over your head just in case. So much for their security. We pushed the cart to the van, slid you in, and we were on the road. I drove and Brigetta hooked the I.V. bags onto the coat hangers in the back and kept an eye on you. She had her stethoscope and blood pressure cuff from nurse's training, and faithfully kept checking on you the whole way home. We had to pick up Brigetta's car, and that was where Mom came in. She was waiting there in the car, and pulled out behind us so we could caravan home."

"My daughter was in on this, too?" asked Emily incredulously, her voice rising in surprise.

"None of us gave her enough credit, I guess, but her sense of family is just as strong as ours. I knew I had to take a chance that she would help us, and she was there within hours of my call. Only Daddy is still in the dark about all this, and Mom plans to keep it that way," said Brigetta.

"Anyway, we took you home for a few days, as Mom had arranged for a hospital bed in the guest suite. We didn't know if the detectives would look for you in another hospital. Dr. Getts came over three or four times a day. When you became completely stable, we arranged for transport to the rehab center. Now you're home, and we're all safe and happy to be all together again," said Mikki.

"Want something to drink, Gran? More coffee?" asked Brigetta, getting up to clear the remaining dessert plates.

"I think I'll have some cold tea, please. That herbal concoction in the glass pitcher, right hand of the fridge, dear," answered Emily. After Brigetta had left the deck, Emily said to Mikki, sighing, "I really didn't want to tell even just you. And now everyone knows."

"Not *everyone*, Gran, just the faithful few," said Mikki reaching for Emily's hand and giving it a squeeze. "Remember, Brig and I had our suspicions about you, our eccentric grandmother; we just had no idea of what was hidden beneath that loveable exterior. No one knows the whole story but me. Brigetta and Mom just think we rescued you from the hospital because we couldn't give away your secret career... and your clandestine, perhaps illegal, behavior. The *private investigative* career. They think you just got drawn into the Dupris thing because you were tracking him for Mrs. Grimes. I told them that the cops somehow were ready to blame you for his death. Just be careful about adding anything else to my story and things will be cool."

"Well, I am quite cool, you know!" exclaimed Emily, squeezing back on the hand now encircling hers, and giving Mikki a wink. "So it's E. Vanderhorn, P.I? Where do I get my new calling cards?"

"You don't. Trust me. You don't." said Mikki.

Both sat back in their chairs and relaxed as Brigetta came bumping through the French doors, holding one side open with her foot as two felines squished their way through the opening. "Hey, you two, were you invited to this party?" she said sharply. "So much for the surprise, Mikki!" Suddenly the two cats ran under the table for safety, escaping from the tray-carrying person who was uttering threats to their lives.

"Oh well!" said Mikki. "Granny Em, here is the new kitten. As you can see, she and Badger are enjoying each other immensely. I got her a separate litter box and put it in the ironing room. That way she shouldn't make any mistakes. I locked her in there for an hour or so, thinking she will believe that is her room."

"She is darling! I love her!" as Emily enticed the orange, fuzzy, half-grown fur ball onto her lap. Carefully and using the weak left hand as merely a balance, she lifted the kitten to her neck, where it began to climb to the back of the chair. The kitten was lying on her shoulder and from its new perch was able to survey her new surroundings. She gazed serenely over her new realm, a princess in her kingdom, and she began to purr loudly. Badger jumped onto Emily's lap for his share of attention, and Emily began to stroke the area below his chin.

"I think I hear a buzzing in my ears," said Emily, as she settled comfortably back into the heavily cushioned chair.

"Yeah, does it sound a lot like stereo cat purring?" asked Brigetta with a happy smile.

"I guess so," answered Emily. "You know girls, I'm quite satisfied with my life, no matter what others might think. I did what I felt I needed to do and, in fact, my biggest regret is that 'extremefavors.com' is no more. I feel no remorse in telling you that I actually enjoyed the work. Not just the fantastic amounts of money, though that was nice too, but the sense of accomplishment, the rush of adrenaline, the excitement. I'll miss all of that, but I know when I have to quit. This was supposed to be the last one, anyway. What happened was just my affirmation. Hopefully after I'm walking better, I'll be happy at the store. I do love that place. The world will survive without this little old lady butting in, maybe even be better off."

Both girls went to the wheelchair and hugged their Granny, squashing the cats in the embrace also.

Badger jumped off Emily's lap indignantly, but the orange kitten seemed to enjoy all the affection and rolled onto her back amidst the hugging, asking for a tummy rub.

"What's her name anyway?" asked Emily, as she obliged the kitten with a gentle massage.

After a pause, Mikki looked her Granny directly in the eye and replied, "Bubbles. You can change it if you like."

"Bubbles? You did say Bubbles?" gasped Emily, so startled she almost flipped the kitten off her lap.

"Well, I told you she was a rescue," said Mikki, looking away, no longer daring a look at those dark blue eyes.

The two young women went inside for more cake, and Brigetta said to her sister, "What was that all about?"

"Remember when we went back to the motel office? We stopped and picked up the cat carrier after we had your car and Granny Em all in tow? I got the kitten from Darla's place after she had died."

"Darla Simmons? The one who knew me from nursing school? The one who had called Lt. Sanderfield?"

"That's the one. It's her cat."

"But how…how did you find the cat? The neighbors said it had disappeared after her death!"

"It disappeared because I had it at the motel. The manager wouldn't let me keep it in the room, but his wife said she would keep it at their house until I checked out. I told them I found it by the road; some one had dumped it off. I bought the litter, cat box, the food, and a collar. Plus, I gave them ten bucks a day just to keep the cat at their place. When I checked out, he knew I would be back that night to get her. When he left for the day, he brought her to the office in the pet carrier to wait for me to pick her up."

"So, as soon as you heard about Darla being found dead, you went back for the cat? Well, that was good you remembered and went back for her."

"Yes, that's me, good-hearted Mikki. I am hoping Granny will still accept her since she knew she was Darla's cat."

"Oh, she will, there's no worry about that. She sure gave you a hard look, though. That was all about the kitten being Darla's?"

Mikki shrugged. "Let's go back outside and give her more cake. Maybe that will cheer her up."

Emily was watching the appearance of stars against the backdrop of evening sky. She had transferred herself to a pillowed wooden rocker with a matching ottoman for her legs. She was looking out to sea, as if contemplating the world and all existence. She rocked slowly and deliberately, stroking both cats in her lap as if to a cadence in time with the waves. A soft and cool evening breeze blew through the tendrils of curly gray hair, raising them gently as she rocked back and forth.

"Gran, are you okay?" asked Brigetta, putting her hands gently on her shoulders, then pulling the afghan from the wheelchair and placing it around Emily's rocking form.

"Fine dear. Just thinking, just thinking," replied Emily.

"I have to get to bed, Gran. Do you want me to help you back to your bedroom and tuck you in?" asked Brigetta.

"Big day tomorrow? Tests?" answered Emily, absently staring straight ahead.

Brigetta nodded and said, "Have to get the most out of this weekend, have a big Microbiology lab test on Monday. Sometimes it's hard to picture the world being made up of little microbes and bacteria and viruses. All those teeny molecules. I am much better with looking at the total picture. How 'bout you, Gran?"

"The whole picture is what I am trying for right now. Just look at those stars, and now--see the moon coming up too? Just gorgeous! Yet, on this same Earth, somewhere, someone is being beaten, robbed, rapped, stabbed, shot or worse. Right in the midst of all this wonder and beauty. That's what I always have looked at. The unfairness, the selfishness, the power-hungry, the greed…it's all there. There's no longer a Garden of Eden."

Not knowing where this was leading or where it had come from, Brigetta gave her Granny a kiss on the cheek and said goodnight. She raised her eyebrows at the door, sending a look of question towards her sister. Mikki just shrugged her shoulders and waved goodnight as the doors closed behind Brigetta.

Now Emily and Mikki were alone. There was more silence as the two sat side by side smelling, watching, and hearing the changing of the tides. Mikki had chosen another rocker and the two were synchronized in motion, but saying nothing.

"You know, I remember that they said the cat was already missing when they found Darla's body."

"I knew you would think of that," answered Mikki, looking straight out at the horizon. "Her photos of the orientation were quite clear and incriminating. Want to see them?"

"No. What happened to her? Darla, I mean, not the cat," asked Emily, still rocking slowly, not looking at her granddaughter.

"I'll bet she overdosed on insulin. That's what they'll find."

"She really was a diabetic?" asked Emily hopefully, turning towards Mikki, at last, to look at her granddaughter's face.

"Probably not. But they found insulin in her refrigerator and syringes in her cupboard."

"You don't need a prescription for insulin," said Emily.

"Or for the needles, syringes or glucose testing monitor. I heard that if you inject too much insulin, your blood sugar could drop to nothing. Extremely low blood sugar brings on rapid unconsciousness and seizures," said Mikki, still rocking the squeaking chair gently. "They found lots of equipment for diabetics in her house…. I made sure of that." After a period of maybe five more minutes of contemplation and rhythmic rocking, the silence was broken again.

"You always were the one most like me, you know," said Emily at last, still rocking and still watching the beach scene. "Not that it's a bad thing!"

"No, Granny, it's not a bad thing at all. And I want to continue to be just like you, in all ways" answered Mikki, now quiet and serious.

"I'm not happy about this, Mikki. But I know I would never be able to stop you. You have a lot to learn. A whole lot to learn. It scares me, and it should scare you too."

"It does scare me a little, but with your help....? I am good at planning and designing, figuring things out," Mikki bargained, "but engineering can be such a bore at times. And I really would like helping out ...doing 'favors'?"

"We'll see, we'll see," said Emily, as she stopped rocking and took her granddaughter's fingers. She gave them a knowing squeeze and a little pat. Then she picked up the young orange cat and turned it to face her, watching the whiskered face intently. "She has lots to learn too. I will call her my Bubbolita. She's had enough turmoil and change in her short life for now. No more drastic changes for her. I will keep her forever safe and protected, cared for, and loved." Saying that, she again reached for Mikki's outstretched hand. Turning back to the cat on her lap, she added, "It's only fair."